THE LIGHTHOUSE KEEPER'S WIFE

THE LIGHTHOUSE KEEPER'S WIFE

JUNE O'SULLIVAN

POOLBEG

This book is a work of fiction. References to real people, events, establishments, organisations, or locales are intended only to provide a sense of authenticity, and are used fictitiously. All other characters, and all incidents and dialogue, are drawn from the author's imagination and are not to be construed as real.

Published 2025 by Poolbeg Press Ltd.
123 Grange Hill, Baldoyle, Dublin 13, Ireland
Email: poolbeg@poolbeg.com

June O'Sullivan © 2025

© Poolbeg Press Ltd. 2025, copyright for editing, typesetting, layout, design, ebook and cover image.

The moral right of the author has been asserted.
A catalogue record for this book is available from the British Library.

ISBN 978-1-78199-676-8

All rights reserved. No part of this publication may be reproduced or transmitted in any form or by any means, electronic or mechanical, including photography, recording, or any information storage or retrieval system, without permission in writing from the publisher. The book is sold subject to the condition that it shall not, by way of trade or otherwise, be lent, resold or otherwise circulated without the publisher's prior consent in any form of binding or cover other than that in which it is published and without a similar condition, including this condition, being imposed on the subsequent purchaser.

www.poolbeg.com

About the Author

June O'Sullivan is originally from Limerick but lives on an island in County Kerry with her husband, three children and one Jack Russell. This is her debut novel; she also writes flash fiction and short stories. She works as a teacher and is a recent graduate of the MA in Creative Writing at the University of Limerick. She always swore she'd be a sea swimmer if she ever lived by the sea but has yet to find the courage. Her other ambitions include learning how to swing dance and walking more of the Camino.

Acknowledgements

I feel so privileged to have been able to bring this story into the world and for that I have many people to thank.

My mother Vickie and sister Avril, who nurtured a love of reading in me from a young age. My husband Declan and children Layla, Dylan and Joni, for their belief in me and their patience when I disappeared for hours into the office.

Francesca Riccardi of the Kate Nash Literary Agency made a dream come true when she offered me representation and I am very grateful for her support.

Every writer needs a tribe and I am lucky to have found mine in the Plague Writers, who have provided advice, encouragement and many cartons of hypothetical eggs.

The writing community in Ireland is very supportive and one of the best parts of this journey has been getting to know other writers in the University of Limerick and elsewhere. We raise each other up and long may that continue. Thanks to Gráinne, Anita and Annmarie, who read an early version and told me it was great!

Skellig Michael is a wondrous place, full of fascinating stories and I have been fortunate to have had access to its unique history through local men with invaluable knowledge: John Golden, Ted Kennedy and Richard Foran. Much gratitude to them for sharing it with me. Thanks also to the guides and workers on Skellig Michael, to Alan Hayden of Archaeological Projects Ltd, and to Frank Pelly and others at the Commissioners of Irish Lights for answering my questions.

Huge thanks to Gaye Shortland for guiding me through the editing process with patience, wisdom and a great sense of direction.

And thanks, finally, to Paula Campbell and all the team at Poolbeg Press for making this dream a reality.

Dedication

To Patrick and William Callaghan

PROLOGUE

June 1868

Eliza lit a lantern and brought it to the table. The flame guttered with the shaking of her hand. She placed it down then went to the window.

'Write it, James – you have to.'

He would write it, there was no other choice. But it hurt him deeply.

'When will the boat come?'

It was her third time asking and he knew the answer no more now than he had before. His hand felt like lead as he lifted his pen and dipped it into the indigo ink that brought to mind the sea on a dark November night when the silvery mackerel rose to the surface at the signal of the moon. The words came easily to his mind where they had sat waiting, composed, indigestible, and with every stroke of the pen his heart broke apart a little more.

Dear Sirs,

I respectfully request transfer to another station as conditions on the island of Skellig Michael are no longer suitable for my family.

I seek your immediate and urgent assistance with this matter.

Yours,

James J. Carthy
Principal Keeper, Lower Lighthouse
Skellig Michael

He placed the pen on the table and looked at Eliza. She hadn't moved but turned her head now as the silence of his pen alerted her that his task was completed.

'When will the boat come, James?'

She lifted the corner of her shawl to her eyes and the retching of her sobs found its way into every corner and crevice of their sad, clifftop dwelling.

Chapter 1

April 1867

'When will the boat come, James?' Eliza clattered her teacup onto her saucer. The breakfast room was empty except for them and their two boys. Joseph was watching the activity outside on the village street while Peter slept heavily in her arms.

'It's already here.' James pointed out the window to the pier across the street where fishermen scuttled along under an upturned boat, only their legs visible, and others mended their nets, tossing them out like washerwomen airing linen. 'The men are loading it.'

Eliza admired her tall husband as he stood, smoothed down his greying curls and straightened his navy, woollen coat. She was sure he was bursting with excitement, taking the job of Principal Keeper of the lighthouse on Skellig Michael, but it would be beneath his station to reveal it.

He smiled at her. 'Stay and finish your tea.'

He took Joseph by the hand and led him outside.

Eliza watched as they crossed to the pier to oversee the final loading of the barrels and crates. James' confident demeanour confirmed to her that he had none of the misgivings she felt about their new adventure.

It would take time to get used to their new surroundings, she knew. Many things were different on the southwest coast. The light, for one thing. Every way she turned it seemed to sift and shift with a startling quality, demanding attention. Of course, the other big difference was the remoteness. From their old lightkeeper's house in Ballinacourty, the nearest town of Dungarvan was reachable by foot. You could set off after breakfast and be there within the hour, with plenty of time to enjoy its bustle. From here, three hours would barely get you to Cahersiveen – not counting the three hours of hard rowing to bring you ashore from the rock of Skellig Michael. Once they landed there, they could only expect to come ashore once or twice a year, weather permitting, and they would have to depend on the local boatmen to bring them in since, as on all rock stations, they were not allowed to keep a boat.

'I'm a lucky man,' James had said last night, as they lay tucked in tight together, listening to the shushing of the waves against the pier wall. 'I know not every woman would agree to live on an island seven miles from the mainland.'

Eliza was clear on her good fortune too, having a fine husband and two healthy boys of two and three years. And being a lighthouse keeper's wife meant comfortable lodgings and generous provisions of food and coal all year round.

From her window she saw a man speaking to James, gesturing at the boat. It must be time to go. She stood up and hefted the sleeping Peter onto her shoulder, laying her shawl across his back. She checked her reflection in a mirror that hung on the wall, making sure her best outfit, a navy skirt and fitted jacket, was presentable,

Her dark hair was still secured in its bun and, although her brown eyes showed the tiredness of the long travel from Dungarvan and the broken sleep, she was pleased with what she saw: the Principal Keeper's wife – slight, neat and fresh-faced.

'Are ye off?' Cáit, the matronly landlady, moved in on her, taking a moment to stroke Peter's hair. 'Good luck and please God it won't be long until we see ye again.'

Eliza smiled, hoping Cáit wouldn't rouse her child who needed this sleep after a restless night.

'We'd a gentleman from an English newspaper who stayed with us a while back. He went out to the Skelligs for a look but he wasn't a bit fond of the islands. "Inhospitable" he said they were.' She cocked an eyebrow at Eliza. 'Sure, I hadn't a notion what that was but he told me it meant unwelcoming.'

'That gentleman was obviously used to a softer life in London, Cáit,' Eliza scoffed, but her stomach tightened into a knot.

'The monks were a bit mad all the same, Mrs Carthy. They started off here on Oileán Locháin.' She pointed out the window, indicating a set of ruins on a tiny island. 'But it wasn't quiet enough for them. Sure, no one would have put in or out on them there either, only the odd gullie. And at least they had the comfort of seeing other souls coming and going, even at a distance. But no, something drew them out to the Skelligs. It would take a lot to draw me out there! But don't mind me, missus, I'm sure you'll be happy out with your handsome little boys.'

Eliza saw Dan, the landlord, giving his wife the eye, beckoning her back in behind the bar. She must make a habit of letting her tongue slip away from her brain, she thought.

She stepped out of the public house onto the street just as a quiet hush fell over it. The fishermen on the pier whipped off their flat caps, holding them tight to their chests, and looked to the ground. From the east end of the village Eliza could hear a high-pitched wail. Around the turn came straight-backed men shouldering a coffin, followed by an old woman, the source of the noise, and a small group walking arm in arm. The old woman's bare feet blurred into the mud and straw on the road and her blackened fingers plucked at her shawl as she cried out her lamentations. The villagers and the men on the pier lifted their hands to make the Sign of the Cross as the procession passed through and rounded the next turn, out of sight, the keening carried away on the breeze.

The pier fell back into action again, the pause to respect the dead finished, and life resumed.

Eliza shivered. She had witnessed funerals with hired keening women many times before, but this had sent a deathly finger crawling down her spine. She shook her head clear as she saw James and Joseph coming back.

'Trant says the tide is ebbing so it's time to push out,' James said. 'Come on.'

He hooked his hand under her elbow and escorted her to the pier. Eliza looked in dismay at the packed wooden boat with twelve men ready to take charge of the six oars.

'James, where are we supposed to fit?'

He laughed and pointed at another team of six oarsmen who were assembling behind in a second boat. He was like lord of the manor surveying all he owned, as Jeremiah Trant stowed the last of their belongings into it.

Jeremiah was an older man, with a good few years on James' thirty-seven, but strong. His wiry frame pivoted and spun as his tanned arms lifted full barrels as though they contained nothing but feathers.

'We're in the second seine boat, Eliza.'

'We do call that one a follower, Mr Carthy,' one of the oarsman said. 'On account of how it follows the seine boat, when they do go fishing.' He looked amused as he delivered this information.

Eliza bridled at his attitude. She longed to set the man straight and let him know that James Carthy was no fool playing at boatman. He had years of experience and had probably travelled wider and rougher tracts of sea than most of the fishermen here. James took Peter out of her arms and handed her into the boat, her heart lurching as it rocked under her weight. At twenty-four, she was well used to the sea but had never lost the fear and respect for the destruction it could wreak.

James passed Peter into her waiting arms then lifted Joseph and climbed in.

Eliza could taste the salt of the sea on Joseph's fingers as she put them to her lips. She blew a slow, steady stream of hot breath to warm them.

The oarsmen fell into their rhythm and Portmagee pier slid away as the boats progressed out the channel, passing a tiny islet.

'*Oileán Locháin!*' Jeremiah called out, nodding in its direction.

The small island in the middle of the channel, with its stone oratory decorated with scallop shells, looked almost homely as they rowed past it. The coastguard station was a welcoming sight as well. Eliza could see a line of white sheets flapping beside the gable and a woman stood up from tending a vegetable patch to raise a hand in salute. It was a fine trio of stone houses. Eliza could imagine herself in one of them. They were certainly a more attractive prospect than the poor fishermen's cottages along the water's edge: one-room, open-fire huts with little to suggest adequate comfort for the gaggles of barefoot children that stared from the doorways.

They were rounding the last bit of headland now, leaving behind all trace of civilisation. She focused on the lookout tower on the high headland but soon they left that behind too and she turned to look at the steel-grey sea ahead. Then she caught her breath at the sight of the two jagged rocks protruding from the ocean on the horizon. They were like brothers. She knew from James that the taller of the two was Skellig Michael. Their destination. The other was the Little Skellig – in Irish *'Sceilig Bheag'*, the 'small crag'. Beyond them, nothing but the wild Atlantic, stretching all the way to America.

The journey seemed interminable. Once the novelty of it all wore off, Peter and Joseph were lulled by the rocking of the boat and fell asleep, Peter in her arms, Joseph on James' lap. At first, the sea chopped at the boat and Eliza's stomach rose and dipped as they crested each wave but eventually she too was mesmerised by the movement of the waves, the rhythmic thud of the oars and the low murmur of the oarsmen reciting the Rosary. She kept nodding off, then starting awake. She'd stare at the fearsome jagged outlines of the Skelligs ahead until her eyes closed again.

She woke with a start when James nudged her.

'Wake Peter, Eliza! We don't want the boys to miss this!'

Peter and Joseph roused and had started to grouch when a loud splash alongside the front of the boat distracted them.

'*Mammy – there's dolphins!*' Joseph screamed.

Sure enough, three grinning, sleek, grey dolphins surfaced and dived in perfect synchronisation.

Joseph leaned over the side of the boat as if to stroke one.

'*Careful!*' Jeremiah shouted.

Joseph turned his red face into Eliza's shawl.

'Apologies, missus, but the water is fierce cold. If the small lad fell in, it's that would kill him before ever he drowned. I had to keep my eyes on this fellow non-stop when he was a young lad and look at him now!' He nodded at the stocky, silent man rowing beside him.

His son, Eliza thought. Now that he said it there was a resemblance, in looks if not in conversational skills.

'The dolphins are lonely out here, I reckon,' Jeremiah said. 'They always pop up to greet us when we're fishing or to-ing and fro-ing from the Rock.'

Overhead the cries of the seabirds grew louder and more raucous.

'We're coming up to the Little Skellig now, missus. A great spot for the gannets and the kittiwakes. Of course you'll get to see the puffins on Skellig Michael soon enough.' Jeremiah was warming to his theme now. 'God Almighty, the monks were great men! Amazing to think what they created out here with their bare hands. It's as sacred a place as you'll find anywhere. There's times you'd swear it was talking to you.' He leaned back, pulling hard on the oar.

The boat grew silent as they neared the two islands. Now that they were closer it felt to Eliza as though the islands had risen from the ocean to the heavens right before her eyes. Two dark triangles, less than a mile between them, growing in size, looming as the boat approached. The men chopped at the sea, bringing them past the Little Skellig, squat, with a cliff-face whitened by the guano of seabirds who made it their home and filled the sky overhead, circling and calling restlessly.

Skellig Michael beyond soared upwards, its twin pinnacles forming an impossible, otherworldly triangle of majestic rock, slate grey with splashes of green. It didn't look to Eliza like a place to live on. There was very little grass to graze animals, no sign of any dwelling place, no flat place for her children to run about, only jagged rock and crashing surf. She struggled to keep her mind steady above the cacophony of the waves and the birds. The dullness of the day lifted as the clouds separated and fingers of light splayed down right onto the rock, daring Eliza to avert her gaze. The sight of it awed and terrified her. This was to be her new home? She did not feel equal to it.

The oarsmen worked in harmony to bring the two crafts as near as possible to the landing at Blind Man's Cove. The waves sucked at the cliffside and Eliza felt that they were being pulled towards the island and repelled in the same motion. The boat tilted and jerked as James leaped ashore. He took Peter from Eliza and motioned for her to come next. Her foot slipped on the wet rim, causing her to stumble hard onto the landing, missing James' outstretched hand. She righted herself, her palms grazed and stinging hot, her knees liquid. Her hands shook as she took Peter, feeling as if the constant suck of the current was threatening to pull them under the boat. She gripped him tightly as Jeremiah put his strong hands under Joseph's arms and hoisted him over the void and onto dry land. She grabbed him too, struggling to balance with the child in her arms and looking around for James to help. He was standing with his back to the boat, hands on his hips, head tilted back as far as it would go, gazing up at the towering rock overhead.

'*Hold tight to those boys!*' Jeremiah's voice was nearly lost in the noise of the kittiwakes circling overhead, calling out their names in a plaintive song that echoed off the cliff walls, creating an inescapable whirlpool of noise.

Eliza gazed up from the narrow landing but her eye met only rock, trimmed here and there by stone steps, then sky, broken by the dark fluttering wings of bird flight. The sight of the men in the larger boat starting to unload their provisions reminded her that in a few short hours these gently spoken, roughhewn men would row back the way they had come, leaving her and her small family alone on this rock, at the edge of the world. A shiver ran through her and she pulled her shawl tighter.

James hefted a bag onto one shoulder, and looked at her with a broad smile.

'Come on! Let's go see our new home.'

Eliza attempted a smile as she hoisted Peter onto her hip. She gripped Joseph by the hand and followed James along the narrow road which skirted the eastern side of the island as far as the southern-most tip where the lighthouse stood. She was relieved to reach a section where a high slate wall, capped by yellow sandstone flags, had been built as protection from the dark sea. There were names carved into the stones and she knew from the AK and PK annotations that these had been inscribed by the principal and assistant keepers who had served here before. She wondered how they had fared.

They climbed upwards, the ocean a sheer drop down, and Eliza had to shake her head to erase Jeremiah's warnings about the treacherous water. At least the lighthouse road felt secure – they were hemmed in by the wall to their left and the ragged cliff-face to the right. But there was another sensation that Eliza couldn't ignore. This narrow road was funnelling them inevitably along, trapping them in. She had to fight a sudden urge to turn back when she came to a large, fallen rock taking up space in the middle of the road.

'*James!*' Eliza called out as she went around it.

'What is it?' He turned and placed the bag on the ground.

'The road is too ... and the rock ...' She pointed at the offending object, feeling like a fool now as she tried to explain herself.

James followed her gaze, looking bewildered.

'It's just a rock, Eliza. You'd better get used to them. This island is one big rock.' He spread his arms wide.

'Well, I'm trying to carry Peter and bring Joseph along too, and he's dragging his feet.'

Eliza tugged at Joseph who blinked up at her in confusion, making her stomach dissolve. What was the matter with her? Why was she getting so irritated and blaming poor Joseph?

James retraced his steps to join them and took the small boy's hand in his own.

'Sorry, Eliza. I was getting carried away with the excitement. You can walk up with Daddy, Joseph, and we'll take our time. The Carthys will walk up to their new residence together.'

Eliza allowed a smile to form. James was funny when he went over the top with pretend pomp. She vowed silently to keep a check on her foolish emotions and followed James and Joseph along the winding road.

They were truly alone. Sea to the left, rock to the right and an endless sky overhead.

Then James stopped.

'There she is!'

He grinned back at Eliza then turned again to gaze at the lighthouse before them. They still had a way to walk but from this vantage point they had a glimpse of the high white tower.

When they at last reached their destination, they rounded the lighthouse and emerged onto a long narrow yard, edged by a wall and paved with more yellow sandstone flags. Alongside the lighthouse was a matching pair of white, two-storey, semi-detached dwellings, each with its own cast-iron porch. The buildings faced west and beyond the wall was a steep rocky drop to a wide cove – Seal Cove.

'Look, Joseph.' James crouched down and pointed. 'That's our house, for Mammy and Peter and you and me. See there, that's an outhouse for the oil stores and sure you know that's the big lighthouse to keep all the sailors and boats safe.'

James shielded his eyes against the sun's glare to gaze up at the light. It would be his responsibility to keep its oil lamps lit and the reflector polished so its beam would be visible from eighteen miles once darkness came.

'Whose house is that?' Joseph was pointing to the dwelling attached to theirs.

'No one's at the minute. The man who was there had to go away. He was a bit bold.' James winked at Eliza.

He had already apprised her of the scandal of the previous Assistant Keeper, a problem drinker, accused of assaulting the former Principal Keeper and relieved of his duties. The Principal Keeper left after the attack, claiming that living on the island could send any right-thinking person crazy. It was an unorthodox situation that meant the Carthys would be alone here until the replacement Assistant Keeper arrived and James would have to cover all duties.

'Will I have to go away too if I'm bold?' Joseph was staring up at his mother with soft, brown eyes.

'Of course not. Sure how could I stay here on this island without you?'

Eliza took him by the hand again and led him up to their house. The weight of Peter on her hip was starting to dig into her nerves. She'd be glad to get them all settled in and comfortable for their first night on the rock.

'I'm going up to the light, Eliza. I'll be down soon to give you a hand.' James indicated the crates strewn throughout the front room that had been brought up earlier by the boatmen.

Eliza, Joseph and Peter were moored in the middle of it all, the boys overcome with excitement. Eliza, overcome. But she couldn't help smiling as James pulled the door hard against a strong gust of wind. He'd be up there for hours, she knew well, like a proud housewife, polishing the glass and brass fittings. Once James got involved with tending to a light he was lost to her.

She stood behind the door and listened to the sounds of her new home. The inside of the house was familiar to her, being of a similar design to other lightkeepers' dwellings with a front room and bedroom downstairs facing the yard, a kitchen at the rear, a single-storey pantry off the gable end, and two bedrooms upstairs. The Irish Lights crest and motto, *In Salutem Omnium – For the Safety of All,* was visible on the ware and other small items. The furniture and white walls almost made her feel like she was back in Ballinacourty. But this house was anchored to the most exposed clifftop she had ever encountered. A strong breeze hurled itself over the wall, rattling the wooden shutters and the glass in the windows. She stood still for another moment, trying to understand what she was listening for but not hearing. Then she realised what was missing. The sound of other people, human voices. It was just her and her children here, cocooned against the wild elements outside.

Eliza turned her attention to the boys. Peter was cruising from crate to crate, grasping the edge of each one. Joseph had rescued a ball of string from one of the boxes and was rolling it over and back on the floor.

Food, thought Eliza. She had lost all track of time but that was of no consequence. Her three men were always hungry. She busied herself in the kitchen, emptying a barrel of provisions. The hooks hanging from the rafters in the pantry still held some dried salted fish and cured meat left behind by the last keeper. They would want for nothing once Jeremiah Trant's boat could visit, weather permitting. James had teased her that the rabbits, puffins and other seabirds were good enough for the monks and he planned to catch plenty of fish when he had free time. But Eliza was glad of the flour, meal, oats, potatoes, fresh eggs, lard and vegetables that were piling up on the sturdy kitchen table now. They would rely on the goats that dwelt there for fresh milk.

She lit the stove, battling against the breeze that came down the flue, guttering the flame, threatening to quench it.

A crashing sound from the front room spun her around.

Joseph cried out, *'Mammy!'*

Eliza ran to where he stood and fell to her knees.

'Where's Peter?' she demanded. He was nowhere to be seen.

Joseph peered from guilty eyes, half-hidden by his balled-up fists.

'Peter falled.'

Eliza scanned the scene and saw what she had missed before. A pile of crates had been toppled, by Joseph, judging from his expression. Tucking her long skirts between her knees she hoisted two of them off the floor, then laughed out loud in relief. There, safe in the crevice created by two fallen boxes, was Peter, his attention focused on a cracked hand mirror that reflected the same curls and blue eyes of his father and his brother. The moment he saw Eliza, he began to cry.

She scooped him up and returned them to the kitchen. She cajoled Joseph out of his tears. There was no need to scold him. This was a new situation for them all and would take getting used to.

Later that evening, with the boys tucked up in their bed, she hauled and carried, unpacked and folded until everything was in its place. The small rooms were neat and starting to feel like home. She stored James' uniform carefully: the heavy overcoat that would be replaced after five years, the shirts and trousers he would wear every day and the cap, jacket and waistcoat that would be required for more formal occasions.

She surveyed her new domain and catalogued the tasks she would have to keep up with every day. The goats would need to be milked, rainwater would need to be collected from the barrels under the gutters, the coal fires in each room would have to be cleaned out and lit to keep the house warm and her baking would be done in the hot bucket.

James had appeared for a short supper then vanished again into a blustery night to keep watch. Eliza had to remind herself not to be jealous – it was a light for God's sake. She was barely aware of him slipping into bed as the daylight crept slowly up the island. She turned and tucked herself in tight against his strong back, savouring the last few moments before the boys woke up.

Chapter 2

Eliza welcomed sleep each evening as soon as her boys were settled, knowing that with the first ray of bright light peeping through the window they would hurl themselves into the new day. Their favourite task was to call the goats for milking. The two hardy, brown-and-white, low-sized creatures seemed to have made the place their own. They wandered at will over the rocky island but would rush into the yard at the sound of oats being shook in a tin bowl. Joseph and Peter loved to make pets of them, keeping them distracted while Eliza crouched and milked each one in turn. They named them Bawneen, 'little white one' and Dorcha, meaning 'dark' for her browner companion. Eliza preferred the taste of cow's milk but there hadn't been a cow on the island since a keeper fell from a cliff trying to gather grass for it to eat.

Within days the boys had exhausted all discoveries within the lightkeeper's dwelling and the small yard outside, enclosed by its high wall, and they longed to spread their wings. Eliza had taken them to the lighthouse on the first day where James showed them around proudly. He led them up the granite steps of the circular staircase and into the lantern room.

'The last keepers left the place in a bad state,' he said, rolling his eyes.

Eliza could see that he had everything shipshape. The bannister on the dizzying spiral staircase was polished to a high sheen. The lantern was neat, with everything in its place and the light reflected the bright day outside, each piece of glass and brass gleaming with evidence of James' efforts. He could do little about the fishy smell emanating from the lantern lamps which were filled with whale oil.

Eliza was keen to visit the monastery she had heard so much about, but with all the demands on her time they had yet to get there.

The arrival of some visitors one morning sent the boys into a flurry of excitement.

Joseph ran in from the yard, shouting, '*There's a fat little bird follying me!*'

'The puffins are starting to arrive.' James clapped his hands. 'There'll be plenty of them to see above at the monastery.'

'Can we go?' Joseph looked to Eliza for permission.

'What do you think, James? Could you come with us for a few hours?'

James paused his rope-mending by the stove to consider. 'I can't, Eliza. Too much to be done. We'll have the Assistant Keeper here soon enough and my time will be freer then.'

Eliza hid her disappointment. This was a lonely station for them but she knew that was outside James' control. She'd take the boys herself, she decided. If they took their time they should be able to manage the climb.

The next morning she prepared some provisions to take with them and they set off, leaving the stove full of turf and their door unlocked. There was no one to trouble their threshold on the island. The day was promising. The surface of the ocean reflected the sparse clouds back to the sky and the pink sea campion growing along the path stirred only lightly in the breeze.

James came out to see them as they passed the lighthouse.

'Are you coming, Daddy?' Joseph asked.

James looked crestfallen. 'No, I have too much to do. I'll come with you as far as the steps.'

He bent to take Peter from her arms, swung him onto his back then reached for her hand. As they strolled along like young sweethearts, he talked about the few landmarks that were visible on the clear day. Eliza could make out the bob of some fishing boats which must have rowed out from Valentia or Portmagee. The sight of them made her feel less alone.

James clamped Peter onto her back. 'Hold onto your mammy. You too, Joseph. I'll keep an eye out for you coming down.'

Eliza stepped onto the stone staircase that weaved its way up and around, out of sight. She paused, uncertain. Was this a foolish venture? No, this new life was demanding her to be brave so she would be. The monks who had carved and hewn six hundred and eighteen steps of this staircase from barren rock with only their bare hands and simple tools would not have balked. She chatted to the boys as the steps led them upwards, pointing out the lighthouse road below them, the fishing boats out at sea, the different seabirds whirling overhead. Her breath grew heavier as she struggled up the ever steeper steps, saving her words now to coax Joseph along. They stopped for a break at the flattest part of the island. The steps they had climbed stretched away beneath them to where the rocks met the froth. James had told her this section was known as Christ's Saddle due to the shape of the dent it formed in the hill.

She sank to the ground, shared out the food, then leaned back on her elbows to take it all in. The blue expanse of uninterrupted sky almost hurt her eyes with its vibrancy. She could see a peak to her right and the unending staircase to the left. When they had rested she secured Peter once more, took Joseph's hand and they resumed their climb. Eventually the incline levelled out to reveal the orderly monastery: round beehive huts and church ruins enclosed by tidy stone walls, the ground punctuated by protruding gravestones that made Eliza think of the appearance of her boys' first teeth.

Joseph let go of Eliza's hand, rushing to explore, his excitement and clumsy feet sending him immediately to his knees. She went to him, blew gently on his scratched knee and wiped away his tears. 'You have to be more careful, pet. Walk slow now and no running.'

She watched as he picked out his steps for a moment or two then skipped off again as though the fall hadn't happened. She looked around at the stone huts, uneven steps and jagged rocks. There was so much here to harm her boys without even contemplating the elevation and the hungry ocean beneath. She knew James would chide her if he were here. He'd tell her not to be worrying, to look at how happy Joseph was exploring.

As if hearing her thoughts Joseph popped his head out of a beehive hut and called to her.

'*Can I sleep here tonight?*'

'*You can!*' she shouted back. '*The seagulls can carry you down in the morning!*'

Joseph disappeared again, following the waddle of the puffins that were gathering in the monastery. Eliza found a patch of grass and sat down with Peter.

'Will I tell you about the monks that built this place?' she asked.

Peter ignored her, too content with beheading daisies.

'Your daddy told me all about it when I met him.'

Eliza had heard the story from James many times but she especially liked to recall the time when they first met, back in Ballinacourty. She, a young woman of twenty, had admired the handsome, weathered face of this man who sat at her father's hearth, entertaining a small group of older men and women with tales of his travels. Some of the men had trodden the same path as James to the many lighthouses around the coast. They were keen to know what changes had come about since their day.

Eliza busied herself making tea and serving slices of buttered bread into their hands, all the while wondering why this tall, older man, with a head of dark curls, kept glancing at her, following her movements, looking into her eyes when she passed by. She smiled, reddening to the ears at this unexpected attention.

Before long, he and Eliza were ensconced by the hearth where they stayed late into the evening. Everyone else had slipped away, winking and nudging at the sight of the two sweethearts.

That was the first time that James had spoken to Eliza of Skellig Michael. He had seen it only from afar while sailing down the coast but had heard tell of it from other lighthouse keepers who had been stationed there. He couldn't explain to her why it held such a fascination for him. Eliza had listened then as he told her of the monks who had sailed out and carved their existence out of the unyielding rock. Their devotion had brought them, a group of twelve, to build their beehive huts atop this island and eke out a meagre living from whatever they could grow or capture. The rest of their time was spent in prayerful observance, often astride the remotest pinnacle of the rock with nothing but sky between them and God. Eliza noted the way James' eyes took on a new depth, darkening the blue, and his voice sank in reverence. She let her gaze sink into the blue-black of his pupils and felt herself being swept away on the tide of his intensity.

Almost afraid of the spell that was being woven she had asked, 'Are you thinking of becoming a monk yourself?'

James had thrown his head back and laughed long and hard. Then his gaze returned to hers and with certainty he said: 'No – I intend to marry.'

Within three months they were stepping into the winter sunlight in Abbeyside churchyard, as Mr and Mrs Carthy.

Eliza closed her eyes for a moment, enjoying the peace. The only sounds were the crash of the waves below and the screech of the birds overhead. She drank it all in. Then she sat up in alarm. Where was Joseph? She had lost track of time since he poked his head out of the hut. She stood up, gathering her skirts and heaving Peter into her arms.

'*Joseph! Joseph!*' she shouted, frightening Peter who started to wail. She tried to hush him. Her heart was in her mouth. '*Stop it now!*' she snapped.

His mouth stretched wider as he put every ounce of energy into his next wail.

'What's wrong with Peter?'

Eliza's feet nearly left the ground as she spun around. Joseph was standing behind her, squinting into the sunlight.

'*Where in the name of God were you?*' She was aware she was shouting but her anger hadn't given way to relief yet.

Joseph's bottom lip jutted out. He was set to join Peter's chorus.

Eliza crouched down and placed a hand on his soft curls.

'I was hiding,' he said. 'I hided so you could find me.'

It was a game they often played in the safety of their own home. Eliza found it bought her a few minutes' peace if she took her time finding the two giggling rogues.

'Why are you cross, Mammy?'

'You gave me a fright. I didn't know where you were.'

'That's cause I hided good.' He was grinning now, delighted that he had concealed himself so well.

'You have to take care, Joseph.'

She closed her eyes and fought back the thoughts of what could have happened. He could have tripped and banged his head on a rock. He could have fallen down the side of the cliff. He wouldn't have been the first. James had told her of another child who had met his Maker in that way and another lighthouse keeper who had disappeared. 'Clifted', presumably. James said he was probably drunk. The reason he was on Skellig Michael in the first place was that he'd been found drunk out of his mind on smuggled brandy with his lighthouse unattended. The thought came unbidden now to Eliza. Why have we been sent here if it is considered a banishment? She cursed the monks for building their monastery here, then stopped, feeling guilty. That would bring bad luck.

She was out of sorts now and their day was spoiled. She swung Peter onto her back and they began their descent, she and Joseph placing their feet carefully on the roughhewn steps. It was harder going down.

She lifted her eyes and gasped. She'd been focused so intently on the steps that she hadn't noticed the sea fog moving in. She pulled her shawl tighter in the cooling air and swallowed hard, her heart beating fast. Would they be able to make it down? She took one more look at the rapidly disappearing horizon. Visibility was shrinking and the Little Skellig was about to be swallowed by the murky cloud. She checked that Peter was secure on her back, grabbed Joseph's hand and continued the perilous decent. Even Joseph, sensing the tension, had fallen silent.

The path drew level as they again reached Christ's Saddle. The mist covered them in a film of cold and wet and she felt Peter snuggling in closer to the back of her neck to stay warm. The mist engulfed every sound. All she could hear was the beating of her heart and her ragged breath. Tears sprang to her eyes. Why hadn't they stayed in the warmth and safety of their house? What a fool she was! She had to push on, as quickly as she dared. She blinked hard to clear her vision and guided Joseph onto the next set of steps. They were wet and as slippery as the green seaweed-covered rocks along the shore. She stepped down hard with her right foot, misjudging the depth of the next step, and cried out as her shoe skidded on the rock. Her body leaned back trying to find balance and Peter let go of his grip on her neck, swinging out wildly from her waist. His fist grabbed at the long, dark plait that she had allowed to hang free, using it to anchor himself.

'*James!*' she screeched.

The four steps below her were all that was visible and she was alone with her boys. She gulped down the fear climbing up her throat and tried to silence the pounding in her ears. She lowered herself down onto the step to settle her racing heart for a moment, drawing Joseph close to her side.

'It's alright, boys. We'll just rest for a minute.' Her voice was thick with tears. She winced, her ankle was throbbing.

'*Eliza!*' James' voice floated up out of the eerie, silent mist.

'Oh thank God! Help us down, James!'

'*Keep coming!*' he called. '*You're almost there.*'

She gathered her courage, stood up and held tight to Peter's bottom, ignoring the pain in her ankle and her scalp as his grasp on her hair tightened, and stepped down and down. Below her James appeared like a spectre and gathered a damp, chattering Joseph into his arms.

They descended together in silence.

James left them at the base of the steps to attend again to the light.

She rushed the boys back to the warmth of the kitchen.

'We must get those damp clothes off you, boys. *Hands up!*' she barked, raising their arms and hauling them out of their garments.

Soon they were wrapped in blankets by the fire, sullen from their manhandling.

'How about some hot milk and raisin bread?'

She felt guilty for being cross with them. None of this was their fault. It had been her idea to go up to the monastery. That was a mistake she wouldn't make again. And shouldn't James have known the weather that was coming in?

Worn out from their adventure, the boys fell asleep quickly that night. Eliza took herself to bed too, dead on her feet. Dawn light was creeping in through the curtains when James climbed in beside her and Eliza made a silent wish that the boys would sleep on a bit longer. James wrapped his arms around her, pulling her head to rest on his collarbone.

'Are you alright?' he asked.

'I am now but I got a fright. We need to be more careful.'

She looked up. His dark eyes were earnest.

'We will, love – sure won't I take care of you always?'

He stroked her cheek with his rough fingers then his lips found hers. She let the kiss go on, alert for any sound from the boys.

James moved his head back to look at her again.

'Now, will you take care of me? I've an awful hard night's work done.'

His hand moved to her thigh, sliding her nightgown up over her hips. Without a word she parted her legs and clung to him as he moved inside her.

Chapter 3

Eliza stopped at the little window on the landing as she made her way downstairs to prepare breakfast. The ocean was sparkling blue, mirroring the clear sky overhead. It was hard to believe they had stumbled their way down from the monastery just yesterday. A sleepy Peter nestled into the crook of her neck, his warm body still holding the heat of his blankets.

'Look, Peter, the fairies are dancing on the waves!'

Her mother had always told her that when she was little and she still loved the notion.

They were just finishing their porridge when the front door banged open and James appeared. 'There's a boat coming, Eliza! I was fishing down at Blind Man's Cove when I spotted it.'

'Who is it?' she asked but he was already mounting the stairs two steps at a time.

Eliza clattered upstairs to the bedroom behind him. Joseph climbed onto the bed, swept up in the excitement. It had been ten days since they had last seen another being.

'Who is it, James?'

'I can't tell.'

He ran a hand across his stubbled chin. Exhaustion showed in his wan face and blackened eyes – he had tended to the light single-handedly since their arrival, carrying the load of two, if not three men, on his shoulders. Instead of the five-hour watch usual for this time of year he had worked almost every minute since they'd arrived, apart from breaks to sleep. Eliza was in awe of how little rest he'd survived on out here.

He finished changing into a clean serge trousers and shirt, pulled on his navy cap and jacket and raced back downstairs and out to the lighthouse.

Eliza and the boys trailed into the yard after him but the only thing visible from there was the vast, blue, uninterrupted ocean. He emerged with a telescope and set off again at a trot.

Now it was Eliza's turn to fret. She hurried the boys inside, washed their faces and hands, buttoned them into their Sunday best and combed their hair hurriedly to squeals of protest. Then she sat them on the bench near the window and told them not to dare move a muscle. She swept the floor and washed and put away the breakfast dishes – that was all she had time to do. Then she rushed upstairs, put on her best dress and brushed and fixed her hair.

As she hurried back down to the boys, James returned, his face bathed in sweat but relaxed into a smile.

'It's Trant's tender boat,' he said. 'I believe you're about to meet your new neighbours.'

'Oh no!'

In her mind she had planned a lovely welcome. The Assistant Keeper's house would be aired, with a fire in the grate and freshly baked bread awaiting them and her own house would be spotless.

Peter unleashed a sneeze, sending a stream of snot from his nose which he then wiped up to his forehead.

'*Oh good God!*' Eliza looked around in vain for a handkerchief. 'How long until they land, James?'

'You have about half an hour, I reckon. I'll meet them on the road.'

When the small party turned the corner and entered the lighthouse yard, a curlicue of smoke was rising from Eliza's chimney and she had warmed yesterday's bread so the kitchen almost smelled of baking. The boys were still perched on the bench, afraid to get off it.

Eliza took a breath, patted her flushed cheeks and turned to the door.

James entered first with a broad smile.

'Eliza, may I present Ruth and Edmund Hunter.'

She shook each hand as it was proffered, taking in her new neighbours who looked to be closer to James' age than hers.

'You're very welcome,' she said, beaming. 'We are so delighted to have you here. I hope the crossing wasn't rough? We haven't seen a soul since we arrived. We were just having breakfast when we heard there was a boat coming, the boys were so excited …' She gestured to the boys who looked more terrified than excited then her voice trailed off into silence as she became aware that she was babbling.

'You rise late on the Rock,' Edmund observed.

His green eyes bore into hers, betraying no emotion, and Eliza could have sworn his neatly trimmed brown moustache had not stirred. Ruth was equally stony, moving only to tuck in a stray wisp of brown hair.

'Not usually but I'm afraid we had quite the adventure yesterday.' Eliza caught James' eye and understood that now was not the time for storytelling.

'Would you like to take tea, Edmund? Or shall I show you the light first?' James asked.

'The light first.'

Eliza had a moment of discomfort as she noted that James was deferring to his junior. As Principal Keeper he had every right to dictate to his assistant the sequence of events. She resolved to remind him of that later.

The men left and Eliza floundered.

'Tea.' It came out as more of a statement than an offer.

'Thank you, Mrs Carthy, but I must decline. I am keen to see our new home and rest after the boat trip.' Ruth's voice was thin, her words clipped.

'Of course. That is understandable. Will you call later?' Eliza's nervous stomach settled. Ruth's refusal had bought her more time.

'That would be lovely.' She smiled faintly as she let herself out.

Eliza's feet were aching by the time a quiet knock sounded at the door but she was happy. She had succeeded in getting the boys to nap so they were in great form. That had given her a chance to prepare everything. The table set for tea with the white-and-blue Irish Lights china, a fresh loaf baked and she was wearing a clean apron.

She swung open the door.

'Come on in. Now, if we're to be neighbours, Mrs Hunter, please feel free to call any time and no need to knock.'

'A man's home is his castle, Mrs Carthy. I would hate to ever intrude on a private moment.'

'Please – call me Eliza. The Lord knows the only thing you're likely to see is these two ruffians laying into each other.'

'Are they quarrelsome?' Ruth faltered by the door.

Eliza sighed. Why was she putting her boys down? They were great lads, bosom buddies and Joseph was kind to his little brother.

'Actually, very rarely. They're good boys.'

Eliza pulled out a chair for Ruth and motioned for her to sit. She prepared a pot of tea and cut and buttered some slices of the warm bread.

Peter and Joseph regarded Ruth in amazement although there was not much to remark on. Dark-brown hair pinned up and a face verging on gaunt in which were set large, brown eyes that would have been pretty if there was a bit of light in them.

Eliza seated the boys and poured the tea then joined her guest at the table and waited for her to begin drinking. Instead Ruth clasped her hands, lowered her head and closed her eyes. When she opened them again she gifted a small smile to Eliza.

'I always say Grace before meals. It is good to be thankful to our kind Lord for all he provides to us. Don't you agree?'

'Indeed.' Eliza glanced in dismay at the boys who had each grabbed a slice of the bread and were chomping with gusto, oblivious as to whether the Lord or the Devil had set it before them.

'How old are your boys?' Ruth asked.

'Peter is just two and Joseph is three and a half.'

Joseph joined the conversation. 'Why does she talk like that?'

'Joseph! Mind your manners. I do apologise, Mrs Hunter. I think he has forgotten how to be around people.' She flashed her eyes in warning at him before answering his question. 'Mrs Hunter is from a different place, up North, so she speaks with a different accent. County Down, I believe – am I correct?'

'That's correct. You have an inquisitive child.'

From Ruth's thin lips 'inquisitive' did not sound like a virtue. Eliza felt she should enquire further about her previous home but feared she would also be condemned as 'inquisitive'.

A strong stink pervaded the air. Peter looked guiltily at Eliza just as Joseph started to laugh.

'*Joseph!*' Eliza snapped, snatching Peter from his seat. 'Excuse me, Mrs Hunter.'

The warmth of his napkin confirmed the origin of the stench. Eliza hurried him upstairs to change, feeling that her first encounter with her new neighbour was a disaster.

When she returned a silent Ruth was regarding a silent Joseph from behind her cup of tea. The atmosphere in the room suggested to Eliza that not a word had passed between them in her absence. How strange, she thought. Had Ruth never been around children before? She decided to release Joseph from his misery.

'Joseph, why don't yourself and Peter go and play?'

They scurried off to the front room.

'This will give us a chance to talk,' Eliza said to Ruth. 'I've been looking forward to it all day.'

She bit her lip. Such a lie! And no chance of a priest to hear her confession any time soon. She poured more tea into their cups and offered a slice of the freshly baked loaf to Ruth who placed it on her plate, then ignored it.

Eliza racked her brain for something to say to her taciturn guest.

'James tells me you were most recently at Inishowen. How did you find it?'

'Pleasant. The Principal Keeper and his wife Rachel were known to us already. We were good friends. She stood for me at my wedding.'

'Are you long wed?'

'Almost three years. April '64. And you?'

'November '62. How wonderful for you, to be a spring bride!'

Eliza studied Ruth's features trying to imagine the dour, pale face and dull, brown hair under a crown of wedding flowers, but she could not. She wondered how old she was.

'I was twenty,' Eliza confided. 'I fear my parents were starting to worry for my chances. But luckily for me James turned up in Ballinacourty and the rest, as they say, is history.'

'Twenty is not so old, I think,' Ruth replied. 'I was thirty-one when I married Edmund. But I had long known that he would be my husband. Our fathers were close friends in the lighthouse.'

'It was arranged?' Eliza couldn't keep the surprise from her voice.

'It's not so unusual. It is often said that it is better than letting the heart rule.'

'Of course.'

An awkward silence spread between them like the sea mist that had enveloped the island the day before. Eliza considered telling Ruth that story but again thought better of it. Maybe when they were friends. If that ever came to pass.

'Were you reluctant to leave your good friend to come here?'

'My feelings are of no consequence. I'm sure you know as well as I do, Mrs Carthy, that for a lightkeeper the light is all and a lightkeeper's wife must respect that. His duty is her duty. We were somewhat surprised that he was not made Principal Keeper but it is only a matter of time and patience. And I have no fear of loneliness. Please God, I may be blessed as you have been.' Ruth nodded towards the boys.

'Oh!' Eliza clapped her hands together. 'Are you …?'

She gestured towards Ruth's stomach. It was entirely possible that Ruth was expecting and it could have slipped her notice. The plain, brown, wool dress she wore was modest in its fitting and could have concealed such news.

Eliza returned her gaze to Ruth's face. She looked horrified. Eliza felt herself blushing.

'I'm sorry,' Eliza began but at that moment Joseph unleashed a wail that pierced her ears. In a flash she was by his side.

He raised an accusing finger at Peter who was grasping a wooden boat.

Peter looked up at Eliza with wet eyes. 'My bo!'

'Peter slapped my face.' Joseph stopped playing victim and took on the role of chief reporter.

'That's very bold, Peter!' Eliza lifted him up.

She went back to her guest, carrying a wailing Peter.

'He's tired. I'm afraid he didn't nap this afternoon.' More lies.

'It's time for me to go anyway.' Ruth seemed to force a smile. 'Thank you for the tea.'

Eliza shut the front door behind Ruth and a few moments later heard the sound of her entering her own house.

James came in later just as she had the boys, in their nightgowns, kneeling by the bed. Eliza said the words of the prayer slowly and the boys did their best to repeat them.

'*Amen!*' they parroted and climbed into bed.

'Is this a new thing? Bedtime prayers?' James spoke with a trace of amusement.

'It is not! We often say our prayers. God knows we could do with them.'

She kissed the boys on the forehead, smiling, as Peter rolled over to cuddle his brother.

James held out a hand, leading her into their own bedroom.

'How is the new lightkeeper settling in?' she asked.

'He's good.' James sat down on the edge of their bed to remove his shoes. 'He certainly knows what he's about. I'll learn a lot from him.'

'From him? Don't forget he's your assistant, James. Not the other way round.'

'Oh! Lady of the Manor, how are we?' he teased. 'You like being the wife of the Principal Keeper, do you?'

Eliza ignored his comment. 'Ruth said they were disappointed he didn't make PK. Is he friendly?'

'Friendly enough. Efficient more so. There wasn't much by way of talk. He was straight into questions about the place, had some ideas about how we can improve the light.'

'That's helpful.' Eliza had to bite her tongue. She didn't want to give in to the temptation to criticise her new neighbours. They had barely landed and there was no choice other than to get along with them.

'How was she? The wife?' he asked.

'I'd say she's pretty efficient as well. I'm so embarrassed I wasn't better prepared. She'll think I'm slovenly. Do you think we'll get on with them, James?'

'It's like this,' he replied, rising to his feet once more. 'We'll have to.'

'Great.' The lack of enthusiasm found its way into Eliza's tone before she could stop it.

'Look on the bright side.' James tipped her chin up so she was facing him. 'You'll get to see a lot more of me now.' He planted a quick kiss on her lips. 'Let's sleep. I don't want to be late for my first shift after Edmund.'

Chapter 4

'I just think she could try harder, James.' Eliza loaded the stove with turf and closed the door with a bang. It wasn't like her to be so out of sorts but the more time she had to herself the more time she had to reflect on the unfriendliness of her new neighbours. 'I don't expect it to be like it was back in Ballinacourty. Those people were kin. Ruth and Edmund are strangers to us but she hasn't even invited me in for tea and it's been two weeks since they arrived.'

James slipped his feet into his boots and checked his pocket watch. His normal punctuality had turned to an obsession since Edmund's arrival. It was as if he feared an immediate loss of position if he kept Edmund waiting for a minute.

'Maybe you put her off you,' he joked.

Eliza rolled her eyes at him.

'They're Methodists, maybe that explains it,' he said.

'James, don't be daft. I was hoping to have some class of a good conversation with you before I'm left to my own devices again. It has nothing to do with their religion.'

'What is it then?'

'I don't know. Don't you find them odd? The way they are so formal and we know nothing about them and you said it yourself he's overly particular with his work.'

'That's not necessarily a flaw. After some of the gombeens I've met down the years, I'll gladly rub along with Edmund Hunter.'

'Well, I don't think it's natural. To be living so close to each other and be so distant.'

Eliza thought enviously of the puffins and rabbits that shared the island's burrows in contentment despite their differences. She felt an affinity with the rabbits – like her, they were outsiders, brought here by a former, well-intentioned lightkeeper. She was tired of being alone with the boys, with just the wide sky and endless sea for company.

She marvelled at the silence radiating from the matching house next door, while hers vibrated with noisy games and occasional battles between Peter and Joseph. She occasionally saw Ruth in the yard, bringing some clothes out to dry, but as soon as Eliza opened her front door Ruth would retreat back to her own house again.

A knock on the door interrupted them.

Eliza opened it to Ruth. Had she been listening? It was eerie her turning up at this moment. Eliza blushed, feeling like she'd been caught doing something wrong.

'Mrs Hunter, come in!'

'Thank you, Mrs Carthy, I won't. I was wondering if you would join me this evening? I must repay your hospitality.'

'That would be lovely. I'll come as soon as the boys are settled. Can I bring anything?'

Ruth seemed lost for a moment then gathered herself. 'We could work on some embroidery.'

'That's a wonderful idea. I'm not working on anything at the moment but I'd be happy to start something new.'

'I shall see you about eight then.' Ruth leaned in past Eliza. 'Mr Carthy, all is well at the lighthouse?'

'It is. Your husband makes an excellent Assistant Keeper.'

She retreated, straightening her skirt. 'Eight o'clock.'

Eliza shut the door. She hadn't mentioned a time and would be very lucky to have her boys asleep by then. The long summer nights were arriving and it could still be bright after nine.

'You see?' James said as he passed her. 'There's your invite now. You were fretting for nothing. I'm sure you'll be great friends in no time.'

'Perhaps. I don't think she liked your comment – him being a fine *Assistant* Keeper.'

'What? I was only speaking the truth. He is a fine Assistant Keeper.'

'And you're a fine Principal Keeper.' Eliza stretched up to kiss him on the lips. 'Be home on time. I don't want to miss my evening out.'

At eight on the dot she slipped out of her door. James had fallen asleep the moment he sat by the fire with his stomach full and now the boys were snoring in unison with their father. Eliza felt almost giddy. The feeling reminded her of younger days, walking miles to Dungarvan for a céilí and miles home again under the moonlight.

Ruth showed her into the kitchen, a mirror image of their own but with a cool stillness.

'I brought my sewing things and some odds and ends of material.' Eliza placed her basket on the ground beside the chair, noticing how tatty it looked. Joseph had taken it apart a few weeks ago and she was still finding items all over the house. She thought to tell Ruth this then silenced herself. She would not speak ill of her boys.

'We'll take tea first. I find I don't sleep so well if I take it too late,' Ruth said.

She poured from a delicate teapot, catching Eliza's eye now and again.

Eliza shifted about on the hard chair, feeling like she was about to be questioned.

'Oh, I have to tell you!' Ruth banged the teapot down. 'I'll burst if I don't tell someone. So far no one knows besides Edmund and I know it's early days but ... I'm with child.' She sat down heavily as if winded by the revelation.

Eliza's glance slipped to Ruth's stomach. She didn't trust herself to respond after her blunder the last time.

'I had an inkling, when we arrived, but we have had some disappointments before and I wanted to be sure. I pray it will work out this time.'

The torrent of words amazed Eliza. A dam had opened and from it flowed a friendlier Ruth. She reached across and took Ruth's hand.

'Ruth, that is wonderful news. When do you expect your baby?'

'Early January, I believe. I have been quite unwell. You must have thought me unfriendly the day we arrived but in truth the boat trip unsettled my stomach terribly. But it will all be worth it. I'm sure.'

'I know what that's like. When I was expecting Peter I was ill every day. We had a neighbour at home, an old woman, who was great for the cures. Nettle tea is a good one, I can tell you and –'

'No. Thank you.'

The dam had shut again and the curt Ruth had reappeared.

Ruth sipped her tea, the sound of the cup settling on the saucer the only sound between them.

'I am more in favour of the new scientific methods than the old *cures*.' Ruth's mouth twisted around this last word as though it was distasteful.

'That may be, Ruth, but having had two boys myself I know a thing or two.' Eliza stared hard at Ruth. She could not believe her rudeness. Would it kill her to feign interest out of civility if nothing else?

'I have no doubt you do, Eliza. But while I may not yet be as experienced as you in the ways of motherhood, I did briefly work as governess for the Hamilton family of Killyleagh. They are connected to the Godfreys of Beaulieu House in Portmagee.' She smiled as if waiting for her pronouncement to take effect.

Its impact was lost on Eliza. She had a vague memory of passing imposing gates that shielded a fine country house outside Portmagee village, but she had not cared to ask its name. Ruth clearly expected her to know of it and to be impressed by her connections.

'Lady Hamilton wrote me a letter of introduction to the Godfreys. They will be in a better position to advise me and no doubt I will see them whenever we go to the mainland.' Ruth looked at her front door as if the mainland was just beyond it.

'Are you worried, Ruth? About having a baby on the island?

Ruth cleared her throat and pushed a loose hair back from her face. 'Indeed I am not! Not one bit. I think myself capable and I pray that I will be. I know Edmund would love a son and it is my duty to provide one if I can. Now, drink up. Your tea is going cold.'

Ruth sat back to sip her own, her hand resting on her stomach.

The thought of what lay before her made Eliza queasy. Being pregnant, so far away from everyone and everything ... indeed, the very idea of Edmund and Ruth ... no! She was being unkind. Just because there was never any public gesture of affection between them did not mean that behind closed doors they weren't ... no! She could not allow her mind to go there.

Eliza had the sneaking suspicion that her queasiness was because she was in the same boat as Ruth. She had lost track of time somewhat but she was almost certain her monthlies were overdue. She replaced her cup with a shaking hand. She couldn't decide if this possibility was something for her to dread or rejoice in.

She glanced across the table at Ruth who had finished her tea and was unpicking stitches from her embroidery, a needle pinched between her lips. This was not the time to share her worries. She wasn't sure she would ever confide in Ruth but, if her suspicions were confirmed, the facts of the matter would speak for themselves soon enough.

Eliza fell into a rhythm as the summer days rolled by. Peter and Joseph delighted in the endless daylight and the new discoveries they made at each turn. She took them along the lighthouse road towards Blind Man's Cove to see what had been washed up onto the rocks from the relentlessly energetic swells or dropped by the seabirds, and they walked home, hands and pockets stuffed with ocean debris that to them were the treasures of the world. The puffins had arrived in their droves and at times it was hard to avoid stepping on them. The sea and skies were vibrant with life. Seabirds whirled in wild abandon across halcyon skies, grey seals flopped and humped in the lazy sunshine and the bottlenose dolphins they had seen from the boat became a common sight.

James thought he spied the water spout of a whale one morning and ran down from the lighthouse to call Eliza and the boys. They spent an hour scanning the horizon with the boys squabbling over the telescope but, seeing nothing, they headed back to the house again.

Edmund was coming across the yard and he stopped when he saw them.

'We were looking for whales,' Joseph told him.

'Whales?' Edmund raised a sceptical eye at Eliza, holding her gaze for so long she was forced to look away, reddening. 'In the lighthouse?'

'Yes,' she said. 'James thought he had seen one and called the boys up. He didn't want them to miss it.'

Edmund eyed Joseph. 'How many did your daddy find to show you?'

Joseph glanced up at Eliza. She knew the child had intuited Edmund's mockery of James and didn't want to betray him. Neither did she but someone had to answer the question.

'None,' she said.

The solitary, cold word felt like an admission of defeat, a betrayal.

'Ah well!' Edmund smirked at Eliza, then continued on his way.

Eliza felt that every time she crossed paths with Edmund – as rare as those moments were – it put her in a bad mood. His sneering, dissatisfied manner irritated her and he had the strangest way of looking at her.

James returned later with a light step, a brace of freshly caught mackerel swinging from one hand.

'What has you in such good form?' Eliza asked him as he flopped the two glistening, staring fish into the sink for her to prepare. She picked up the sharpest knife and slid it under the gill then from backbone to tail. She put the exposed backbone and head into a bowl for James to throw out to the seagulls. The smell of blood and metal and raw fish hit her nostrils as the wet remains slopped into the bowl and her stomach twisted. She put her hand to her mouth that had suddenly filled with sour saliva and closed her eyes for a moment, willing herself to swallow it back down.

James continued speaking. 'My esteemed Assistant Keeper was fulsome in his praise of my improvements to the light.'

'Was he now? That's not like him.' She took a deep breath, controlling the sick feeling.

'To praise?'

'Or to be fulsome.'

'Oh, he was fulsomeness itself today. Did you not encounter it yourself? He said he had a "grand wee chat" with you and the boys.'

'A "grand wee chat"? He did not. He was mocking me, and you.'

'You took him up wrong. He was in mighty form because he had mighty news. Ruth is expecting their first child. Isn't that wonderful?'

He sat down at the kitchen table.

'I feel Skellig Michael is good for us, Eliza. It fills me with energy every morning from the moment I place a foot upon it. I'm so happy here, doing my work in the lighthouse, taking pride in it all. It's a simple thing but when the oil lamps are full, the glass polished and the wicks neatly trimmed I'm a happy man. This island is brimming with life.'

His joy and enthusiasm were pleasing to see but Eliza felt tired and sick and her breasts were aching. Gutting fish rarely bothered her, except when she was in the family way. She lifted the calendar card from the dresser, considering how many weeks had passed since they arrived on the island. More than seven. She realised that her monthly rags were still in their linen bag hanging in her wardrobe, unused since they had left the mainland. Her mind turned in confusion – there was too much to consider, too many plans to make and too many feelings to examine. But her heart felt happy and light.

Before she had time to think the words were out.

'So am I, James.'

He gazed in confusion then gradually the realisation hit. His face filled with joy and in two strides he was lifting her into the air and twirling her about.

Eliza squealed and Joseph and Peter ran in from the front room.

'Are you crying, Mammy?'

'No, Joseph, pet. I'm laughing!' Eliza wiped the tears of happiness away.

A knock at the open door made them spin around.

'Am I interrupting?' Ruth stood there, taking in the happy scene.

'Not a bit. Come in.' James escorted her to the fireside armchair and she sat down. 'Eliza was just telling me some wonderful news. The second piece I've had today. And the same news for all that. The same news as your husband was telling me earlier.'

James was tied up in knots trying to convey his message delicately.

Eliza stepped forward to put them both out of their misery. She placed a gentle hand on top of Ruth's.

'I'm having a baby as well, Ruth. A little later than yours is due but I've no doubt they'll be firm friends, please God.'

At that, Ruth stood up from the armchair, looked around the room as though she'd never seen it before and fell to the ground in a faint.

James cast around wildly as if he didn't know where his place was in this room with a collapsed woman.

Eliza shouted, '*Run and get Edmund!*'

She crouched beside Ruth and was about to go and get her some cold water when she felt her stirring.

Carefully, she guided her back to the armchair then asked the obvious, but dreaded, question. After all, Ruth had mentioned earlier 'disappointments'.

'Is everything alright with the baby?'

Ruth whispered, 'Yes, I think so.'

Then not another word was spoken. Eliza couldn't think of a single, solitary thing to say and Ruth seemed intent on gathering her strength. She gulped in shaky breaths and wiped at her eyes.

The two boys stared, the awkward silence of the room broken only by the noise of Peter's thumb-sucking.

Edmund arrived moments later, his expression grim as he took in the scene before him. His wife, weak and distressed, being consoled by the Principal Keeper's wife. He remained just inside the open door and nodded at Ruth.

'Let us go home. I have no desire to disturb Mrs Carthy further and James is awaiting my return.'

'Oh, heavens no! Ruth might need to sit a while longer,' Eliza began to protest. 'And James won't mind in the slightest if –'

He raised a hand to silence her. 'It is my shift. I am on duty. Come along, Ruth.'

Ruth rose to her feet, not meeting Eliza's eyes.

'Thank you, Eliza. I feel better now. I'm sorry for intruding on your evening.' She smiled weakly then walked out of the room a few steps ahead of her husband who nodded once in Eliza's direction, before shutting the door.

Eliza was still in her seat by the stove when James returned.

'You're back already? Don't tell me Edmund went straight back up to the lighthouse!'

'More or less. I didn't expect him so soon either but he must have sorted whatever the trouble was.'

'He did not! He turfed her in next door and resumed his precious shift. That woman might need to go ashore to see a doctor. Honest to God! I don't think I've ever seen such an unfeeling specimen of a man! Poor Ruth, to be married to a man like that. And do you know? It was arranged by her father. What must he be like?'

'*Eliza.*' There was a warning in James' tone.

'What?'

'You have to stay out of it. It is their own business and that's that. There's no good going to come from you having an opinion on what goes on behind their closed doors.'

Eliza huffed in frustration and stood up to start the supper. She was desperate to discuss it with someone. With a pang she realised she was missing her mother and aunt. They were great women to talk with when they were all under the same roof. She could almost conjure up the three of them working in harmony to churn the butter, screeching in delight at the latest scandal, her sides aching from laughing. She hadn't had that in the years since her mother died of typhus, only weeks before she married James and Katie married a sheep farmer in the Comeragh Mountains. But in this moment she missed them more fiercely than she ever had. Her eyes filled with tears.

James took her arm and pulled her into a tight embrace.

'I don't mean to be cross with you, love. I just want us all to get along. Won't you have enough to be doing when our own little girl arrives?'

'You think it's a girl?'

He lowered his voice to a conspiratorial whisper. 'Don't tell the boys but I reckon we could do with a little girl now to complete our family.'

Eliza smiled up at his handsome face. That sounded lovely. Her whole being felt suffused with warmth and the loneliness left her.

Eliza knocked on Ruth's door the next day. She told herself she wasn't ignoring James' warning. She wasn't interfering in the Hunters' affairs. She was just checking on a neighbour. It was the right thing to do.

Ruth's response made her wonder why she had bothered.

'I must have eaten something that didn't sit well with me. And I haven't been sleeping well with the baby getting bigger. I'm fine now.'

The half-shut door, held firmly by Ruth, countenanced no further discussion and Eliza decided to forget it. The alternative was to drive herself mad with speculation. She returned to her own house, resolving to adopt James' attitude of staying out of their neighbours' business, and busied herself with taking care of the boys and knitting for the new baby.

Chapter 5

In August the Irish Lights steamship, the *Princess Alexandra*, came to the island and Eliza brought the boys down to nearby Cross Cove to watch as oil, dried goods and coal were winched up by the derrick. The powerful chain was swung out from the Rock to the waiting ship where the barrels were hooked on one by one. Then Edmund and James operated the winches to haul them onto the island. Eliza watched with awe at the ingenuity of the mechanism and dread at the thought that any one of them might need to be lifted on or off the island by the same method if necessary.

The ship sailed away, not to be seen again until the spring. Eliza felt even more grateful for Jeremiah's tender boat that brought them updates from the mainland and fresh supplies to add to their store whenever it was possible. She and the boys often walked back down to the boat with Jeremiah who was always keen to hear how they were faring.

Towards the end of September he told her, 'We won't be seeing as much of ye from here on out, missus. They're saying the winter is to come early this year. The birds have started to move south already and the animals are coming down out of the high places. 'Tis a sure sign. But we'll be out to ye every chance we get and we'll leave plenty to keep ye going in the meantime.'

Jeremiah's predictions were proved right by an October that blew in hard from the Atlantic, churning the ocean and threatening to blow them inland with it. Eliza had her hands full keeping her boys occupied within the house and the walls of their confined yard. There were many days when they couldn't step foot outside their front door due to the blowing gale and pelting showers. James often had to crouch low under the wall, running the length of the yard, to get to the lighthouse without being thrown about by the wind. It was hard to tell at times what was rain and what was the sea itself, reaching up and over the island to drench them all.

She saw little of Ruth and was conscious of the closed shutters next door and that her neighbour might be disturbed by the racket her boys made. But what could she do? She had to let them run off some steam whenever they could. She had knocked on Ruth's door a number of times to no avail and when she enquired of James all he had to offer was that Edmund said she was resting a lot and no more.

The harshness of island life was becoming even harder with the bad weather and Eliza's pregnancy. The growing bump made her daily tasks slower and more wearying. She could barely crouch down to milk the goats. She tried standing them on an upturned crate to make it easier but they saw that as a game and leapt off, spilling her bowl of hard-won warm milk. She had nearly cried the day before when a strong breeze swept all her clean washing from the line and she had to cart the heavy basket of wet clothes in for rewashing. She didn't risk putting them out again and the kitchen filled with the damp of the clothes drying before the stove.

Her queasiness had settled down in the last week, she was thankful for that, although James' plans of trapping some of the rabbits on the island for a stew had threatened to set it off again.

A day of blue skies appeared in the final week of October. Eliza couldn't stop looking out the window at the still, blue ocean mirroring the almost cloudless vista overhead. She had nearly forgotten that a day like this could exist after the weeks of blustering wind and rain. She rushed to wash as many clothes as possible, to take advantage of the good drying breeze, then took a bucket of water outside to wash off the salt that crusted the outside of their windows. The boys played, chasing each other in the yard, enjoying their freedom after so much time cooped up. They thought it was summer again and threw off the heavy woollen vests they wore over their shirts.

When she was finished cleaning Eliza brought a chair outside, sat down and rested her head back against the wall. She closed her eyes, allowing the heat of the autumnal sunshine to wash over her face.

'Hello, Eliza.'

She started. She hadn't heard Ruth's door opening yet here she was in front of her like an apparition. The swell of her stomach was undeniable now and the pallor of her face was testament to the weeks she had spent indoors.

'How are you?'

Eliza smiled and rubbed at her neck which was stiffened from its position. How was she? She was so busy she never stopped to think about how she felt but each night as she climbed into bed her body reminded her that this was her third pregnancy: heavy breasts, swollen feet, stiff legs, aching from carrying a bump that felt larger already than it had ever been with the boys.

But she answered simply, 'I'm well, Ruth, and you?'

'Yes, quite well. Though I am glad of this brightening today. How is James? And the boys?'

'Oh, the boys are the same as ever. I can barely keep up with them now.'

With a sickening jolt Eliza registered that Joseph and Peter were no longer in the silent, empty yard. She jumped up, grabbing at Ruth's arm.

'Where are they? Have you seen them? I must have dozed off.'

Without waiting for a reply she ran into her own house calling their names. She could sense they weren't there – why would they be? She rushed out again past Ruth who had taken her spot on the sunlit chair.

She reached the lighthouse tower and shouted from the bottom of the stairs.

'James! Have you seen the boys?'

'No!'

His answer propelled her out of the yard. With difficulty she made her way down the lighthouse road, cursing the twists and turns that prevented her from having a clear view of the way ahead. Maybe she should have sent James. What would Ruth think of her, losing her children? She rounded another bend and let out a cry of relief. There they were. Joseph leading Peter by the hand, with Edmund, of all people, who was carrying a barrel.

Eliza stretched her arm out to the rock-face and leant on it to catch her breath and steady her heartbeat. She found her voice as they reached her.

'What do you two think you're playing at? I nearly had a heart attack. I didn't know where you were.'

'These two great wee boys came down with me to help and let their mammy sleep.'

Edmund smirked at Eliza who had to resist the urge to push him over the wall.

She looked at Joseph who knew he was in trouble.

'I was helping.' His hopeful eyes widened as he tried to gauge just how angry she was and held out a bundle of rope. He presented it to her like a suitor with a bouquet of flowers.

'You cannot go anywhere without telling me first. Do you understand me, Joseph Carthy?'

He nodded.

'The same goes for you, Peter. Come on.'

She took them by the hands and began the walk home. Edmund kept pace with them in silence. Then he spoke.

'It must be difficult to keep two small boys safe out here.'

Eliza held her tongue. She couldn't tell if he was being sincere or criticising her mothering. He shouldn't have taken the boys without telling her.

'I know it's on Ruth's mind,' he continued. 'Having a baby out here, so far from everything. No doctor or handywoman to assist with the birth. Then trying to rear it in safety on top of a rock, in the middle of the Atlantic Ocean. Sure you can't take your eyes off them for two seconds or they'll be gone.'

A heavy silence lingered in the aftermath of his words until he spoke again.

'I'll leave you now. And you'd better get back before those clouds come in.'

He was right. Dark rain clouds were gathering. She gathered the boys to her and together they hurried back up the path. Their day in the sun was at an end and her encounter with Edmund had left her even more uneasy.

Chapter 6

For the next few weeks the island was subsumed once more into a permanent cold fog. Eliza felt the pressure of being shut in by the omnipresent cloud. She fought the urge to open all the windows as she knew it would give access only to the damp and not the fresh air she craved.

The tender boat made no appearance at the landing and Eliza was relieved she had put aside some supplies. She and the boys saw little of James. The darker evenings and shorter days had him working long hours. Each watch was eight hours and the recent bad weather meant that both he and Edmund were busy every day making repairs to the tower, the wall and the houses. It crossed Eliza's mind that the island was determined to rid itself of anything that didn't naturally belong there.

Eliza took the boys to the lighthouse to pass some time and get them out of the house after a long day confined within its four walls.

'This is a nice surprise.' James' words were welcoming but his clipped tone suggested otherwise.

Edmund only nodded in their direction. He shot a querying look in James' direction. It was plain that he didn't find their visit pleasing or appropriate.

'Daddy, can I help you light the light?' Joseph tugged at his father's trouser leg.

James scooped him up into his arms. 'Not this evening, Joseph – we have too much work to do.'

As if to emphasise the point, Edmund said, 'We need to take another look at the lamp, James. I think the beam has weakened.'

James put Joseph down, giving him a slight push in Eliza's direction.

'I'll see you at home later.' He looked sad as he spoke.

Eliza understood this was serious work and there was no time for distractions but she felt that Edmund could allow them a few minutes together. Whatever problems there might be with the lamp they didn't seem to have James unduly worried.

She knew that James missed their company as much as they missed his. Often, when he finally got to bed, the last conscious word to leave his lips was 'Sorry'. She understood that he couldn't change things but, to tell the truth, she was bored and lonely. There was only so much she could do with the boys to pass away the inclement days and weeks and stop them from fighting. Lately, she had been joining them for naps in the afternoon. She was glad of the rest and Peter needed more of it too. He had been troubled by a runny nose and barking cough since the damp weather came in and it woke him, and her, most nights. She often wondered how she would manage if it continued after the baby was born. But she couldn't allow her thoughts to stray in that direction. All of her concerns were in a locked box in her mind and she knew that once she lifted the lid she would have to face up to all her fears about delivering and caring for a baby on this island.

Once the boys were tucked up at night she would position herself in a chair by the window in the front room from where she could see the yard. She was trying to knit a new vest for Joseph for his birthday but most nights she woke from a slumber, the needles on her lap and more stitches dropped than made. It wasn't the most exciting birthday present for a small boy but it would suffice if she couldn't make it into the Cahersiveen Fair Day before November.

Eliza was woken from her slumber in the chair by a noise outside. She put aside her knitting and peered at the darkened window but all she could see was her own reflection. Her hair was like a bird's nest and she tried to smooth it down by licking her palms and patting the errant wisps. She leaned closer for a better look. Then jumped back in horror, shrieking, as a face loomed up in front of her. She ran to the fireplace, snatched up the poker and raised it, ready to strike. She had no idea if the face belonged to a man, woman or demon but she was ready to hit it a wallop.

A loud knock rattled her door, then the doorknob turned and Ruth peered in.

'It's me, Eliza.'

'Jesus Christ Almighty, Ruth! Are you trying to kill me?'

Eliza lowered the poker and staggered to the fireside chair. She placed a hand on her chest, wrestling with the lingering horror and embarrassment.

'My heart! You frightened the life out of me.'

Ruth raised a hand to her mouth to stifle a snigger and Eliza felt a rush of anger.

'What in God's name are you doing creeping around out there and peeping in at windows?'

'Were you really going to hit me with the poker?'

'I didn't know it was you. I thought at first it might be James but then your face –'

'No – James is still above at the lighthouse. I just left him.'

'You just left him? What do you mean?' Eliza felt the sting of jealousy.

'I grew tired of my own company so I thought I would visit with him and Edmund. But Edmund was gone to check the oil stores. I wanted to see if you were up before I knocked. That's why I looked in at the window.'

Eliza was baffled. Ruth rarely left the house and when she was indoors she must tip-toe around it for there was never a sound. Now here she was flitting around the island in the dead of night, paying social visits to another woman's husband and frightening his wife half to death.

'I have found these last few weeks long. Haven't you?' Ruth strained her back against her hands, then began to pace around the room.

Eliza was worried that she'd crash into the furniture with her sizeable bump.

Eliza had to agree. The flat, fog-bound boredom of the last few weeks had been broken only by the minor celebration of All Souls. She'd carved out an old turnip to place a candle inside it but it was already half-rotten and she'd had to throw it out. The boys had cried with disappointment so she tried to appease them with ghost stories around the fire. That plan backfired and she ended up with both boys in her bed, wrapped around her in terror. Whatever she might have to say about Ruth, this was something they could agree on. They all needed something to break the monotony.

An idea came to Eliza with a sudden clarity.

'It's Joseph's birthday on the twenty-second of this month. He'll be four. Why don't we have a little party?'

'I never care much for birthdays. Mine was in September and we didn't mark it. But now that you say it, Edmund's is on the twentieth. We could surprise him too.'

'Surprise him with a party?' Eliza couldn't hide her doubt that this was something Edmund would enjoy.

Ruth nodded as if Eliza had just agreed that it was the best idea she had ever heard. 'James can persuade him to come.'

She's hysterical, thought Eliza. Before she had a chance to respond, the door opened once more and this time it was James.

'James! We're going to throw a party for Joseph and Edmund!' Ruth exclaimed. 'Isn't that a wonderful idea?'

'Are you alright?' James approached Eliza, placing his hand on her flushed cheek. 'You look shook.'

'I'm afraid I gave her a bit of a shock. I looked in the window unexpectedly.' Ruth looked around the room like she had been sleepwalking and was just coming to her senses. In a quiet voice she muttered, 'I'll leave you to your evening now. I've taken up enough of your time.'

She slipped out of the house, her spirit flattened, all the energy gone from her like the wind from a mast's sails.

James smiled at Eliza. 'We're to have a little celebration?'

'It was to be a party for Joseph but Ruth has decided it should be for Edmund too. I think her mind is slipping, James. She's either shut up like a clam next door or wandering around looking for company. Did you see how quiet she got when she decided to go? She's like a spring day – hot one minute, cold the next. You never know which way the wind is blowing with her.'

'I find her friendly enough. We had a nice chat above in the lighthouse.'

'Is that so?'

'Now, now! Don't be like that,' James teased her. 'Aren't you lucky to have such a fine husband for other women to covet?'

Eliza smiled and rolled her eyes. She didn't want to spoil this rare time together with bad feeling.

'Show me Joseph's vest – how is it coming along?'

James retrieved the needles from the floor and held the work-in-progress to his neck, sizing it up.

'You'd want to get knitting, woman. Or hope that Joseph starts shrinking.'

'Maybe I should turn it into a scarf?' she retorted and smiled as he burst out laughing.

Five days later, the boys and Eliza were ready for their guests. The weather had worsened since morning and a curtain of heavy rain shrouded the island. Despite this, Eliza had made a big effort. The front room was cosy with chairs positioned around a blazing fireplace and the side table set with a few treats that the boys were ogling: boiled sweets, slices of buttered soda bread, dried fruit and pound cake.

Ruth arrived, her cheeks flushed in the gloom, then the door opened again and James brought a blast of cold air into the room with him.

'God Almighty! It's wetter than it looks out there! Is this where the party is?'

'Yes, Daddy!'

Joseph had brought Ruth to the table to see the spread. For once, she was responding to his chatter and admiring each item.

As James turned his back to the fireplace, to warm the damp out of his clothes, Eliza beckoned to him surreptitiously. He followed her into the kitchen.

She stepped close to him and murmured, 'Where is he?'

'The other "Birthday Boy"?'

She frowned a warning at him. She didn't want Ruth to overhear and think they were mocking her.

'He won't come down,' he muttered. 'Said he has work to do and that's that.' He threw his eyes to heaven.

'Oh God!' Eliza groaned softly. 'What will we tell her?'

'I'll just have to tell her what he said.'

Back in the front room, Eliza seated Ruth and James by the fire and poured tea for the adults. She handed them a cup each and then started to pass around a plate of buttered soda bread.

Ruth studied James' face. 'Will Edmund be down soon?'

James had just taken a large bite of bread and took an extra moment to swallow his food. Eliza could see he was buying time.

'Well, it's like this. He said he won't seeing as how he's in the middle of a job and –'

'That's quite alright,' Ruth interrupted. 'His work is the priority.' She forced a smile and took a slice of bread with a shaking hand.

Eliza felt sorry for her. This party was meant to be a break from the mundanity of the long winter days but Edmund seemed determined not to enjoy anything.

Ruth bit into the bread, chewed slowly and sipped at her tea. The sound of the rain hammering down and the strengthening gusts of wind rushing past the gable of the house masked the awkward silence in the room.

Eliza was about to say something when Ruth exclaimed, 'Oh, I almost forgot!'

She reached into the pocket of her dress and produced a single, miniature, wooden train carriage. 'I found this in our house. It must have been left behind by the last AK, or maybe a visitor. I thought you might like to have it, Joseph. For your birthday.'

Joseph reached out, snatching the carriage from her hand.

'Joseph!' Eliza warned. 'Say thank you!'

'Thank you,' he mumbled. He promptly got off his chair and lay on the floor, pushing the carriage up and down across its surface.

Ruth frowned. 'It's really a souvenir, more for looking at than playing with.'

'Young boys'd break iron.' James smiled, watching fondly as Joseph became the train driver.

Eliza glared at him. It was hardly a reassuring statement.

They finished their tea and bread and wished Joseph a happy birthday with slices of pound cake.

James went repeatedly to the window, watching as the wind and rain lashing at the island intensified.

'The swell is getting fierce,' he said and as if to prove him right a spray of seawater topped the yard wall and flung itself against the window, rattling the pane. There had been no shortage of wild and windy nights since they moved to the island but it was the first time Eliza had seen the sea breach the wall. The wall that was their sole protection from the devouring ocean below.

'Why don't we go into the kitchen?' she suggested.

The rear of the house might feel safer and at least the window there showed them nothing except the impassive rock-face behind them. Ruth started to help her gather the plates. James remained at the window, staring out at the rain cutting into the steel-grey ocean. Eliza could sense his worry. The birthday party was a frivolous distraction now. He went to the porch and pulled on his overcoat.

'I'll go up again now and leave ye at it.'

A gale of wind blew down the hall as he opened the front door. They watched from the window as he crouched under the wall and ran, head down against the cold rain driving in hard.

Eliza and Ruth were gathering the last few items in the front room when the door flew open again. It was James with Edmund behind him.

Ruth's face brightened. 'You came!' She produced a small brown parcel from her pocket and offered it to Edmund.

'What is that?'

'A present. For your birthday.'

'Have you read the calendar wrong, woman?' A deep red flush spread across his cheeks.

'No,' Ruth replied, her voice shaky. 'But I didn't mark your birthday yet so ... open it.'

'Not now.' He turned away from her.

Ruth's face fell. She slipped the parcel back into her pocket.

The atmosphere in the cosy room suddenly lost all its warmth but Eliza could feel the heat of her temper rising. Why did Edmund have to be so rude?

James broke the silence. 'It's nasty out there. The stores are taking an awful hammering. We're going to try and secure them until the storm passes over. I left some rope by the stove.' He headed for the kitchen, leaving them in a tense silence. Edmund was staring into the flames and Ruth turned her face to the window but not before Eliza saw her hand swiping away a few tears.

A blast of wind tore one of the shutters from the window. Eliza started and gave silent thanks that she and her boys were safe from the steely rain that was hammering down as though it wanted to shatter the glass.

James returned with the rope and the men made to leave.

James turned back to Eliza. 'Go into the kitchen and don't stir anywhere until this passes over.'

In the kitchen Joseph and Peter were engrossed in playing with their new toy. Ruth had brought a chair to the window where she now sat, her head against the wall, staring out unblinking at the rock-face, as if awaiting rescue. She had been so excited about the party but Edmund's reaction had stripped any joy from it.

Eliza was spared the need to speak as the rain clattered down on the roof, drowning out all other sound.

A while later the two men burst into the kitchen.

Ruth stood up, her face pale. 'Is everything alright?'

'*For God's sake, woman, can't you keep quiet? This is serious business!*' Edmund roared.

The blood rose in Eliza's face. She looked at James. Would he say something to Edmund? Surely he'd step in?

James raised his hands and spoke quietly to Edmund. 'What do you think?'

'The cover is off the barrel on our side. We'll have to test it. And we'll have to cover it for now the best we can. The barrel on this side is shattered.'

With a sickening twist of her stomach Eliza realised what they were talking about. The rainwater barrels. Their only source of drinking water on the island. One destroyed and one possibly contaminated by the saltwater. If even a small amount got in, it would be undrinkable. There was no hope of collecting more during this kind of weather and even less hope of Jeremiah being able to come out. Unless they secured their supply now they could be left without any. And how long could they survive that?

Eliza went to the cupboard and took out a small steel plate. She handed it to James silently. The men left and came back almost immediately, James carefully carrying the plate with a puddle of water on it, drawn from the barrel. He sat it onto the stove top and they all watched in silence as the water evaporated.

Eliza drew in a deep breath. *Thank God.* There was no white residue. This barrel was still good.

Edmund and James disappeared once more into the wild storm. They came back with the barrel and together they manoeuvred it into the porch for safe-keeping.

Eliza watched them from the hallway.

'I need to go up now and get the lamp lit,' Edmund said.

It was true. In all the panic about the water, the light had faded from the day and the sky was darkened further by heavy storm clouds.

'I'd hate to think of a boat out in this.' James glanced at Eliza.

'If there is, they'll be left to their own fate.' Edmund's words were cold.

Eliza couldn't believe it. As lightkeeper he had a duty to protect life at sea. There wasn't much they could do for a boat in difficulty, besides keeping the light lit, but Eliza was chilled to hear the callous way he dismissed human life.

James looked down at his boots. 'I'll come up too.'

Edmund had first shift tonight but Eliza knew that James would feel less than useless sitting by the fire with the women and children on a night like this. She returned to the kitchen, shut the door and took a seat by the stove, her back to Ruth who had resumed silent vigil by the window.

'This party was a silly frivolity,' Ruth said eventually.

'Ruth, I'm sorry. This is all my fault. After all, it was my idea.'

'Oh I know!' Ruth snapped. 'It *is* your fault. My fault was in letting you talk me into having it!'

Eliza was stunned at Ruth's words. That wasn't what happened. Hadn't Ruth been enthusiastic about it? *She* had suggested making it be a celebration for Edmund too. Words of protest rose in her throat but she didn't want to argue in front of the boys.

Ruth slid to her knees with difficulty, clasped her hands under her lowered chin and began to recite her version of the Lord's Prayer. Some of the words were unfamiliar to Eliza. If she had been with her own people she would have led the Rosary. Instead she knelt to pray her own words in silence – much more meaningful than the formulaic words she had just heard. She issued a heartfelt plea to God, the saints, the angels and anyone else who might be available. *Please protect my James and send him home safe to me. And Edmund.* Her hand went to her full belly as she thought for a moment of the terrifying prospect of being a widow and mother to three small children alone. She chased the thought from her mind. It was unimaginable.

Eliza paced the room. James and Edmund had been gone for hours and the silence was testament to her and Ruth's anxiety. Peter had fallen asleep and Eliza had put him and Joseph to bed in the downstairs bedroom. She wasn't sure if that was a good idea. If a large wave overtopped the wall it could reach into the house. But the rafters upstairs were creaking wildly in the gales.

Finally the storm eased and the rain settled into a steady, weary pitter-patter. The kitchen door opened and Edmund came in.

Ruth started out of her seat and went to his side.

'Come on,' he said. 'I'll take you home. It has calmed but there's still a rogue gust now and again.'

'Is everything alright?' Eliza asked. She'd rather get her information from James but he wasn't here. 'James?'

'Fine. A wave topped the light. It shook the panes and I thought they were going to give but they held.'

Eliza shut her eyes in relief.

'Goodnight to you.' Edmund began to close the kitchen door behind him, then paused. 'There's no sign of the goats. We might have lost them.'

Eliza sat down heavily in the fireside chair. She felt tears fill her eyes. She was exhausted and worn from worry. First the drinking water and now the goats, her boys' little pets, were missing, lost. In a matter of hours the island had shown her just how quickly it could take whatever it wanted.

Chapter 7

Days passed with no sign of Ruth. She had retreated once more into silent hibernation next door. James would not discuss the Hunters with Eliza, closing down the conversation at every attempt and so she gave up and turned her attention to her own affairs. She had told the boys a version of the truth after they stood in the yard rattling the oats in the pan for the goats.

'They went off in a fright during the storm,' she said. Then she told them a lie. 'They'll come back.'

Every morning, before she forced herself out of bed she lay for a few minutes with her hand on her bump to feel her baby moving. She cherished this special, private moment that was hers alone and it gave her such a feeling of joy to know the baby was healthy and active. November would soon become December and she began to contemplate Christmas on the Rock. She hoped she could get to the mainland beforehand and maybe she could make it to Mass. She had always loved it as a child in Waterford. The little church in Abbeyside, where she and James were wed, would be full to the rafters, with the men gathered at the back, spilling out into the porch and the yard outside where they could mutter news to each other and not draw the priest's ire. The church was always bathed in guttering candlelight and there was a sense of peace and joy. Even in the years when the numbers in the congregation were visibly shrunken by death and emigration, there was comfort to be found in the coming together of the community.

Eliza had noticed the small, wooden church in Portmagee and longed to be there, not for the spiritual connection so much as the human. She craved the physical presence of other human beings, outside of their tiny group on an island in the middle of a vast ocean.

The weather improved suddenly and Eliza woke to blue skies and a calm sea. It was still biting cold but it felt as though the island had been transported by magic to another, kinder climate overnight.

'James, do you think we can make a visit to the mainland?'

Eliza placed his breakfast on the table then slumped into the chair opposite, moving it back to create ample space for her belly.

'I'm not sure, Eliza.' James furrowed his brow before breaking into a smile. 'Are you sure you wouldn't sink the boat?' He dodged to the left as she flung a piece of crust at his head. 'I don't see why not,' he continued. 'This fine weather is due to last. Jeremiah could be out to us again one of these days. Be ready – yourself and the boys can go back in with him in the tender. Why don't you see if Ruth wants to go?'

Eliza's heart soared. The thought of escaping the island for a night made her giddy even if Ruth did accompany her. She couldn't keep the smile off her face as she said a silent prayer that Jeremiah would come soon.

The next day she knocked on Ruth's door. She hadn't seen her since the storm and it was clear from the shuttered, darkened windows that Ruth didn't want company. The door creaked open.

'Eliza ... come in.' She opened it wider to make room and they moved inside like billowing sailing ships.

The women took a moment to gauge each other's bumps. Ruth's was bigger and lower down. Eliza tried to remember what her mother always said about that. Was it a sign of a boy? Ruth had lost weight so her belly protruded from a tiny figure too slight to support it.

'Are you well, Ruth? We've hardly laid eyes on you this past while.'

'I've been very tired, Eliza. So tired it's all I can do to waken long enough to eat.'

'You poor thing!' Eliza felt guilty at how well she had been feeling. But it had been the same with her first two pregnancies. At about this point she got a burst of infinite energy and felt like a young girl again. She knew it wouldn't last forever and no doubt near the end of her time she would be dragging her feet like Ruth was now.

Ruth slumped into the nearest chair without asking her guest to sit. She flung her arm across her eyes, her head thrown back and Eliza feared she would doze off before she could broach the idea of the trip ashore.

'Ruth, I'm planning to head to the mainland the first chance I get. Just me and the boys of course. James will have to stay. Would you like to come with me? We could be ready to go the next time Jeremiah comes out.'

'Go in to the mainland?' Ruth lowered her arm and sat up straight. 'I would like that! I could pay a visit to the Godfreys at Beaulieu House. I would like to see their doctor.' She put her hand on her stomach, a shadow of concern flitting across her face before it brightened again. 'When do we go?'

Eliza went to the window and opened the shutters. The room filled with bright, winter sunshine – the housewives' betrayer, it showed up a layer of dust on every surface that it touched.

'The weather is perfect so I'd say we'd want to be ready to go at any moment.'

Ruth pulled herself up to standing, a hand on her lower back. 'I'll prepare my bag.'

Eliza nodded and left to make her own preparations.

'Will you come away from that window, Eliza? You'll have the glass worn out. And sure you can't see the boat from there anyway.'

Eliza was in no mood for jests. To her utter disappointment, Jeremiah had failed to appear.

Every morning, before she got out of bed, she said a prayer that the good weather would hold and Jeremiah would come. Every day she was granted half her wish but no Jeremiah arrived.

'Wouldn't you think he'd make use of this fine weather though?'

'I'd say you're dying to get away from me, is that it?' James put his arms around her.

Eliza sighed into James' chest. She'd made the mistake of telling the boys about the trip and every day now they wore her down asking when they'd be leaving. She pushed herself away from James.

'I'll go make some dinner for you.'

'Thank God – I thought I'd be left to starve while you gawped out the window. I'll go down to the stores at Cross Cove. I need to bring up a few things.'

Eliza and the boys had just sat down to eat when James returned.

'Your wish has come true!' he announced.

Eliza turned, half expecting him to be teasing her again. 'Is it Jeremiah?'

'It is. I met him coming up the road just now. I told him you're travelling.'

Eliza's heart skipped a beat and her mind scattered to everything she still needed to do.

'Will you knock at Ruth's door and tell her to be ready?' she said. 'Come on now, boys, we need to hurry.'

James put his arm around her waist. 'He won't go without you – go easy!'

Eliza went to move away but he held her fast. He turned her face to look into her eyes.

'I'll miss you,' he said in a low voice

'It's only one night, James.'

'Still – if the weather turns you might be gone longer. It will be lonely here knowing you and the boys aren't waiting for me in our little home. That bed will be too big and cold without you in it. So hurry back to me.'

'We will.' Eliza smiled. She knew all about loneliness out here but she was surprised that James felt it too. She'd thought that with his work in the lighthouse he didn't have time to dwell on such things.

He released her, tousled the boys' hair and left.

Eliza wrapped the boys up in every warm garment they had, picked up their travelling bag, and led them outside. The sun was shining but there was a nip in the air and she knew they'd feel the brunt of it once they were on the open sea.

She placed the bag at her feet and shut the door after them, saying a silent prayer that they would return safely. Then she started at the sight of Ruth who was standing stock-still outside her own, closed front door. Her bag, larger than Eliza's, was at her feet and her gaze was towards the ocean.

'All set, Ruth?'

'I'm ready to go,' she answered, still not taking her eyes from the horizon.

'What a pity James didn't think of taking our bags down. Can you manage it? Maybe Edmund will come down and give us a hand.'

Ruth turned her eyes from the sea to Eliza.

'He's working.'

Eliza swallowed down some angry words. Working! On a still calm day with not a puff of a breeze? Would he watch, she wondered, from the lighthouse as his heavily pregnant wife struggled to the pier with her bag that any gentleman, husband or not, would be mortified not to assist her with? That man had no heart – this was the final piece of proof Eliza needed of that.

'Joseph, hold hands with your brother and walk down easy ahead of us.'

She put her own bag in her right hand and took one handle of Ruth's to share the burden.

'Here, we'll manage it between us.'

Now she hoped Edmund was watching and might feel a pique of shame that not one but two pregnant women were struggling down the lighthouse road.

The going was slow and Eliza exclaimed in relief as they turned the corner and met a red-faced James running up the steep incline against them.

'I'm an awful eejit,' he puffed out between breaths. 'It was only when I got down and talked to Jeremiah that I remembered your bags. Sure I could have brought them on ahead. Give them to me here.' He grabbed a bag in each hand and strode down the road.

They reached Blind Man's Cove and there was Jeremiah waving his hat at them.

'*Hello!*' he called.

Eliza and the boys waved back and the other oarsmen raised their hands in greeting.

'How are my boys?' Jeremiah asked when they reached the pier. 'Come on aboard, missus! I'll give you a hand there. 'Tis good to see ye after that storm. We were praying for ye.' He grasped Ruth's arm, steadied the boat, then helped her down into it. Eliza went next, then took Peter from James and finally Joseph.

James looked down at them from the landing. Eliza was sorry now she hadn't embraced him one last time.

Jeremiah winked up at him.

'There must be something fierce in the water out here.'

Eliza blushed. She knew he was referring to their full bellies.

'Now so. Move up there, lads, and we'll row these fine ladies and gentlemen ashore. We'll have stories and songs to pass the time away. Am I right?'

Eliza laughed and Joseph clapped his hands. Poor Tom trained his gaze on the floor of the boat. Given his mute appearance until now, Eliza doubted they'd get much of a story or a song out of him.

Jeremiah pushed them off with his oar and within a few pulls they were away from the island. Off its soil for the first time in five months.

Soon Eliza's shoulders relaxed and she turned her face to the winter sun. Her boys were giggling and trying to join in with a rhyme that Jeremiah was teaching them. Everything felt good in the world at that moment as her body aligned with the gentle rhythm of the calm sea. The only chill came from Ruth who sat in stony silence, her back to the island, never once looking back.

As they pulled up to the quay in Portmagee, Eliza marvelled at the men's stamina, especially Jeremiah's. The whole journey he had kept her boys entertained with stories and songs. He pointed out every bird that passed overhead and told them what was likely to be passing under their boat in the wintry waters. Eliza had been lulled to a contented trance. Ruth had closed her eyes and not one word had passed her lips.

Joseph and Peter were tired now. Joseph leaned into her shoulder and Peter cuddled into her chest, sucking his thumb.

The oarsmen eased the boat alongside the quay wall and Tom leaped out to secure it.

Jeremiah called up to him. 'Go across to O'Connells' and make sure they've a room for the night. These boys are dead on their feet. Will the one room do ye, ladies, or will ye be needing two?'

Eliza was about to answer when Ruth spoke in a clear voice. 'I won't be lodging in O'Connells', Mr Trant. I am to visit with the Godfreys in Beaulieu House and I expect they will invite me to lodge with them.' She recited the last sentence as though it had been rehearsed. Was she sure of this invitation, Eliza wondered, or just hopeful?

'Right so, missus.'

Jeremiah turned away to finish mooring the boat but not before Eliza caught sight of his raised eyebrows. This was the haughty Ruth that Eliza knew, her attitude sharpened by her personal ties to the biggest land-owning family in the area.

'Will you go there now, Ruth, or will you have something to eat first?' Eliza asked. 'And how will you manage your bag?'

'I'll go there directly, thank you, Eliza. I'm sure they'll send a boy over for my bag. Could you leave it into O'Connells' for me, Mr Trant?'

She stood, awaiting Jeremiah's assistance to get her out of the boat, with a regal air that caused Eliza to choke back a laugh.

On the pier, Ruth straightened her clothes, then marched off in the direction of the village.

Eliza and Jeremiah exchanged a wry glance but Eliza broke it after a second. It didn't seem fair to Ruth, even if she was behaving with awful arrogance. Of all the people on this quay and in this village, only Eliza knew of Ruth's troubles and sadness on Skellig Michael. If she chose now to bear them under a shield of haughtiness then more power to her.

'Mrs Carthy! We're delighted to see you again!'

Dan O'Connell was weaving his path down the busy quay, skirting around the fishermen mending their nets and pots.

'It's a while since we had you with us. Was that the other lighthouse lady I passed just now?'

Eliza couldn't answer him until she was handed up onto solid ground in a joint effort by Jeremiah and Tom.

'Yes. That was Mrs Hunter. She's making her way to call to Beaulieu House.'

'Is she now? Well, we've two fine rooms being readied by Mary Kate.'

'I only need the one,' Eliza interrupted. 'It turns out that Mrs Hunter plans to stay at Beaulieu House.'

Dan repeated the raised eyebrows of Jeremiah but, in true publican diplomacy, moved the conversation to safe harbour.

'Well, we're delighted to see yourself and these fine young men. I see the South Kerry sea air is suiting you all – you're after getting so big!' Dan reddened as his eyes landed unintentionally on Eliza's belly.

Eliza pulled her winter cloak around her as far as it would go.

'Well, long life to you and yours anyway, Mrs Carthy!' Dan bent to pick up the two bags. 'Come on! Cáit is dying to lay eyes on ye and I've no doubt she has a fine fire on to thaw ye out.'

The little procession weaved up the quay, with Eliza responding to greetings from all sides. She felt the proximity of human contact wrap around her like a cocoon. It was as if everyone here knew who she was and she loved it.

The boys hid behind Eliza's legs as she followed Dan into the public house and through to the dining room.

Cáit was just putting the final touches to the table setting but turned to greet her like a long-lost relative. 'Oh, you cratur! How are you getting on? I said prayers for you many a day when the wind and rain were lashing in on top of us here. And that storm, God Almighty! I said to Dan, what about that poor woman and her two babas out on top of that rock? Didn't I, Dan?'

'You say a lot of things, Cáit, but I give a lot of it plenty of no notice. I'll take this bag up to your room, Mrs Carthy. You can be telling Cáit the news.'

'News?' Cáit's face brightened.

News to her must be like oxygen to a flame, Eliza thought.

'Mammy is having a baby,' Joseph jumped in proudly.

Cáit bent down and took his face in her hands, squeezing his soft cheeks. 'Well, God bless you all! Will you mind your mammy and the new baby?'

Joseph looked at Eliza in horror then back to Cáit. 'No. Mammy will mind the baby. I'll help Daddy.'

'Ah, I see, another lightkeeper in the making. Sure isn't it a fine job? How are things out on Skellig Michael anyway, Mrs Carthy?

Plenty of gullies and sea breezes, I'm sure? How you don't crack up with the boredom, I don't know. Although I suppose you've a bit of company now since the other keeper and his wife arrived. What are they like?'

'Well, they're very pleasant …' Eliza began to answer but Cáit was in full flow.

'I know I shouldn't say really but they stayed here a night before they went out to ye and I said to Dan did you ever see a pair so well met? One of them as odd as the other. They hardly said a word to anyone here and even less to each other. Was that her I saw trotting up the road with a big belly out in front? A miraculous conception that must have been anyway – God forgive me!'

Eliza almost snorted in shock. Cáit halted briefly to bless herself and wipe away her blasphemy. The gesture sobered her somewhat and she remembered what she was about. She pulled a chair out for Eliza.

'Sit down there now, let you. Give me that cloak. You must be wiped out from the journey. Lads, ye come with me into the kitchen and we'll see what we might find.'

With that, she and the boys were gone, leaving Eliza in the sudden silence. She stretched her arms out wide then closed her eyes and rotated her neck. She felt good. The journey had been long but she was glad to be here. She placed a hand on her stomach. The baby kicked as if in a greeting. Eliza smiled at the lovely, secret thrill. She hadn't much longer to go now but she almost wished that she could pause time, keep the baby inside of her where she knew it had warmth, nourishment, security. She couldn't guarantee that for the rest of its life, once it came into the real world.

Her thoughts were interrupted by Cáit returning, carrying a tray, the boys trotting after her.

'Mammy, we see'd her chickens,' Joseph said.

Eliza laughed. 'Saw,' she corrected.

'We saw'd them. Come look.'

'Leave your mammy stay off her feet while she's able. You can show her later. I've a pot of spuds on for you all and a bit of cured bacon and here's a few cuts of bread to keep you going for now.'

'Thank you, Cáit, you're great.' Eliza cut up a slice of bread for Peter who crammed two pieces into his mouth together then struggled to keep them in as he and Joseph dissolved into silly giggles.

'You'd swear they never saw a bite!' Eliza was mortified.

Cáit was lingering, no doubt angling for more news. Sure why not, Eliza thought, she'd been craving a good natter for months.

'Will you join me for a cup of tea, Cáit?'

'I will, sure! I normally take a cup around this time.' Cáit pulled out a chair beside Peter and sat down.

Joseph looked at her in alarm. 'What about our dinner?'

'Joseph!' Eliza admonished.

'Don't worry. Mary Kate is looking after your spuds. Eat up your bread now like a good man.'

Poor Mary Kate, thought Eliza, run ragged no doubt. 'Is she your daughter?' she enquired.

'No, she's my brother's child. He married a sickly one from the Glen and, God help us, she's taught the child nothing. So she's with us for a bit of training to see could she get a bit of work as a domestic. There's plenty of work in Valentia now with the new cablemen moving down and looking for girls to keep house.'

Eliza had heard about the new cable. Everybody had. She wished she had more time to tour around the mainland and see the new telegraph building in Foilhammerum and all the improvements on the island. She wondered if the telegraph would ever make it to Skellig Michael. Imagine being able to send messages like that, like magic! No more isolation.

'Dan tells me Mrs. Hunter is to lodge at Beaulieu House,' Cáit said.

Eliza nodded. So this was what she wanted to discuss. What harm? She was curious to find out more herself.

'Yes. She was anxious to call on them – the Godfreys, I believe?' Cáit nodded.

'They have a mutual acquaintance,' Eliza added.

Cáit nodded again, more slowly. She seemed happy to let Eliza talk on but Eliza was reluctant to break any confidence Ruth had placed in her. There wasn't much more she could tell anyway. And Cáit no doubt knew more than she did about the neighbouring gentry.

'What are they like? The Godfreys?' she asked.

'Oh, a fine family! And a fine house. Any important person who comes to Portmagee is to be found at Beaulieu.'

'Is it a large family? Oh thank you, Mary Kate!'

Eliza paused to smile at the wispy girl who placed the plates in front of her and the boys with shaking hands. Her fingers were red raw. Eliza blushed as Mary Kate caught her looking at them. She snatched her hands away and her fingers disappeared up inside her sleeves.

'Go and see after the pigs, then take your own tea in the kitchen,' Cáit commanded.

With a whispered thanks Mary Kate was gone.

Eliza busied herself helping the boys with their food but she hoped Cáit wouldn't forget her question. She was intrigued now about the Godfreys. Maybe she would call there herself tomorrow on the pretext of meeting Ruth for the boat back out to Skellig Michael?

She needn't have worried. Cáit was primed with information and ready to share it.

'Let me think now. There's old Mrs Godfrey. Her son, Michael, and his wife and they've had six children, five living. It's a busy household. I hope Mrs Hunter finds rest there – if that's what she's after.' She paused, eyebrows cocked at Eliza then continued. 'The eldest daughter Maria must be, what now …? Eighteen, I suppose. Then Bella, she's only a year younger and a nice-looking girl but they do say she's a bit mausy. What's the fancy word they use for it again? Melan-something?'

'Melancholia?'

'The very one. What does it mean to you?'

'Well, someone who gets pulled down by life, I think.'

'Pulled down by life. That's a nice way of saying it. The next one is a boy, John – a fine lad, about fourteen, a pure Godfrey. And the next girl, Lucy, is the same. Where am I now? Is that four? The last one is the baby, Michael Junior, but he must be seven now or near it at least. Their first boy, Robert, died in the cradle. May he rest in peace. 'Twas very sad to see the small coffin going for burial.'

Cáit made the Sign of the Cross and Eliza followed suit. The image of a tiny coffin, made for a tiny baby, flashed into her mind with such clarity she almost felt she had seen it with her own eyes. She blessed herself again, like a charm, to ward off any harm and keep her own baby safe, her three babies.

'Will you call to Beaulieu yourself, Mrs Carthy?'

'I might, Cáit. If I get the chance tomorrow before the boat goes back. I never asked Jeremiah the time.'

'I'll find that out for you. Now I'd better shift myself or Dan will be giving me dark looks.'

Cáit strained up from the table and smiled at the two boys who'd fallen into a food stupor.

'Did ye like that? Ye can have some lovely runny eggs in the morning. Can I get anything else for you, Mrs Carthy?'

'Thank you, Cáit. Not for tonight but I was wondering about Mass, for the Feast of the Immaculate Conception? Is there any chance we could get into town tomorrow?'

'Why don't you kill two birds with the one stone? I'll call you early and you can be in with Dan, get Mass inside and you'll be out again in plenty time for Jeremiah. I'll let him know your plans. How does all that sound?'

'Cáit, you're a godsend!'

Cáit laughed, naked delight on her face. 'My usual clients aren't so *flathiúlach* with kind words like that. Sure you might decide to stay here altogether.'

Eliza smiled but she thought immediately of James returning to a silent house and a cold bed.

Cáit read her mind. 'You don't like to be away from himself. I can see it. Isn't it marvellous? I said to Dan when ye were here last, there's a fierce *grá* between them two. Not like the two odd fish that came after ye – God forgive me.'

With that she was gone, calling out for Mary Kate.

Eliza was still smiling as she herded her two small men up the stairs. God must be kept going with all the forgiveness that Cáit needed.

Chapter 8

Joseph and Peter woke early the next morning, keen to be downstairs with the funny chickens and the nice, runny eggs. The dining-room was empty, apart from Dan who was mopping his plate clean with a hunk of bread.

'Well, now.' He beamed at the boys. 'Look who the cat dragged in. Did ye sleep well? Was that you I heard snoring the house down?'

Joseph giggled.

'I thought so. You want to travel into Cahersiveen with me, Mrs Carthy?'

'If it's no bother, please, Dan.'

'No bother at all. Sure I'll be glad of the company. It will save me talking to my dumb *asal*.'

Joseph creased into laughter again at the notion of Dan chatting to a donkey.

'Sit down there by the window and have a sup of tae to keep the chill out of your bones. 'Tis a fine day but there's a breeze that'd skin you.'

Eliza looked out the window. She hadn't thought yet to check the weather but was relieved to see that conditions were fine. They should be able to make it back to Skellig Michael without incident.

She felt like she was suspended between two worlds. It was a strange feeling, a type of exile. Longing to leave a place then, in the next breath, longing to return to it.

'I'll have the cart out front, Mrs Carthy, and we'll be on the road after your breakfast.'

Half an hour later Joseph and Peter were perched between Dan and Eliza, bellies filled. The donkey set an easy pace and Eliza was glad the going was gentle. Dan pointed out things of interest as they passed, like the small row-boat that served as a ferry across to Valentia Island, and the Protestant Church just outside the village.

As they crossed a small bridge, he said, 'Keep your eyes left now and we'll be passing Beaulieu House.'

The road curved around to the right. Eliza could see some outhouses by the water's edge but nothing more. The land here looked good, well-fed cows roaming in well-tended fields. She felt like she was seeing the colour green for the first time, the lush grass was such a contrast to the island that was turned to brown by the harshness of winter and would remain so until the summer. The road straightened then curved left again. Dan slowed the cart to a snail's pace as they drew level with an imposing stone entrance.

'Beaulieu House?' Eliza said.

'The very one.'

As the cart began to move off again Eliza had a clear view up the driveway. The large limestone piers and iron gate gave way to a curved driveway flanked on both sides by blackberry bushes.

'It looks very fine,' she said.

'Oh, that it is! On the other side of the house they've a walled garden with a pond that has fish in it only for looking at, not for eating, and a water wheel turned by a small stream.'

Eliza nodded. She felt envious now at the thought of Ruth enjoying all that Beaulieu had to offer. Was she taking a turn around the walled garden at this very moment as Eliza plodded by on a donkey and cart?

'Might we call on the way back, Dan? To see if Mrs Hunter is ready to leave?'

'We can, of course. As a matter of fact when the houseboy came for the bag yesterday he gave the message that I was to call today.'

The town was showing signs of liveliness as they arrived, as Friday was Fair Day and there were many carts travelling in the same direction.

Dan stopped and tied up the donkey, consulting his pocket watch.

'Look at that for timing! You're just in time for Mass. Go in now, let ye, and get a seat. I'll stay near the door, keep an eye on the cart.'

Eliza smiled to herself. She doubted the cart needed to be watched over. No doubt, as usual, the older men would gather near the church entrance and exchange their news in hushed whispers. And they said women were bad for talk!

Inside, she led her boys by the hands up to the midpoint of the church. She could feel eyes on her back. A stranger in town, they'd be trying to place her. She just hoped Joseph and Peter would be good and quiet. The last time they'd seen the inside of a church was before they left Ballinacourty. She sometimes felt like time was standing still on Skellig Michael but when she saw the changes in Joseph and Peter she couldn't deny its passage. The boys were looking around, taking in the thatched roof, the damp stone walls, the simple altar with the startling gold of the tabernacle.

Eliza bent and pulled them close so she could whisper. 'If you're very good now and stay quiet for Mammy, you'll get something nice after.'

Joseph's eyes widened. He had a better understanding of what that promise might mean. He frowned at Peter and raised a finger to his lips. Peter did his best to copy his brother, with comical results. Joseph had to stifle a giggle with his hand.

The arrival of the priest brought hush to the loud whispers of the congregation. Eliza paid little attention to the priest's words. She knew the service by heart so could follow along without thinking. The routine was comforting and she allowed her mind to wander to the people who had filled in around her. They could just as easily have been her own parish folk back home. Of course there was no mutual recognition, no slight smile, or nod of the head. But she was glad to be among them all the same.

The boys behaved impeccably and, as soon as they re-emerged into the frosty morning, they clamoured to know what their reward would be.

They made their way up to Main Street where the traders had their wares on display. Eliza tasked Joseph with finding a nice trinket for his daddy and a small toy for himself and Peter to share. This freed her up to carry out her own business, secreting away a few Christmas surprises for the boys. She was revelling in the voices all around her, cresting and falling in Gaelic. They made a change from the incessant racket of the seabirds. On days when she was feeling good she loved to listen to the birds and identify them by their call. But there were often days when she just wished they'd quieten down.

Joseph was at her elbow now, pointing to a pretty display at the next trader's stall. 'Look, Mammy – for Daddy!'

It was a clear bottle, inside of which was a tiny and intricate ship. Eliza knew lighthouse men in Waterford who whiled away the hours making such things. She wondered if James would like to have it or not, but Joseph was insistent and she gave in. The boys agreed on a bag of marbles between them and their spree was complete.

Eliza scanned the crowd for Dan. He hadn't been outside the church when she came out. There was no sign of him here either but she figured he'd be able to track her down. Up ahead on the left she saw a sign for tea-rooms and she led the boys in. They warmed their hands on mugs of sweet tea and devoured currant buns.

They were just finishing when a barefoot boy burst in, sweeping his hat off to reveal a head of ginger curls.

'Are you the lighthouse lady?' he asked.

Eliza was so startled she answered before she'd had a chance to consider whether or not she should. 'I am.'

'Dan O'Connell is waiting for you outside Bowlers'. He says to come down to him in your own time. He's there now.'

Eliza smiled. Clearly the message was come in your own time but ideally that would be straight away. She beckoned to the serving girl and settled up, then stood to gather her purchases.

The boy stepped in. 'I'll give a hand with those, missus.'

Eliza was grateful. She felt a bit guilty about how much she had spent already and no doubt this young man would be expecting something for his trouble. But her lower back was killing her and it felt like her bump had grown, the skin was so stretched tight around it. She longed for her own bed and gritted her teeth at the thought of the donkey and cart, the boat ride and the long walk that stood between her and it.

'Thank you,' she said. 'What's your name?'

'Paudie Bréannain.'

They set off down the town, Peter and Joseph gawping at Paudie, hanging on his every word.

'Have ye heard of Daniel O'Connell?'

Eliza nodded. Who hadn't? That was like asking if you'd heard of the Queen of England.

'He came from here, you know. He lived in a grand house out in Derrynane but he was born here. There's talks of building a fine church in the town and calling it after him.'

Eliza's eyes widened. Calling a church after a politician, not a saint? Unlikely! But she let Paudie gabble on.

Dan was standing by the donkey and cart, rubbing his hands together to warm them. The redness of his cheeks suggested he'd warmed his insides already.

Eliza looked around for Paudie. He had disappeared.

'Where did Paudie go?' she asked Dan. 'I wanted to give him a coin.'

'I've taken care of that, not to worry. His father owes me a few pound so Paudie runs errands for me when I'm in town.'

Dan helped her into the cart then lifted the boys in too.

'He's a great lad for the tall tales,' she said.

'How's that?'

'Talk of a church being built here and named after Daniel O'Connell!'

Dan blessed himself as he climbed up to sit beside her. 'May he rest in peace! 'Tis true. There's talk of that alright.'

'Really? A church named after a layman, not a saint?'

''Twould be a novelty alright.'

'Will it happen?'

'Sounds like it will. Mind you, I only come into town for the news and a good half of it I pay no heed to. But sometimes the maddest-sounding schemes are the ones that come about.' He sat smirking, looking out to the road ahead as his donkey plodded its familiar path. 'He's a relation of mine, you know.'

'Paudie?'

'Yerra, no! Daniel O'Connell! Did you not notice we have the same name? Do you think Mrs Hunter would have stayed with us if she'd known that?' Dan laughed loudly.

Eliza smiled but her heart sank. She hadn't thought about Ruth much in the last few hours and she didn't relish the thought of her company again.

The cart turned in at the entrance to Beaulieu House and started up the drive.

They hadn't got far when a skinny girl came running to meet them.

'Joanie – how's things?'

'Good now, Dan, thank God. I've a message here for the lighthouse lady, from the other lighthouse lady – the one inside with Mrs Godfrey.'

'Oh?' Dan seemed nonplussed. 'Are we not to come in so?'

Joanie looked down at her feet and shook her head. 'I don't think so. The lighthouse lady is resting upstairs and not leaving today and Old Mrs Godfrey isn't well. She had Doctor Shanahan out already this morning. I was told to give ye these.'

She handed two envelopes to Dan then took off again towards the house.

Dan muttered under his breath as he wheeled the cart around again to face the road. He handed Eliza the two envelopes, his jaw clenched.

A quick glance told her one was addressed to her and one was blank.

They moved off at a quick trot. The boys laughed in delight at the jostling of the cart and Eliza gripped the seat under her.

'Did you ever hear the likes of it? That was some welcome!' Dan was outraged.

She held the envelopes tight without looking at them again. She was dying to know what they said but she'd wait until she was alone.

The winter sun was glinting off the water in Portmagee village as they reached it. Eliza thanked Dan and hurried inside. Leaving the boys with Cáit, she went upstairs to her room.

Sitting on the bed, she looked the two envelopes over, then opened the one addressed to her.

Beaulieu House,
Portmagee,
8th December 1867

Dear Eliza,
Please excuse me for not meeting you in person today. I have made a decision not to return to Skellig Michael until after I have had my baby. The Godfreys have kindly invited me to remain at Beaulieu House. I will return to Skellig Michael when I am able.
I beseech you please to give the other letter to Edmund.
Yours in gratitude,
Ruth Hunter

Eliza stared at the unopened envelope. She was to give this to Edmund, knowing what it contained? Was she the cause of this? If she hadn't planned this trip would Ruth have remained at her husband's side? She thought of James warning her to stay out of the Hunters' business. Well, she was well and truly in it now whether she liked it or not.

Chapter 9

Jeremiah and the oarsmen manoeuvred the boat in until it was snug against the landing. The swell was more pronounced today and they had to time their leap ashore well or risk an icy plunge. The banter hadn't been as free-flowing on their return journey and Eliza sensed the men were intent on getting back to safe harbour.

There would be no time for Edmund to pen a reply to Ruth. She could barely imagine the torture of having to wait to communicate your feelings to your deserting wife. Or, maybe it was worse to sit and wait on the mainland and get no response to the missive that announced your desertion.

Eliza turned back to Jeremiah once she was on firm ground.

'Thank you, Jeremiah. We'd be well and truly lost out here without you.'

Jeremiah climbed down into the boat and waved a large, calloused hand to dismiss her thanks. 'Don't mention it,' he answered. 'Don't the Commissioners pay us well for our trouble? And sure I love the bit of exercise. It keeps me from seizing up. You mind yourself now, missus. Please God it will all work out.'

The men pushed off and pulled hard on the oars.

'*Daddy!*'

Joseph let go of her hand and ran up the road. Eliza turned and her heart rent in two. One half floated with joy at the sight of her own James. The other sank at the sight of Edmund. Should she hold off on giving him the letter until they were at their own thresholds? No. What could she possibly say when he asked why Ruth wasn't with them?

James was smothered by his two boys, Joseph talking a mile a minute.

Edmund passed him by and stopped in front of Eliza. He scanned the horizon a moment as if Ruth might be en route in some other craft.

Then he looked straight into Eliza's eyes.

She saw the briefest flicker of grief and anger and then acceptance.

'Ruth?' he asked.

'She's well. There's nothing wrong with the baby or anything but ... I'm sorry.' She handed him the sealed, blank envelope. 'That's for you,' she added, feeling foolish.

He stared at the blank surface. Then he slid it into the pocket of his overcoat, nodded at Eliza, turned and walked back up the lighthouse road, alone.

Eliza made a quick supper for the boys. They were nearly asleep on their feet after the journey but rallied to give James his ship in a bottle. He covered them in delighted kisses and helped Eliza settle them to bed. Then he led her to the seat by the stove. He knelt down and removed her boots.

Eliza sighed. No wonder she'd been dying to come home.

'You must tell me about Ruth.'

'I will in a minute – pass me that parcel from the table.'

He handed it to her. She eased the twine off and lifted out a crocheted baby hat.

'Do you like it?'

'It's lovely but I don't think it will fit me.' He sat it on top of his head and twisted and turned for her to admire him.

'Stop! It's for the baby.'

'What are you buying hats for? Aren't you well able to crochet yourself?'

'Are you cross with me?'

'Don't be silly!' James pulled up another chair to face her. He lifted one of her feet onto his lap to stroke it.

Eliza groaned in pleasure.

'I was buying things for Christmas and I felt it would be nice to get something for the baby too.'

'Of course. Now I suppose you'd better tell me the big news. Why did Ruth not travel back with you? I presume she stayed in Portmagee. Oh God, Eliza!' He sat up in mock alarm. 'Don't tell me you pushed her out of the boat on the way home!'

'May God forgive you, James Carthy. I don't dislike her that much. I just find her hard to figure out. She gave me a letter as well.'

She passed it to James and he read it in silence.

'That's that then.' He remained quiet for a few moments. When he spoke again there was a new seriousness in his voice. 'What about you?'

'What about me?'

'Would you like to go ashore to have the baby?'

'And surround myself with strangers? No, thank you. But I did wonder about maybe bringing a handywoman out. Just to help when the baby comes and for a few days after. I meant to enquire with Cáit, she'd know of someone, but somehow Ruth's letters knocked it out of my mind.'

'Of course, Eliza. I'm all for that. God knows I'll not be much use to you at the birth. I'll send word with Jeremiah the next time he comes.'

Eliza rested her head back. She felt a strong sense of relief. A handywoman would come when she needed her.

Chapter 10

Eliza saw little of Edmund over the next few weeks. According to James, he was his usual taciturn, efficient self. Typical of the man. She didn't expect Edmund and James to have heartfelt exchanges up at the lighthouse but surely it would be natural to make some mention of the fact that his pregnant wife had left on a boat and not returned?

She turned her attention to Christmas preparations. The house needed to be cleaned and decorations had to be found or made.

She was dusting the shelves of the kitchen dresser the day before Christmas Eve when there was a knock on the front door. She opened it to find Edmund, carrying a crate.

'I thought I'd leave these in with you. You have more mouths to feed.'

She stared at him, lost for a moment. She glanced at the contents of the box: cured beef, dried fruit, some boiled sweets and more. His Christmas provisions that had come out with Jeremiah's boat.

'But won't you want these?' she asked.

He looked down at the floor. There was a long pause and it felt to Eliza like they were both holding their breath. There was no harm in what she had said except it had reminded them both of the solitary Christmas that lay before Edmund.

He looked up at her, expressionless.

'I won't require much. If I'm short of anything I'll call.'

Eliza couldn't think what to say so she nodded and then he was gone.

By the time James returned from duty the house was transformed. Eliza had decorated the fireplace with sprigs of bright red-berried holly and some garlands of ivy that she had brought from Cahersiveen and kept in water and she was ensconced by the warm stove, feeling festive.

James looked at her with concern. 'You're pale. There's nothing stirring, is there?' He placed his hand on her large belly.

Eliza laughed. 'No, I think this baby is happy to stay put. I should be fine until sometime in February, after Saint Brigid's Day.'

'Stay where you are and I'll make our tea.' James opened the pantry door and let out a low whistle. 'Mother of God! Who's going to eat all this? We'll be fat as fools.'

'Edmund brought in a box to add to our own Christmas stuff – he insisted that he had no need of it. Isn't it awful, James? To think of him next door with no one and us in here, all together and happy.'

'I don't know, Eliza. I see that man every day and I can't say that Ruth leaving has knocked a stir out of him.'

'But it must have all the same. And at this time of year. Well, it makes you remember, doesn't it? I've been sitting here thinking back on Mammy and Daddy when we were small and Daddy coming home from Dungarvan with the cart loaded up with fine things. All this warmth and togetherness makes you feel the absences all the more.'

James nodded. 'Let's ask him in.'

'For dinner?'

'Yes, we'll have to share watch from five, but …'

'Will you ask him so? I'd feel a lot better about it.'

'I will. Now let's sit up for our tea.'

Eliza poured out full cups while James settled the boys to the table. Her heart was glad. They were blessed and it was only right that they would share their good fortune.

'Mammy, tell us again about the angels and the Baby Jesus.'

Joseph was hunkered down in front of the small crib, unable to take his eyes off the sacred figurines. It had been her mother's and one of the few personal things she intended to take with her, wherever James' job took them. Eliza had broken with tradition by including the Divine Infant before Christmas Eve night but the boys were in awe of it.

Eliza leaned across Joseph's head to adjust a sprig of holly that had gone askew on top of the crib.

'They say that there's an angel in every spike of the holly leaves and that they're watching over the Baby Jesus and all of us and any prayer you say tonight will be answered.'

Joseph's eyes widened.

'What will you pray for, Joseph?' she asked him.

'I don't know, Mammy. I'm thinking.'

'What are you thinking?' James brought a gust of wind in with him.

'He's trying to decide what to pray for.'

'Well, I'm praying for a bite to eat. This fasting lark is well and good if you haven't hard work to do.'

Eliza laughed at the pinched, starved expression on her husband's face. She'd never known anyone to enjoy their food as much, yet there wasn't a pick of fat on him. She swept her arm towards the laden Christmas Eve table. The boys had been as good as gold all day and had allowed her to get on with cooking and now they would break their fast in style. James let out a low whistle.

'I knew I did well in letting you marry me.'

'Oh, you let me, did you? I recall it a bit differently. You'd have been an old bachelor if I hadn't taken pity on you.'

James placed a kiss on her forehead as she fought to keep the smile from her lips.

'I'm a lucky man. Now, can I sit to eat?'

'You cannot. We've another job to do first.'

Eliza retreated to the kitchen then returned with five candles in candlesticks. She put the largest one in the centre of the windowsill with two smaller ones on either side.

'*Me see!*' Peter was trying to clamber up her leg.

James hoisted him up and brought Joseph to the front so they could all watch.

'These candles are for Mammy and Daddy, and these are for you two.' Eliza lit each in turn.

Joseph broke the reverential silence, pointing at the largest candle. 'Is that for the baby?'

'No, pet, that's the *coinneal mór* – that's for all the family. Peter, you must light that one seeing as you're the youngest, for now.'

James let Peter hold the taper with him. The lit candles made a mirror of the darkened window. Eliza allowed herself a moment to admire the handsome tableau they created before they all sat to eat together.

As soon as he finished, James went to take first watch, groaning that he'd never be able to stay awake after that fine feed.

Eliza cleared away the remains of their meal while she waited for Edmund to arrive. She hoped it wouldn't be an awkward evening. What would they talk about? And how would she avoid mentioning Ruth?

'God bless all here and a Happy Christmas!' Edmund shut the door with more force than was needed. The draught created by his arrival caused the *coinneal mór* to extinguish.

'*Mammy!*' Peter began to cry and buried his face in her legs.

Edmund stood, frozen to the spot.

'Peter, don't worry,' Eliza said. 'We'll light it again.'

She smiled at Edmund but felt a ripple of concern deep in her stomach. She was a practical woman but the old superstitions were hard to ignore completely and it was considered a bad omen if the *coinneal mór* was accidentally quenched.

'I'm sorry,' Edmund said. 'The wind ...'

Elia relit the flame, reassured by its dancing warmth.

'It's no bother, Edmund. Is it a bad night out?'

'It's a bit blustery, but there's no cold.'

'Well, that's good at least. Have a seat here at the table.'

'I don't know about that.'

Eliza stopped in her tracks, confused. Was he refusing to eat?

'Up around our way they don't fancy a mild Christmas.'

Eliza understood. He meant the weather.

'Why's that?'

He sat and Eliza placed a glass of whiskey in front of him.

'They say a green Christmas makes a fat churchyard,' he said. 'You see, a cold, crisp one gives you a lovely spring and there's less sickness about.' He raised his glass then wet his lips with the whiskey. 'Your health!'

Eliza widened her eyes. Was he going to be miserable and spoil the evening with his talk of illness and graveyards?

'Well, we're all in good health, thanks be to God.' She put a plate of food in front of him.

'And you're well with the baby?' He nodded in the direction of her stomach.

'Yes, thank you, all is well.'

'That's it, Mammy!' Joseph stood up on his chair.

'What's what? Sit down before you knock something.'

'My prayer!' Joseph was too excited by his announcement to sit. 'I'll say a prayer for our baby, that it'll be here soon and it'll be a boy.' He sat down, delighted with his decision and gazed at the adults, awaiting their approval.

'That's a lovely prayer, Joseph.'

Edmund opened his mouth to speak but Joseph shot to his feet on the seat again.

'I forgot something. I'll say a prayer for your baby too.' He looked straight at Edmund. 'Do you want a boy or a girl?'

The silence grew thick as Eliza waited for Edmund's response. Joseph's innocent blunder had pulled back the curtain on Ruth's absence. She rubbed at a spot on the table, avoiding Edmund's eyes.

'I don't mind, young man, once it's healthy. I hope the baby and its mother will be with us all ... soon ...' He faltered. When he spoke again his tone was softer. 'Although I suppose I like the idea of a son.'

Eliza was shocked to see his eyes shining, just as she was surprised to hear him say, 'the baby and its mother'. Not 'my wife' or 'Ruth' or even 'Mrs Hunter'.

'Eliza, this food looks delicious. Let me say Grace.'

He bowed his head and blessed the food in a strong, clear voice. *Be present at our table, Lord. Be here and everywhere adored. These mercies bless and grant that we may feast in fellowship with Thee. Amen.'*

Then he lifted his fork and began to work his way around the plate of food with no apparent enjoyment, pausing to chew each mouthful studiously before embarking on the next.

Eliza was glad to have the excuse of putting the boys to bed, leaving him to finish his meal alone.

Joseph and Peter settled down to sleep with their bellies full of apples and sweets. Eliza returned to the table, fearful that Edmund would stay to pass the evening with her. An awkward silence would be unbearable but it would be even worse if she couldn't trust herself not to mention Ruth. The loud ticking of the mantel clock drew attention to the silence engulfing the room.

Eliza felt compelled to say something but to her great relief Edmund rose and put on his coat.

'Mrs Carthy, I wish to thank you for that wonderful meal. You have been most kind.'

'Don't mention it, and please, for the love of God, will you call me Eliza?'

'Right so – Eliza it is from now on,' Edmund replied, with warmth in his voice.

Eliza wondered if it was brought on by the whiskey he'd drunk. His green eyes penetrated her own and she had to look away.

'You know, I've been observing you, admiring you, I suppose,' he said. 'And I think you're a good woman. James is a lucky man. I wish I was as lucky as him. I wish I had what he has.' He leaned down so close to her face she could feel his breath on her cheek and half-whispered, 'I'm glad we've had a chance to spend this time together, Eliza. I feared it might be inappropriate without your husband present but I see now that's as you wished.'

Without warning he lifted her hand from the table and held it, lightly stroking it with his thumb. He held her gaze for longer than necessary, then with a slight squeeze he released her hand, smiled and slipped out the door before she managed to reply.

She stood up abruptly, knocking the chair to the ground behind her. Her stomach churned. She could not believe what he had implied. That she had arranged the evening to be alone with him? Had she understood him correctly? He knew damn well that both he and James couldn't leave the lighthouse at the same time. The strange moment left her feeling sick and she struggled to turn her mind to anything else. She banged the crockery into the kitchen sink, harder than she intended. The brief exchange felt like a transgression although she knew she was blameless. It was infuriating.

She went to bed but spent a sleepless night revisiting the events and wondering if she should tell James.

Christmas morning was bright and dry. Eliza struggled to keep her thoughts on the boys as they squealed with excitement over every little surprise.

James woke late, having gone to bed in the early hours. She watched him move about, wondering if she should mention what had happened with Edmund but she didn't want to spoil their morning.

'Will I take them out for a while to give you a chance?' he asked.

'Oh yes. I'm worn out from them.'

James pulled her close and kissed her. 'Happy Christmas, Eliza. Isn't it great to think that this time next year we'll have three lovely babas at our table?'

'Please God.'

'You're a good woman, Eliza.'

She burned red at his echo of Edmund's sentiments, glad that James couldn't see her face. 'Is Edmund coming in for dinner today?' she asked. She hoped her tone wouldn't betray her.

'No, I tried to insist on it but he was adamant. He said he had encroached on our hospitality enough last night and was grateful for it. He's offered to do my shift as well as his own so I don't have to be in the lighthouse until the morning.'

'Did you accept?'

'Well, I wasn't going to. I wondered if it looks bad for a Principal Keeper? Then I thought of you down here alone with the boys. If you had someone to keep you company, Ruth, even … So I said yes. I'll take him up some food later on.'

'Speaking of food,' Eliza removed herself from his embrace, relieved to hear she wouldn't have to face Edmund again, 'I'd better get on or there'll be no dinner.'

James gasped, his face in mock horror, then he called to the boys.

'Joseph, Peter – we'll go for a walk. Mammy said if we don't get out from under her feet she won't feed us.'

Eliza lifted the lid from the pot of spiced beef that had been simmering on the stove all morning. The rich scent of sugar, cloves and warm meat filled the kitchen, reassuring the boys that there would be food, despite Daddy's messing.

When she finally finished her cooking, she set the table and sank into the soft cushions of the rocking chair beside the stove. She shut her eyes and put her hands on her swollen belly.

'Hello, baby,' she murmured. 'Happy Christmas.'

Her eyes shot open as the baby moved, deep within her. She laughed as she felt a hard lump press against the inside of her taut skin. She thought it was a hand or maybe an elbow. The baby was still head up then, she would have a few more weeks at least.

'Stay where you are awhile, pet. Mammy is not ready for you yet.'

She kissed her fingers then pressed them to her bump, smiling.

The door nearly came off its hinges as her three men burst in.

'Ye must have guessed I was sitting down,' she teased.

'Stay there. I can put the dinner up,' James said.

'You cannot! After all my hard work. Wash your hands and you can carve the beef.'

When all the food was on the table, Eliza sat down across from James. Joseph and Peter couldn't keep their eyes off the food.

'Can we start, Mammy?'

Joseph's hand was already reaching but James placed his on it to stop him.

'We'll say the prayer before meals first, Joseph. Close your eyes.'

Eliza could see that it took every ounce of his powers to obey his father. James winked across at her before he shut his eyes and adopted a serious tone. He thanked God for the food, his work, their health, the boys, the new baby.

Eliza opened her eyes, sure he was finished, but he continued.

'We thank Edmund for doing Daddy's work today and allowing him to take this meal with his family. Amen.'

The boys echoed his amen, then clamoured to fill their plates.

'Ah, lads – your eyes are bigger than your bellies. Go easy!' James laughed.

Eliza's appetite had deserted her at the mention of Edmund's name. She tried to enjoy watching them all wolf it down, while she forced herself to eat a little. She rubbed at her bump in an absent, circular motion.

At last, James pushed his empty plate away from him and scraped his chair back.

'God Almighty, that was a fine feed.' He rubbed his own protruding belly. 'Look, boys! Who am I like?'

Joseph dissolved into giggles, followed by Peter who had no idea what was so funny but was caught up in the giddy moment.

'Are you having a baby too, Daddy?' Joseph could barely get the words out and he squealed even more when Eliza flung crumbs across the table at James.

'Stop! Eliza, stop!' James laughed. 'I'm not joking. I won't eat again for a week, I'd say.'

'Really? So you don't want any pudding?'

James dropped his head as if to consult with his belly.

'There's a small bit of room left for pudding.'

Joseph was given the honour of setting the brandy-soaked pudding alight. By rights it should have been Peter, being the youngest, but Eliza didn't trust him with a lit match and alcohol. James disappeared briefly to the lighthouse with a plate of food for Edmund. When he returned they settled by the stove as the evening gathered in.

The boys begged for a story and Eliza dozed while James told them how Christmas was spent when he was a young boy. They wilted, first Peter, then Joseph, so James carried them to bed. Eliza snoozed in the firelight before making herself climb the stairs to bed where she slept, her secret untold.

Chapter 11

The days following Christmas ebbed away. Eliza marked *Nollaig na mBan*, the special celebration for women on the sixth of January, with a quiet prayer for the women in her family. She'd give anything to have them by her side now. She wondered what Hanora would have to say about Edmund's behaviour on Christmas Eve. She was older and more fiery and Eliza's heart sank at the thought that her sister would have dealt with the situation there and then and not have it bothering her ever since, as it was bothering her. Hanora would probably write it off as the idiotic fumbling of a drunken eejit. Having so much time alone, with just the boys for company, wasn't helping Eliza. She found herself replaying the scene over and over in her mind, trying to understand what had happened. She had given him no invitation surely, had she? She batted the thoughts away and tried to keep her mind busy.

When she wasn't mulling over Edmund's improper approach, she thought about her baby. She tried not to focus on how her body felt. She knew she could drive herself crazy trying to read into her aches and pains. With every day that passed she was no closer to securing a handywoman. And with every passing day she was closer to the birth. She promised herself that she would keep calm. The baby would come when it was ready and she had to trust in herself.

Joseph had been three weeks early, taking them all by surprise. Especially Eliza, as every older woman the length and breadth of the place had told her first babies are always slow to come. Peter had arrived as expected but it was a difficult birth. She had been glad of the handywoman's expertise and the herbal poultices that helped her to heal. She thought of Ruth, in the lap of luxury no doubt in Beaulieu House, with houseboys and girls at her command and nothing to do but nurse the baby and rest once it was born. She envied her for a moment. But then she pictured the austere, grey stone of the place, and the stilted talk in a house full of strangers.

Eliza felt that she was getting slower on her feet and the boys were getting faster. Peter was sure and steady now and pushed himself to breathlessness to keep up with his older brother. Joseph was starting to grate against the confines of the yard and asked Eliza a thousand times a day if they could go into the lighthouse, down to the pier, up to the monastery. Eliza had laughed out loud at that request. Wherever she managed to waddle to she was certain it wouldn't be up six hundred and eighteen steps. Joseph took to playing lighthouse keeper, with himself as Principal Keeper naturally, and Peter as his assistant. On fine days they ran around the yard launching ever more complex rescues that required rope, empty crates for boats and planks for oars. When the mist came down hard Joseph took up position inside the front window with a small round stick as his telescope and reported his sightings to Peter who soon lost interest in this version of the game.

They screamed with joy one day when a bedraggled white goat returned to them, bleating plaintively. It was Bawneen, Little

White, the sole survivor by the looks of things. Eliza was relieved that it meant no more black tea for her.

She tried to tune out Joseph's constant chatter in an attempt to soothe a menacing ache behind her eyes. She had slept badly, finding it impossible to get comfortable. As soon as she did and was starting to doze, James crept in from his shift, dropped straight to sleep, and lifted the roof with his snores.

So Joseph had to repeat himself more than once before she registered what he was saying.

'*Jeremiah and Tom!*'

'What?'

'They walked past the window.'

'Where?'

'They're going to see Daddy.'

No, thought Eliza. They're going to see Edmund.

'Mammy, come on! We want to see Jeremiah!'

He pulled at her hand, trying to shift her bulk towards the door. Eliza felt for him. She knew exactly what he was feeling. They hadn't laid eyes on another soul since before Christmas and Jeremiah's visits always meant something new and exciting: provisions, tall tales, a new song or some news he'd picked up. He was their lifeline, their reminder that life on the mainland still went on and that there was a whole world out there.

Eliza was wary. He must have news of Ruth, otherwise he'd have called to her first, as he always did. What if it wasn't good news? Babies didn't always arrive in rude health. She had passed by enough *cillíní*, burial grounds for unbaptised babies, to know that. And Edmund was as unfathomable as ever. Even if it was good news, who knew how he might react? He might jump for joy or the news might affect him as lightly as the water washing over the rocks below them. She didn't really want to see him either, having successfully avoided meeting him since Christmas.

'Why don't we wait here, Joseph?' she said. 'Jeremiah will come and see us when he's ready.'

Joseph hunched his shoulders up to his ears and stuck out his lower lip. But he didn't have long to wait as a few minutes later the front door opened and James bounded in.

'A girl!' he announced. 'Clara! A bit early but fine and strong and doing well. The doctor was called for yesterday morning. The little girl arrived in the evening, a fine pair of lungs on her they say and all is well, thanks be to God!'

'That's good news.' Eliza felt herself relax. 'Edmund must be delighted.'

'I suppose so. All he said was "Good, that's good". Jeremiah shook his hand and gave him an envelope, a letter from Ruth I'm guessing. It got kind of awkward then with us all standing around and Edmund saying, "good", over and over. So I thought, we'll have to make a toast! Wet the baby's head! I said I'd come down and get a drop to do the job."

'Will you tell Jeremiah to call down to us for a cup of tea when he's ready?' she asked.

'I will.' James blew her a kiss as he headed back out the door with a whiskey bottle and four glasses.

She prepared the tea with a thousand questions running through her mind. How was Ruth? Did Edmund even ask? When would she come back? Would he go to the mainland? She'd ask

Jeremiah some of them but others were the kind of question only a woman could answer.

Jeremiah entered with 'God bless all here!' and removed his peaked cap. Tom remained in the yard, lighting his pipe and leaning on the front wall, surveying the grey sea. The other oarsmen never ventured up this far, preferring to stay with the boat.

Joseph and Peter ran to Jeremiah, nearly flattening him in the process.

'Tell us a rhyme!' Joseph demanded.

Jeremiah laughed. 'Wait till you hear this one!

'One, two, three,
Me mother caught a flea,
She put it in the teapot
And made a cup of tea.
The flea jumped out,
Me mother gave a shout
And in came Daddy
With his shirt hanging out!'

The boys fell about the place, giggling. The sheer nonsense of it thrilled them and Eliza couldn't hold back her own smile.

'Will I pour you a cup of tea, Jeremiah? No fleas in this pot!'

'Do, so.' He laughed.

'And Tom?'

'He'll be in in a minute. All the excitement was too much for him.'

Jeremiah took a large swallow of his tea. Eliza buttered thick cuts of bread, fighting back the urge to throw all her questions at him at once.

Tom came in, nodded and stood with his back to the stove, warming his hands.

'There's tea poured here for you, Tom,' Eliza said.

Tom joined them, winking at the boys who were trying to repeat Jeremiah's rhyme.

'You brought good news, Jeremiah,' Eliza prompted, unable to wait any longer.

'I did. Any new baby born is good news for sure.'

'Have you visited Beaulieu House?'

'Oh God, no!' he laughed. 'Cáit went over, with a few things for Mrs Hunter and the baby but she got no further than the front door. All we know is what the house girl told her.' He drank his tea and took big bites of the bread.

Eliza held back for a few minutes, giving them a chance to eat and drink. When she couldn't wait any longer she said, 'Edmund was pleased, I take it.'

Jeremiah put his cup down and looked her in the eye.

'He said nothing more once Mr Carthy left to get the whiskey, only kept on writing in a big book.'

'The log.' Eliza wondered was he recording the birth of his first baby or the day's weather.

'I suppose so. When Mr Carthy came in with the bottle of *uisce beatha* to wet the baby's head, Mr Hunter said he wouldn't take any! Can you believe that? His own child! No one said he had to get blind drunk, only wet his lips. So what could we do? Myself and Tom and Mr Carthy took a drop and Mr Carthy wished the child good health. And all the while the child's father was behind us scratching away in his – what did you call it? Log? As if we weren't in the room! I don't mind telling you but I'm glad that child is born and I'll be gladder still if I've no more messages to relay for him, or her.'

Eliza nodded. Jeremiah was clearly annoyed. There was no point making any more enquiries about Ruth. But there was one question she needed to ask.

'Jeremiah. Do you know any handywoman?'

'There's Margaret O'Donoghue.'

'Would she come out to me, do you think? I'm surrounded by men out here. I'd be very relieved to have a woman by my side when my time comes.'

'Sure, that's natural. I can ask her. When is – when will – when do you need her to come?'

He turned a deep red, gesturing at her belly. Eliza looked down at it herself. The poor man. She didn't mean to embarrass him. Maybe she should have let James ask but she couldn't risk him forgetting.

'Not for another month anyway. Would she come out around Saint Brigid's Day, do you think?'

'I'll ask for you. I'm sure she'll have no problem with it. Her own husband is a fisherman and she goes out with him at times so she'll have no fear of the trip.'

Eliza swallowed. She hadn't even considered that the handywoman mightn't travel by boat! She fought to calm her fears. Jeremiah would look out for her, she trusted him. He rose now and put on his cap. Tom rose too as if in response to a signal.

'We'll be off. Thank you for the tea and God bless.'

They were no sooner out the door when James stormed in, letting it slam behind him. Joseph and Peter stared with round eyes as their father banged four empty glasses and an almost full whiskey bottle onto the table.

'*You won't believe this.*' He was red-faced with temper.

'Jeremiah told me.' Eliza put her hand on his arm to steady him. She didn't like the boys seeing him so riled up.

'Told you what? That that oddball turned his nose up at a drop to wish his baby good health?'

'Yes.'

'Well, that's only the half of it.'

'Go on.'

'He said nothing else until Jeremiah and Tom were gone and do you know what he said to me then?' James was apoplectic. 'He said he didn't think it was proper for a keeper to take a drink while on duty. And that he knew of keepers who were relieved of their position for such behaviour. Can you believe that? The cheek of him! He's above there writing in the logbook, probably making a note of my misbehaviour. Jesus Christ! Wasn't I only being friendly and trying to make the most of things?'

'I know.' Eliza understood his anger. The thought entered her mind that she should tell him now of Edmund's behaviour towards her. But she feared it would send him over the edge. He had earned his position the hard way and she didn't want anything to threaten that. She had replayed the scene so many times since that she was starting to question her understanding of it. And what would James make of her not telling him sooner? Would he think she had encouraged Edmund?

James closed his eyes and took a breath. When he opened them again he smiled at the boys. They smiled back, relieved.

'Don't mind me. I'm only giving out. I'm due to inspect his dwelling this week. I'll be sure to give the place a good going-over. No harm to remind him who's PK around here.' He chuckled, but there was no warmth in it. 'Now I'd better go up again before he records me as missing in action.'

Eliza followed him to the door, her opportunity missed. She knew now that she would probably never tell him. It would bring too much trouble to their home.

'I'm sorry,' he said, smoothing a few strands of her hair. 'I shouldn't bring my bad humour to you. He vexed me something unreal. Is there any chance, I wonder, that he'll follow his wife to the mainland and seek another post?'

Eliza thought about it. It was possible. Ruth didn't have much good to say about living on Skellig Michael. She might not even return. Then Edmund might leave. That would be a relief to them all.

Chapter 12

Eliza was glad when Saint Brigid's Day came around on the first day of February. It hadn't been a bad winter but she was glad that spring would soon arrive.

'Brigid!'

'What's that?' James was finishing his last sup of tea before going up to relieve Edmund. Eliza had her head bent over the sink, struggling to rinse the soap from her hair with cups of water. The large bump was impeding her progress and she sighed with pleasure when James took the cup from her hand. His large hand riffled gently through her thick hair, stroking her scalp, as he doused her with scoops of water. She shut her eyes to savour the sensation then carried on.

'I'm just thinking. If it's a girl, what about Brigid?'

'I thought you'd decided on Mary for a girl? That's what you had in mind the last two times.'

'Yes, but I was thinking of maybe changing it.'

He squeezed the water from her hair then she felt him lay a towel across her shoulders. She straightened, wrapping it around her head.

'Go with the name you've always had in mind. There's bad luck in changing that now.'

He kissed her, then slipped out the door as the boys clattered into the kitchen.

She had promised they'd gather some rushes for the Saint Brigid's Cross. The day was fine and a gentle breeze caressed their uncovered heads as they followed the road down towards the landing. They started up the south steps towards the monastery, their progress slow.

'*Mammy, I found some!*' Joseph doubled back to her with a tuft of grass.

'Good boy, we'll see can we find a few more.' She tucked the useless blades into her apron and puffed her way up the steps behind him, holding Peter by the hand. Her lower back ached and she could feel every morsel of the food she had eaten threatening to rise up her throat.

'Wait, Joseph, we won't go too much further.'

He returned to her side, hopping from foot to foot. She knew he was dying to go up all the way to the monastery, or to Christ's Saddle at least. Peter tugged at her hand, urging her on.

'Oh look, there's a fine bunch!'

To the left of the steps was a small bunch of rushes, just enough for a cross. Joseph wrenched them from the earth and skipped down ahead of her. As she neared the final steps she could hear him chattering on.

'And we're going to make a cross now. Mammy said it will keep us all safe.'

'A cross?'

It was Edmund. Eliza wiped her forehead with the corner of her apron. She was hot and flushed and in no mood for company, certainly not Edmund's.

'Hello, Edmund.'

'Hello, Eliza. Joseph here was telling me about the cross you're making. You're very adventurous to be up those steps at this time.' He smiled and let his gaze slip to her belly.

Eliza flushed again but this time in annoyance. Was he telling her how to take care of herself? How patronising! Did he never tire of telling people how they should carry on? She crossed her hands over her bump.

'I'm able for it, thanks be to God.'

He continued smiling at her and she was grateful when Joseph broke the silence.

'You have a new baby.' Joseph spoke as though announcing it for the first time. 'When can we see it?' He squinted against the sunlight that cast Edmund's face into shadow.

Eliza couldn't see Edmund's expression but the silence spoke for itself.

'Soon, I hope. Mrs Hunter and the baby will return soon.'

Mrs Hunter. The baby. It was odder he was getting, Eliza decided.

'We'd better let you be getting back,' she said. They were going the same direction probably but Edmund would move faster.

'Will we make you a cross?' Joseph asked.

Eliza was lost for words again. Was every encounter she had with this man doomed to awkwardness? 'Joseph, I don't think Mr

Hunter wants a cross.' His faith held no such beliefs as far as she knew.

'Well, that would be lovely. But I'd say you have just enough there to make one fine cross for your house. I tell you what. I'll come and see it when it's done.' Edmund smiled at Eliza. 'How about that?'

Eliza reeled. She did not want this man in her house again, certainly not without James present.

Edmund set off down the road at a quick pace. Eliza kept her eyes on his back until he disappeared around the bend. He was like a man without a care in the world. Like a man whose wife was not miles away and whose first-born child he had yet to meet. He was as unreadable as the sea around Skellig Michael.

Eliza's legs were a dead weight by the time she got home. She longed to rest but the boys wanted to make the cross straight away. She laid the rushes out on the table, selecting the longest and straightest to start with. She wove them around each other and was transported back to her mother's kitchen watching her weaving crosses for the entrance to the house and the cowshed, believing it would guarantee the wellbeing of all in the house in the months to come.

She was pleased with how it came out. She sprinkled it with holy water and Joseph said the prayer, then she put it on the mantel out of harm's reach. She didn't trust herself to climb onto a chair, so James could hang it over the doorway when he returned.

She was hungry again and so were the boys. As she prepared their meal she hoped they'd settle early – her bed was calling to her. The baby was pressing on her, lower down than before. She racked her brain trying to remember how it had been in her final weeks before Joseph and Peter arrived but the memories were lost to her. There was one thing she did recall from before. When it started, she would know.

Eliza woke. The black sky outside the bedroom window bore no bright stars. The waves crashed on the rocks below and the slate roof tiles were rattling in the wind. The weather the last few weeks had been very unsettled, with choppy seas and strong breezes that kept all boats from their landing. Every night she prayed that the morning would bring a clear sky and her handywoman. But now the wind had strengthened into a storm. That must be what woke me, she thought.

As her mind moved towards wakefulness she felt wet beneath her. Had Joseph or Peter climbed in beside her and wet the bed? No, she was alone. James was on duty at the lighthouse. Her stomach flipped over as she realised what had happened. Her waters had broken. The baby was on the way.

Swallowing down the panic, she rose, shivering, making sure not to wake the boys. She peeled off her soaked nightgown and put on another, stripped the sheet from the bed and crept downstairs. She tossed it into a basin in the back kitchen and stood still in the dark silence, wondering what she should do now. She had heard of women whose babies didn't come for a long time after their waters went and others who were delivered within the hour. She had no idea how this would go. All she could do was wait. She moved toward the armchair and, feeling the chill in the room, wrapped a blanket from the chair around her shoulders and crouched down to light the stove. As she did a wave of pain crashed down upon her, moving across her abdomen and lower back. She cried out, gasping for breath. It stopped as suddenly as it had begun. She wiped tears from her eyes. She hadn't known she was crying. She longed to give in to the tears now that she was aware of them but she knew she had to stay strong. She was alone. On an island. The baby was coming and no tears could change that. With a trembling hand she lit the kindling in the stove and sank back into the chair. Another pain hit her, this time deeper and longer. She panted hard until it passed, reminding herself that it would end, it couldn't go on forever. Just as she felt she would have to scream out, it stopped.

'Mammy, what's wrong?'

Joseph and Peter appeared in the doorway, their too-big nightgowns trailing nearly to the ground. Peter leaned into his brother, sucking his thumb, half asleep still. Joseph was wide awake, wide-eyed and scared.

'It's alright, boys. I was lighting the stove and I burned my hand. Why don't you go back to bed awhile? It's not morning yet.'

'I'm hungry.' Joseph watched her with a wary eye as if he sensed the fear in the room.

'Come in, so. Peter, lie down there a while.'

Peter stretched out on the settle bed under the window and fell back to sleep straight away. She covered him with the blanket.

'Is your hand alright?' Joseph's eyes followed her around the room.

'Yes, pet. Don't worry. I've the fire going now so I'll make your porridge.'

The edges of the sky were tinging with faint light. It looked to Eliza like the day would be dark and broody. An intense squall of wind swept around the house and the flame in the stove dipped, then flared.

'The storm woke me.' Eliza smiled at Joseph.

She stirred the oats, feeling like they would never cook, then finally put the bowl down in front of him. He lifted a spoonful, blowing hard to cool it fast.

She paced up and down the room, on the alert for another pain. It came on her without warning, sending a ring of fire down her spine. She clenched the back of a kitchen chair and bent double, letting out a deep, guttural groan.

'*Mammy!*' Joseph shouted. '*What's wrong?*' He started to cry.

The noise woke Peter who took his cue from his frightened brother and started to wail even louder.

Eliza caught her breath and straightened. She felt weak and sat down hard on the chair, wiping the sheen of sweat from her face.

'Boys, *shush*! Don't be scared.' She managed a smile. 'The baby is coming, that's all.'

Joseph's gaze shot to the door as if expecting a baby to walk through it.

I have to get the boys away from the house, she thought. It was bad enough having to labour alone. She could not face it with two frightened boys in her care. What could she do? The kitchen clock showed seven. James wasn't due down for another three hours. Edmund must be next door asleep. She'd have to rouse him so he could go and get James. She threw her hooded cloak around her shoulders and slipped her bare feet into her boots.

'Stay here,' she told the boys. 'I'll be back in a minute.'

She opened the door and a gust of wind swept in, wrenching it from her grip and slamming it into the wall. Joseph cried out and Peter skittered across to slide into the seat beside his brother, who put an arm around him. Eliza struggled to pull the door shut behind her and stumbled out into the wild morning. The cloak slipped from her shoulders and within seconds her hair and nightgown were drenched by the heavy rain driving in from the demented ocean.

She staggered to Edmund's door, trying to pull the cloak around her for decency. She knocked on, then hammered at, the door with the flat of her hand.

'Edmund!'

Her voice was no competition for the swirling, howling gale and she despaired that he would even hear her. Just as she raised her hand to bang again, the door swung open and a shocked Edmund stood there, rubbing at his eyes. He took in her bare legs, unlaced boots, soaked night clothes and terrified expression.

'I need your help!' Eliza shouted. *'It's the baby!'*

His eyes went to her swollen belly and the blood drained from his face. He stepped back from the threshold, pulling her in out of the storm. He pushed the door shut behind them and scanned the room as if he could find what she needed there. Eliza wished again that she had the company of an experienced woman. Men were useless in these situations. She'd have to spell it out for him.

'The baby is coming. James is at the lighthouse. The boys are awake and I need him.'

Edmund pulled on his coat and boots, springing into action.

Eliza screamed as another pain started to build. Then she was inside it. It was its own world and she was no longer in Edmund Hunter's house. She groaned, emitting a noise that she never knew was within her. When it passed she opened her eyes to see that she had gripped Edmund's arm throughout and he was frozen to the spot. She removed her hand as if scalded.

'*Go!*' she commanded. '*Be fast!*'

Edmund shot out into the dark morning and she struggled through the driving rain to her own door.

The boys hadn't moved from their spot and watched her in silent terror.

'It'll all be fine now. Edmund is gone to get Daddy.'

She struggled upstairs to her room and changed out of her wet clothes once more. She felt weary and it had only just begun. How would she get through this? Her eyes settled on the rosary beads hanging on the mirror. They were worn, wooden beads, scented with rosewater, that her mother had given her. She was ashamed to admit that they were rarely used by her. It was her mother's fervent fingers that had burnished their smooth roundness. But they looked like solace to her now. She took them down and sat on the edge of her bed, running her thumb and forefinger across each bead. The front door slammed.

'*Eliza!*'

She could have sobbed with relief at the sound of James' voice. He crossed the space to the bed in one stride and wrapped his arms around her.

'Eliza! What do you need? What can I bring you?'

She felt calmer already in his presence and didn't have to pretend to be brave anymore.

'A handywoman.' She tried to laugh but it came out as a sob.

'I know, I know. Sure, you would have her only for this blasted weather. But look, you'll be fine. You've done this before. And I'll help. My God, you frightened Edmund half to death. I'd say he'd welcome a drop now for his nerves. Duty or no duty.'

'You better go down to the boys. They're terrified. Put water on to boil. Bring up some linen.'

'Right. On the way.' James mock-saluted and moved to the door. He turned and looked back at her. 'I love you, Eliza.'

Then he was gone.

The wind outside had picked up again, sheets of rain were being blown sideways and a ferocious shower of hail battered Eliza's window.

When James returned she asked him to light a candle for her. The warm glow of it brought her comfort. He watched as she paced around the room.

'*Go!*' was all Eliza could manage as another pain swelled, crested and broke across her body. She rode it to its end. When she was out the other side she looked at James. His knuckles on the doorknob were white.

'Stay with the boys. If I need you, I'll call,' she gasped.

She drank her tea standing at the window, massaging her lower back. Between the pain and the blind panic she could feel something else. A sense of power. Outside her window, nature was riotous, destructive. Inside her another storm raged but it would be creative. The next pain disabused her of that notion. She was not in control of her labour, she was at its mercy. She took her mother's beads and sank to her knees beside the bed. She lowered her head onto her outstretched arms and began to recite the Rosary. She rocked backwards and forwards and prayed loudly through the next pain and the next. She was shivering and sweating at the same time. She had just begun a fourth Rosary an hour later when she was overcome by an urge to push. She didn't want to do it and it was all she wanted to do. She surrendered to it and felt as though she would be rent in two. In the next still moment she pulled clean linen onto the floor beneath her knees and then she had to push again, bearing down. She allowed her fingers to explore and, yes, she could feel the baby crowning. She was almost there. The next push brought her to the limits of her universe. The pain was infinite and she thought she wouldn't bear it but then with a whoosh she felt emptied.

The baby's head was free and with the next push she reached her hands back and into them was delivered a wet, sticky being.

She sank to the floor, laughing and crying. Ten fingers and toes, a little girl. A strong, mewling cry filled the room and Eliza sobbed with joy. Her baby was perfect. She wrapped her in a blanket and pressed the bundle to her chest. In response the baby started to nuzzle, seeking out a nipple on instinct. Eliza opened her nightgown and the baby latched on. Eliza allowed her head to fall back against the bed. She was exhausted. The only sound in the room now was the suckling of the baby at her breast. The storm had eased and it felt as if the house around her was holding its breath.

'We heard a cry.' James pushed the door ajar, averting his eyes.

Eliza surveyed the disarray around her. She was grateful for his discretion.

'We have a baby girl.' Her voice was husky, raw. 'Bring me a new blanket, and a scissors.'

'Right.' He was gone, clattering down the stairs.

'That's your daddy,' she told the baby who regarded her with a serious gaze, her tiny, red fists feeling the air of her new world.

Eliza and the baby dozed for the next few hours, rousing only to feed. She summoned enough energy to put the room in order. James followed her instructions to dispose of the cord, blood-soaked linen and afterbirth in the fire. As soon as she struggled into a clean gown and climbed into bed a wave of exhaustion swept her away. The rest of the day and night were like a fever dream, punctuated by brief moments of lucidity. James placing a cool hand on her forehead. The baby's wet mouth on her nipple. Joseph and Peter's excited whispers.

'Are you alright, Mammy?'

'I am.'

'What's she called?'

'Mary Carthy,' Eliza breathed out before slipping under again.

She woke in the dead of night, somewhat restored. James stirred but didn't wake as Mary's wailing filled the room. She lifted her to the end of the bed and changed her napkin, relieved to see the wet. Her heart swelled with love and pride. Her baby was here, alive and doing great. She dressed her, humming softly, then sat in the chair by the window to feed her. She guided her searching mouth, wincing as it clamped down on the raw nipple. Tears sprang to her eyes. She remembered this from Peter and Joseph. The initial euphoria of feeding well, followed by days of agony before it settled down again. She stroked her little finger along her baby's downy cheek. She would endure it all. It was worth it. Mary's head lolled, sated, already asleep.

Eliza put her back in the bed beside her snoring daddy, arranging the blankets around her so she was safe and snug. She stepped gingerly towards the boys' bedroom. They were knotted together in a tangle of limbs, sweaty foreheads and soft night noises. She smiled, then retreated as her stomach growled angrily. She was starving. She went to the pantry and smeared butter onto chunks of bread before stuffing them into her mouth. Her hunger amazed her. She felt as though she was outside of herself watching this ravenous she-animal who couldn't be satiated. Finally she drew breath and surveyed the damage. It looked as if a fox had got in. She tidied up and tiptoed back up the stairs.

The stars had all gone in. She lowered herself onto the bed, trying not to disturb Mary. She wished James would wake. She wanted to talk to him, to share the magic of the day, to relive the miracle of their beautiful new baby. She stared at the side of his face, willing his eyes to open but they did not. She looked at Mary, sleeping with her arms abandoned over her head, frowning. What did she have to frown about? Eliza shut her eyes. She was tired. She longed to gaze at Mary all night long. She was in love.

Chapter 13

'Eliza, there's someone here to see you.' James shook her gently awake.

Her eyes felt as though they were filled with sand and as her body came to life she started to feel the aches of childbirth. Her lower back was stiff and her breasts ached. Beside her on the bed, Mary slumbered. At the end of the bed stood a woman she had never seen before. Tall, with a strong chin and bright eyes, she had a reassuring, quiet confidence about her.

'This is Margaret O'Donoghue. Jeremiah brought her out, first chance, when the weather cleared.'

'A day too late, I see. But it looks like you managed well without me. Thank you, Mr Carthy.'

James got the subtle message and left the room.

'How are you feeling, Eliza? We'll go by our first names if that is alright with you?'

Margaret removed her cloak, placing it on a chair. She put her bag on the end of the bed and opened it.

Tears sprang to Eliza's eyes from nowhere and she covered them with her hand.

'Mother's tears,' Margaret spoke with kind pragmatism. 'You'll see more of them, no doubt. But this being your third you'll know that anyway. Now I'll take a quick look at you and then I'll see how the little girleen is doing. You called her Mary?'

'Yes, that's right.' Eliza felt like a helpless child in the face of Margaret's efficiency. She became aware of the messy room and its stale smell.

Margaret stood beside her pillow waiting, for what Eliza had no idea.

'Shift yourself down the bed now and I'll have a look.'

'A look?' Oh ... she meant to examine her.

Eliza blushed a deep red. She slid down until she was flat on her back. Margaret folded the blankets down, lifted Eliza's nightgown to her waist and parted her legs. She made quiet noises as she pressed and probed with still-cold fingers. Eliza tried to lie as still as possible with her eyes shut tight. She knew it was necessary for Margaret to check her, especially as she had been unattended for the birth, but she hated the discomfort and intrusion into her most private places.

'Right.' Margaret straightened up and turned away. 'You can fix yourself up there again.'

She opened the bedroom door and called down.

'*Mr Carthy! Could we have a bowl of warm water, please, and some linen?*'

Eliza winced as she moved around trying to cover herself up. Everything hurt.

'Does he know where to find things?'

Eliza nodded.

'You're lucky so. Many's the house I go into the man couldn't find the kitchen, let alone anything else. Tell me about the birth. Were you labouring for long?'

'Yes. Actually, no, I don't think it was that long. I can't recall, to tell the truth.'

Margaret laughed. 'That's a thing all handywomen will tell you. The way women forget their pains as soon as the baby is out. That's how we keep having them. I've five myself.' She threw her eyes to heaven.

'There was a storm.' Eliza wasn't sure if she was describing the weather or the birth. 'I was afraid.'

'And why wouldn't you be? God help you. I said to my husband when I saw the bad weather coming in – that poor woman out on the Rock with her baby coming any day and she waiting on me to land. I included you in my prayers that the baby might wait but sure didn't it turn out grand? You'll be back to yourself in a few days and you have a fine baby. You didn't think of coming in to the mainland? Like the other lady?'

'Mrs Hunter? No.' Eliza shook her head. 'I don't know anyone in the village and my place is here.'

'There's many women wouldn't have stayed here, you know. Fair play to you! Now, will we take a look at her ladyship? Come here to me, peteen!'

Margaret lifted the sleeping baby and started to strip her. Mary protested as the cold air touched her skin.

'A fine pair of lungs anyway, God bless her. She's a fine baby. Is she feeding for you?'

'Yes.' Eliza smiled. She was so proud.

Margaret dressed Mary again and handed her over. She watched as Mary launched herself at the nipple and Eliza grimaced in pain.

'That will ease.'

Margaret opened her bag and withdrew a small bottle. She dabbed her fingers on the open top and traced a cross on Mary's forehead. Then lay a white cloth across her for a moment. The *Bratóg Bríde*, a ribbon soaked in dew on St Brigid's Eve.

Eliza felt reassured by the combination of scientific practicalities and traditional *piseogs* that Margaret seemed to rely on.

'I'll stay around for a few days and give you a hand. Once you're on your feet I'll go back in. Jeremiah said he'll come out for me if the weather holds.'

Eliza felt the tears coming again. She supported Mary's head with one hand and reached for Margaret's hand with the other.

'Thank you.'

Margaret was a godsend. The boys got on great with her. James was happy going to the lighthouse knowing that Eliza had help. The thought crossed Eliza's mind many times a day – how would she ever have managed without her? Mary was thriving but waking throughout the night to be fed. Eliza often woke in those days to find Margaret up and about, with the house tidied and the boys fed and dressed.

But the good weather held and the day that Eliza had been dreading arrived, bringing with it Jeremiah to take her right hand away.

'Thank you for everything, Margaret. I don't know what I'm going to do when you're gone.' Eliza was close to tears. She palmed some shillings into Margaret's hand.

'You'll do just fine. Don't we all? But if I don't get home to my own gang they'll be feral. Now, mind my girleen!' Margaret planted a kiss on Mary's cheek as she slept in her cradle near the stove. 'And those two lovely boys. I've grown fond of them all. Make sure when you come ashore to bring them to see me.'

Eliza waved Margaret off, leaning against the doorway. Her respite was at an end and she'd have to find the energy somewhere to go on alone. She was startled as the Hunters' door opened and Edmund darted out.

'Is she gone? Have I missed her?'

'Only just. You'll catch her easily.'

Edmund ran out of the yard, leaving his front door wide open. Eliza spotted a white envelope in his hand – a letter. A letter for Margaret to take ashore to Ruth? The sound of the boys bickering drew her back inside. She smiled in at Mary, somehow still slumbering through the racket.

'We'll have to get you christened soon, missy,' she said.

The thought formed an idea and a plan that lifted her spirits. They had a reason to take a trip into the mainland. She'd discuss it with James later. And with the coming of spring there should be no shortage of opportunities.

Chapter 14

Five weeks later, on the eve of Saint Patrick's Day, the Carthys were down at the landing, waiting to get into Jeremiah's boat. Eliza could hardly believe that three months had passed since her last trip to the mainland. Jeremiah had joked that day about her and Ruth's full bellies. Now her little baby was tucked in warm against her chest, oblivious to whether she was on land or sea. Jeremiah had brought with him the supernumerary relief keeper who would cover James' duties during his short absence. James had given Jeremiah a letter to send on his last trip out to them. His request for a temporary absence had been answered quickly and Eliza was glad she wouldn't have to make this trip alone.

The relief keeper was a lanky man who looked to Eliza to be closer to her age than James', with dark hair and a tidy moustache.

James extended a hand to him as soon as he leapt from the boat.

'James Carthy, Principal Keeper.'

'Arthur Nelson.'

They shook hands. Then a silence hung between the men.

James seemed to be waiting for Arthur to say something more. When nothing was forthcoming James spoke. 'You're from up north? Have you been down this far before?'

'Aye.'

'To the Skellig?'

'Not the Skellig, no.'

Eliza coughed to suppress a giddy laugh she could feel coming on. She was so excited to go to the mainland and the awkwardness of the conversation between the two men was comical to her.

James glanced at her and tried again to engage Arthur.

'Well, we're happy to see you. My wife and I are taking our new baby ashore for her christening.'

'Aye.'

'You'll be here with Edmund Hunter, my Assistant Keeper. He's up at the lighthouse. I'm sure you'll rub along fine.'

At this the man came alive. 'Edmund and I know each other well. Our paths have crossed before. A *finer* light-keeper I've yet to meet,' he said, with heavy emphasis on 'finer'.

Eliza looked from one man to another. There was so much being said between them without words.

James drew himself up to his full height and nodded. 'It's good to know I'm leaving the light in capable hands.'

Arthur turned his back to James before he had even finished his sentence and took his bag from Jeremiah. 'We'll have it in tiptop shape when you get back.'

'It's already in tiptop shape.' James sounded defeated.

Eliza stepped closer to him and laid her hand on his arm.

'Well, I don't doubt it is with Edmund Hunter around,' said Arthur. 'I'm surprised he's not made PK yet. It won't be long, no doubt.'

James bristled. He watched the retreating Arthur making his way up the lighthouse road then shook his head. 'What an ignoramus! You'd think I'd offended him but, sure, I've never even met him before.'

'It sounds like he's a good friend of Edmund's,' Eliza offered by way of explanation. It was to be expected that he'd be strange and surly was what she meant to imply.

James frowned and took charge of Peter and Joseph, seating them low in the boat to protect them from the spray.

There was a swell and the crossing promised to be rough but Eliza was too excited to worry. She climbed into the boat beside her boys.

She watched over her shoulder as Skellig Michael receded. She sighed happily and thought of all the things she was looking forward to. A night in Dan and Cáit's, another night in the College Arms in Cahersiveen, a visit to the shops, Mary's christening.

There was the 'churching' for her too but she'd done it twice before and knew to take it in her stride. She smiled, remembering the kind, whispering voice of her old parish priest in Ballinacourty. Father Cantwell had been around a long time, had given her all her sacraments and even married her. He was so old by the time Peter was born she felt she would have to prompt him so he wouldn't forget the words: *'The Earth is the Lord's and the fullness thereof.'* It had felt more like a fatherly blessing than a cleansing of her sin. What was the sin anyway? To love and to bring a child into the world didn't strike her as sinful. She hoped the Cahersiveen priest would be as kind. She tried to recall him from Mass on their last visit but found he had made no impression on her.

Mary started to stir inside Eliza's shawl. She had fed well before they left and Eliza stilled now, hoping her baby would settle back to sleep in the warmth.

'God bless the child, missus!'

Jeremiah was smiling, his blue eyes bracketed by his seafarer's wrinkles. The rhythmic movement of his arms pulling on the oars didn't knock a stir out of him and he spoke as though it cost him no effort.

'Thank you, Jeremiah. She's a good girl, thank God.'

Eliza smiled down at the tuft of brown hair peeking above her shawl. It was vain of her but she loved the chance now to show Mary off to the few people she knew. Dan and Cáit, Jeremiah, Tom, and Ruth. Her heart sank a little. She didn't know what to do about Ruth. It would be rude not to call but then Ruth hadn't sent as much as a note since her unexpected decision to remain on the mainland. Edmund had been awaiting a reply from the letter that travelled in with Margaret O'Donoghue. He had asked James to enquire with Jeremiah if he had any letter and to bring it to the lighthouse if there was. There was no letter.

James kept his eyes on Skellig Michael as if he was trying to guess what Edmund and Arthur might be discussing, or plotting, in his absence. With every pull of Jeremiah and Tom on the oars they were leaving them behind and Eliza had the sense that James would rather stay on the island.

'We were all worried for you when the weather turned near your time,' Jeremiah said. 'I was fierce anxious to get Margaret out here to you. I'm only sorry we were too late but you made out alright in the end.'

'I did. Sure, it couldn't be helped. Is there word of Mrs Hunter? Is she still with the Godfreys?'

'Indeed and she is. We don't ever see her in the village. Some do say she goes to service with them on a Sunday but the baby don't be with her.'

Eliza grimaced. She knew that some women, especially in the upper classes, left the care of their children to others. But, much as she often longed for five minutes to herself, she couldn't imagine leaving Mary from her side.

'She's well though? And the baby?'

'Oh, she is by all accounts. A fine, healthy baby. All the women working there are mad about her. It's been a while since they had a little one at Beaulieu to dote over.'

Eliza felt a pang of jealousy. She had yet to lay eyes on Clara Hunter but she was willing to bet that Mary Carthy was every bit as adorable, if not more.

As they neared the mouth of Portmagee channel James rose to his feet, shielding his eyes with his hand.

'They've made some improvements, Jeremiah?' His attention was focussed on the Telegraph Field. From their position the roof of the building was just visible above the cliffs in Foilhummerum Bay.

'A few changes alright. But I don't know that they're improvements.'

'It's incredible.' James sat, leaned on the side of the boat and looked down into the depths as if hoping to catch sight of the telegraph cable. 'To think of all those words moving across the ocean floor beneath us at this very moment.'

Eliza smiled, glad to see that James had put the earlier unpleasantness out of his mind. The telegraph industry was becoming an obsession with him. She thought it would be nice if he was a cable man instead of a lightkeeper. Then she would be living in one of the fine new houses built for the cable workers in Valentia and enjoying the high life.

Mary was stirring in earnest now. Eliza felt her breasts swelling in anticipation of the next feed. She pulled her shawl up higher around her baby, hoping to delay it until she was in the warmth of O'Connells'.

Dan and Cáit greeted them like family. Before Eliza knew it Mary was gone from her arms and passed around to be admired and blessed. Cáit handed her back just as she started to whimper.

'Why don't you go and see to her in the front room there? I've a good fire going. I'll look after these boys for you. Are ye hungry, lads?'

Joseph and Peter nodded, wide grins spreading across their faces.

'James,' Eliza said, 'make sure they mind their manners.'

As she left the room Dan placed a creamy pint of porter down in front of James, settling in with one for himself to exchange news. James seemed more at ease now. No doubt he would be glad to spend some time away from Edmund and the tension that pervaded wherever he was.

They passed a fitful night in O'Connells', their sleep broken by the sounds of the pub and the pier. They had grown so used to the thick silence of Skellig Michael that it was hard to settle without it. The only one who slept well was Mary.

'She knows it's her special day,' Cáit said, tucking a silver coin under the white christening shawl for luck. 'Dan is ready with the cart to run ye in now. Make sure and call tomorrow before ye go back to the island.'

Eliza sat behind James and Dan with the boys. She craned her neck for a good view as they passed the gates of Beaulieu House but the glinting windows gave nothing away. She'd made no arrangements to call yet but she knew she'd have to.

As they disembarked on Main Street she spoke to Dan.

'Would you mind calling to Beaulieu House on your way out, Dan? Let Mrs Hunter know that I will visit with her tomorrow?'

'I will indeed, missus.'

'Thank you, Dan. And you'll come for us in the morning?'

'Straight after the breakfast.'

He wheeled the cart around and took off.

Joseph and Peter stared in amazement at the hustle around them. They might as well have been in Dublin or London. The street was full with Mass-goers dressed in their best for Saint Patrick's Day, with white crosses, shamrocks or green ribbon on their clothes. Eliza had found some green ribbon in her sewing box. Peter and Joseph had griped about wearing it but now they saw they were in good company.

'James, you'd better go and speak to the priest.' Eliza took hold of Peter's hand as a large group passed by.

'I know what I'm at, Eliza,' James said, his tone sharp. 'We'll take our things up to the hotel first and get settled in, then I'll go.'

They made their way up the steep incline of High Street and into the College Arms. Eliza found a spot inside the window so the boys could watch the comings and goings. She shut her eyes. She could feel the beginning of a headache. She missed the peace of the island. The pace of this day was so hectic already. And James' bad humour was spoiling it.

A serving girl had just put a pot of tea down for her when he returned, flush-faced.

'Come on. He said he'll do it but it has to be now, before Mass.'

'Now?' Eliza looked in dismay at the tea.

'Yes, now! He didn't want to do it at all only I explained that we'd come in from Skellig Michael and that we don't know when we'll be in again. He said we picked a bad day but he's waiting for us now so let's go.'

They hastened back down High Street to the stone church. The priest was waiting at the entrance in his vestments, tapping his foot and watching their progress. Eliza noted his impatience, his lack of interest in the boys or even Mary as she handed her to James. As she followed him inside the front door, she realised she didn't even know his name. A hard lump formed in her throat as she pulled her shawl over her head and knelt before him. He handed her a lighted candle and rattled off the words, sprinkling holy water in the form of a cross. She stumbled to her feet, reaching for the hem of his stole to hold as he turned on his heel and stalked towards the altar with Eliza following. She knelt again and he blessed her with more holy water then gestured for her to stand. It was over. She was churched, cleansed of her sin of childbirth.

'Where's the child?'

Eliza went outside and summoned James. He hurried to the font with Mary. Eliza watched the priest as he took her precious baby like a sack of stones and daubed her with holy oils and water. She stood poised, ready to snatch Mary out of his arms. He passed her back when she screamed with the shock of the cold water. Eliza wiped her head with the shawl and soothed her. She turned back to thank the priest but he was facing James with his hand outstretched for payment.

'Thank you, Father,' she muttered then led the boys to a seat.

James joined them, leaned forward onto the pew in front and sighed. 'I wonder now should I have left you and the boys to it? Was there a need for me to come ashore at all?'

Tears threatened Eliza's eyes again. James' disinterest, the rudeness of the priest and the memories of Joseph and Peter's christening days when they were surrounded by friendly faces made her feel lonely. She didn't hear a word of the service.

A fine feed of lamb and potatoes and a stroll around the busy streets tired the boys out. Eliza wanted to get them back to the hotel before the streets got too rowdy. The pubs were packed with people and the singing and dancing was starting to spill out onto the street.

That night the boys and Mary fell asleep quickly but the racket kept Eliza awake until the early hours. The sound of glass breaking, laughter, cursing, a failed attempt at a chorus – would it ever stop? Eliza wondered if any of these people had to be up in the morning. At some point in the night James turned his back on her complaints, sighing that he couldn't understand why she wasn't happy, then snored to the high heavens.

A hotel worker was busy sluicing down the path outside the front door when they came down for breakfast. The familiar face of Dan O'Connell appeared in the dining room as they finished. He was looking a bit green around the gills and didn't speak a word as he loaded their bags onto the cart.

'Are you well, Dan?' James smirked. His spirits seemed to be restored now that the time had come to return to the island.

'I've been better. There was a fierce session last night. The back of my head hardly touched the bed before I had to rise out of it again. Well, what did ye make of your night in town, lads?'

Joseph wrinkled his nose. 'It's smelly.'

Dan roared with laughter. 'You're dead right, boyeen! 'Tis much better where we are in Portmagee and God knows nothing can compete with the fresh air of the Skelligs.'

They set off at a fast pace. Dan must be keen to get back to his bed, thought Eliza.

'Did you give my message to Mrs Hunter, Dan?'

'I did that. She said call when you like.'

Eliza looked down at her dress and shoes. Was she presentable enough for Beaulieu House? Her shoes were good quality but scuffed and stained from the visit to town. But she decided she'd have to do, as Dan directed the cart between the impressive limestone pillars.

Chapter 15

The avenue curved to the left between rows of hedges that kept the house from view until the final turn. Three storeys, whitewashed, with a pretty bay window.

Dan stopped and Eliza climbed down, taking Mary from James.

'Can we come in, Mammy?' Joseph looked like he was about to leap from the cart to join her.

'No, Joseph,' James said. 'You'll come back with myself and Dan. We'll go and talk to the fishermen down the pier.' He turned to Eliza. 'Should we wait for you? Will you be alright?'

She nodded. 'I can walk back after or I might ask Ruth to organise a trap for me.'

She'd give anything to leave with them but Ruth was expecting her. She'd probably seen her by now anyway or been informed that her visitor had arrived.

Eliza took a deep breath and knocked on the imposing wooden door. A flushed, lanky girl of about fifteen years, with brown curls escaping from her bonnet, answered so quickly that Eliza suspected she had been watching from inside the door, anticipating her knock.

'Good morning. I'm here to see Mrs Hunter.'

Eliza heard an affected voice coming from her own mouth. Cop on to yourself, she thought, no need to be putting on airs and graces.

'Good morning. Mrs Carthy, isn't it? I'll show you in.'

Eliza recognised her now. It was the girl who'd come out to give them the letters from Ruth the last time they called. Eliza followed her and was disappointed not to see more of the house as she led her straight into a reception room at the end of a short corridor. The room was nicely furnished but what caught Eliza's eye was the large window that framed the sea beyond it, capturing the still blue of the channel.

'It's lovely, isn't it? Even nicer in the summer. But I suppose you get enough views out on the island. How old is your baby?'

'Six weeks. She was christened yesterday – Mary.'

'Ah! God bless her! She's lovely and quiet. Not like the one we have here.' She rolled her eyes. 'Sit down there for yourself and I'll go get Mrs Hunter.'

Eliza couldn't help smiling as the girl left the room. She was so forward. She couldn't be long in service and she wouldn't be much longer either if she didn't change her tune.

Eliza had a moment to admire the room again. Heavy mahogany furniture gleamed, the cream wallpaper gave the room a homely warmth and the upholstered chair she was in wrapped itself around her as if to encourage her to stay a while longer. Her disturbed sleep had made her tired and she could feel herself getting drowsy.

The sound of footsteps coming down the hall alerted her and she sat up straight.

'Now, Mrs Hunter, your visitor is in here.'

The girl's voice had changed. Eliza smiled. She wasn't the only one putting on airs.

'Thank you, Joanie. I know where to go.' Ruth clipped her words.

'Can I bring you some tea or anything?'

'No, thank you.'

The footsteps stopped outside the door.

'You can leave us now, Joanie.'

Ruth was clearly trying and failing to shake her off.

'Well, if you're sure you won't need ...'

'I'm quite sure. If Clara wakes, dress her up nice and warm and bring her down here to me.'

One set of footsteps retreated, followed by silence and a long sigh. Eliza held her breath. Ruth entered and Eliza stood up to greet her. It was a much changed Ruth from the one who had stalked, forlorn, through the village last December. She had lost the baby weight of course but was plump around the face, not as drawn, and there was good colour in her cheeks. She looked more at ease with herself.

'Eliza. Welcome.'

She leaned in to get a closer look at Mary, snoozing in her blankets. Up close Ruth smelled of scented powder. Eliza was aware of her shabby appearance and certain that whatever smells she had brought out from the town, scented powder was not among them.

'Is she always this quiet?'

Eliza tensed. Was there something implied in this question? She was already on the alert, anticipating offence.

'Yes, she's very good. Although she showed us what fine lungs she has yesterday when she was christened.'

'Of course. That's why you came ashore?'

'Yes. That and the churching.'

Ruth sat opposite Eliza who settled back into her comfortable chair again.

'Did you have a difficult time?'

Eliza was lost for a moment. Was Ruth enquiring about the churching?

'On the island, I mean. When the baby came. The women here were full of news about the storm and your handywoman not being able to travel.' She frowned at Eliza.

'Oh, yes. Everything worked out.'

'Good. I had Doctor Shanahan attending to me. I can hardly look the man in the eye since. I'm ashamed to admit the terrible things I said in my agony. I travelled through the pains of Hell, Eliza, and I truly thought my God had forsaken me. And do you know what I decided in that moment?'

Eliza was glad that the brief pause allowed no time for a response.

'I decided then and there that I had to find my own strength. And I did. I found a strength I never knew I had and I leaned upon it and it got me through. I think back to the woman who left Skellig Michael and do you know? I pity her. She was weak and didn't know what she was made of. Well, I do now and I'll tell you it is a different Ruth Hunter that's coming back to Skellig Michael with you today. I am a mother now and that changes everything.'

Ruth fell silent. Her brown eyes pierced into Eliza's and a faint sheen of sweat coated her forehead.

Had Eliza heard her correctly? She was coming back to the island?

'And I have a beautiful baby for my troubles. Ah, there she is now!'

A raucous scream rained down on them from somewhere up above. Eliza couldn't pinpoint the source as it filled the house right up to the rafters. The sound of it woke Mary who began to cry.

Joanie entered the room, struggling to soothe the red-faced creature that wriggled in her arms. She handed the bundle to Ruth.

'I don't know what's the matter with her, Mrs Hunter. I didn't do anything but you'd swear I scalded her.'

'I'll settle her, Joanie. Off you go.'

Joanie stalked out of the room and Ruth shushed Clara until she quietened.

Eliza drew in closer for a look. Clara had the same green eyes as Edmund and Ruth's pale colouring. She buzzed with energy, shifting about in her mother's arms as if she longed to take off.

'She's beautiful, Ruth. I think she has Edmund's eyes.'

Eliza realised that was the first mention of him. How strange that Ruth hadn't asked after her husband.

Ruth's body shifted so that Clara was out of Eliza's line of sight. Her shoulders set and when she answered her voice was colder. 'No, Eliza. You're wrong. She's all mine.'

Eliza walked around the room, jiggling Mary out of nerves more than necessity, while she waited for Ruth to gather her things upstairs. She was unsettled by the news that she was returning to Skellig Michael with them. Of course, it was to be expected. Ruth had said as much in her letter a few months previously but Eliza hadn't expected it would be today.

She tuned into the unfamiliar noises of the house. Laughter, voices winding their way through the corridors and unseen rooms, crying. Yes, there was the sound of someone sobbing. An adult, not a child. Eliza stopped walking and jiggling and listened. She could hear a voice, quiet but firm, responding to the crying but she couldn't make out what was being said.

Ruth walked back into the room and Eliza jumped, embarrassed at being caught eavesdropping. Ruth looked perturbed, her colour high again as she fussed at her sleeves.

'I'm ready to go, Eliza. The trap is waiting for us and we're to have another passenger – the girl Joanie.'

'To the village?'

Ruth was avoiding her eyes.

'I mentioned to Mrs Godfrey that I might look for a girl to help me with the house and Clara and she has insisted that I take Joanie. She has spent quite a bit of time with Clara so …' Ruth sighed and looked behind her, towards the door, where the sobbing had quietened to a pathetic sniffle. 'I'm actually very vexed but what can I do? The girl is useless and I suspect the Godfreys want rid of her. Both her parents are dead, her aunt placed her here, and unfortunately she's just not suited to service. But the Godfreys have been good to me – they probably feel this is a kindness as well, sending me off with a mother's companion. I'll have to take her. There's nothing for it. Maybe island life won't suit her either. I'll look for a replacement once it's decent.'

She looked for no comment from Eliza. Her speech was simply to allow herself acclimatise to the situation.

'Shall we go?' she said.

Outside the front door the Godfreys' trap was waiting, laden with Ruth's bag, a small bundle and a red-faced Joanie, sniffing and holding Clara with as much tenderness and enthusiasm as if she was a turnip.

Ruth climbed up and took Clara into her arms. She tutted. 'Joanie, do not have me listening to that sniffle. Pull yourself together.'

Joanie swallowed loudly and buried her face in her hands where at least the sound was muffled.

A sharp breeze came against them as they trotted toward the village, making idle chat pointless.

The driver deposited them at the pier where Eliza could see the boat was nearly ready to depart, the oarsmen taking their places. She started to make her way over to O'Connells' when James and the boys came out to meet her. He took in the collection of passengers with a glance.

'Is that Ruth? What's she at?'

'Coming with us. That's her companion, Joanie. Say nothing to the girl or she'll be in floods of tears again.'

His expression darkened. 'Go up to Cáit there. She wants to see you before you go.'

As Eliza made her way to O'Connells' she heard someone calling her name. She turned to see a smiling Margaret walking towards her, carrying her handywoman's bag.

'Eliza! I heard you were in. I'm dying for a look at my little girl.'

She peeked inside the shawl where Mary was snoozing. 'Ah, bless her! She looks fine and hearty anyway. She's doing well? How are you and the boys?'

'We're all well.' Eliza smiled.

Thoughts ran through her mind of Edmund's strange carry-on and how Ruth was returning all of a sudden and bringing another stranger into their midst, and the unpleasantness of the supernumerary keeper and how James had no patience with her since they came ashore but there wasn't time for all that now. She felt a reluctance to return to the island and relinquish the chance to get to know this woman more. To have a good talk. To have a friend.

Instead she said, 'The boys are in the boat if you want to say hello.'

Margaret's face fell. 'I'd love to but I'm on my way to a delivery. The Walsh girl from Kilkeavaragh – you wouldn't know her, of course. But I really shouldn't have stopped to say hello to you even. She needs me fast. Give the boys a big squeeze from me. We'll have to make time for a proper visit next time you're in.'

She rushed away, waving to the boys who stood up in the boat, waving back frantically and earning themselves cross words from James.

When Eliza returned to the boat with a warm loaf of Cáit's brown bread, everyone had boarded. Joseph and Peter were staring at Joanie who sat, gripping the edge of the boat with one hand, and the seat with the other, shaking her head in disbelief at the sudden change in her situation.

Eliza passed Mary in then took a seat beside Ruth.

'Right so,' Jeremiah declared.

At his signal Tom undid the mooring ropes and jumped in, pushing off the pier wall with the oar.

A loud wail filled the air, causing Joseph and Peter to cry out and huddle close to Eliza. The sound was coming from the slip. She could see a stooped, shawled figure waving one hand in their direction. Everyone on the pier and the slip came to a standstill and Joanie cried out in terror.

'*Oh Jesus Mary and Joseph, we're all going to die!*' She began to sob.

'James?' Eliza looked to her husband for an explanation but he seemed as lost as her.

'It's the Kiely woman. She must have finally lost her mind,' Jeremiah said.

He maintained a steady rhythm with the oars but Eliza could see the colour had drained from his face.

Eliza looked back towards the woman. The sound was growing fainter as they moved away but with a jolt she recognised her. It was the keening woman she had seen with the funeral the first day they had left for the island. But now there was no sign of a funeral.

'I've seen her before, Jeremiah. What is she doing?'

'She's keening.' Joanie stared at Eliza, her lips quivering.

'I know. But why?'

'We're going to die!'

Ruth tutted while Eliza tried to assume an air of indifference but her heart was pounding in dread as they left the safety of the harbour.

Joanie began to pray under her breath and kept it up without pause. Eliza was soon tempted to tell Jeremiah to turn around and row her back in. It was a rougher crossing this time and the keening had frightened the wits out of Joanie. That's if she had any to begin with, thought Eliza. Every time the boat rose on a wave and landed with a thump her voice rose with it and a '*Dia!*' or '*Muire!*' escaped her clenched lips. Joseph and Peter looked as though they didn't know what to make of her, or Ruth and the new baby.

'God bless the child!' Jeremiah called out above the din of the oars and the prayers. 'Mr Hunter will be glad to see her no doubt, and yourself.'

'Indeed, Mr Trant.' Ruth sounded indifferent. 'Do you have many children yourself? Besides Tom?'

'I do. Tom is my eldest. I've three other boys and one lovely *cailín*.' He smiled. 'They're a lot bigger than your baby there but I remember those days well.'

'Who does your girl take after?' Ruth enquired.

'Oh, her mother's side, thanks be to God. I've no claim on her and isn't she better off?' Jeremiah laughed.

The boat rocked as the team of rowers drew them close to the island.

'Edmund has us spotted, I'd say.' James pointed up towards the lighthouse road where a glinting light suggested a telescope or binoculars. The swell was high, requiring Jeremiah and Tom to abandon their first manoeuvre. On the second attempt they drew level with the landing and James jumped out to hold the rope. Eliza followed him and helped Joseph and Peter.

She looked up the road. Strange that Edmund wasn't coming down to meet them, or the supernumerary keeper.

Joanie, Ruth and Clara were still in the boat.

Ruth nudged Joanie with her foot. 'See now? Nobody died. Get out there and I'll hand you up the baby.'

Joanie didn't budge. Her eyes scanned first the cliff-face towering above the little boat, then the churning waves beneath them, as if considering her fate. Ruth glared at her.

Tom spoke. 'Will you be alright, Joanie? You don't have to stay.'

It was the most Eliza had ever heard from him and she was shocked by the tenderness in his tone.

It snapped Joanie out of her stupor.

'What choice have I?' she spat at him, refusing to meet his gaze. She clambered out, took Clara and turned to face the road ahead.

'Thank you, Mr Trant.' Ruth accepted Jeremiah's hand to disembark.

A rogue gust of wind whipped her skirts and cloak around her and she kept a tight grip of his hand. She shouted to be heard above the wind. '*When will you come again?*' She sounded almost as forlorn as Joanie.

'A few weeks' time, missus, please God.'

'That'll do.' She released his hand and nodded thanks at the other rowers.

'I'll go and round up that Nelson fellow,' said James. 'It would be a shame if you had to leave him here.' He scanned the horizon where dark clouds charged towards them, a sinister cavalry.

As if summoned by James' words, Arthur Nelson appeared at the bend in the lighthouse road, tearing down it as if a pack of wild dogs was on his heels. The group stood in silence, watching his frantic approach.

He was shouting as he ran. *'Hang on! Don't go without me! I want off this cursed island!'*

Eliza held Mary tighter to her chest and nudged Joseph and Peter behind her legs. Arthur's face was pale, with black circles under his eyes and his trousers was ripped up one side. It was a stark contrast to the impeccable, self-assured man they had left here two days before. He brushed past the women and children and flung his bag into the boat, almost clocking Tom on the head with it.

'Steady on, man! What's the panic for?' James took hold of his arm.

'Let me go! Let me go!' Arthur's voice was laced with terror.

James released his grip on him and held up his hands. 'I've no bother letting you go. But what in the name of God is wrong with you? You're frightening the children.'

Arthur looked around him at the small group gathered on the landing as if seeing them for the first time. He shook his head and stepped closer to James. He spoke in a low voice but the wind carried his words to them all.

'You're a fool bringing your children to a place like this.'

'What are you on about?' James leaned in and sniffed the air. 'Have you been drinking?'

'I have not. I don't imbibe alcohol.' Arthur straightened up. He was coming back to himself again. He looked at Eliza. 'I don't mean to frighten anyone. But this island is no place for women or children. Or anyone for that matter.'

Eliza heard Joanie whimper and Ruth tutted loudly at her.

'Where is my husband?' she demanded of Arthur.

He looked at her, completely lost. 'Your husband?'

James explained. 'This is Mrs Hunter.'

'Well, sure that's part of it.' His voice quivered. 'I have no idea. I went up to the lighthouse last evening for my shift and when it was over he never showed up to take over. I was too terrified to leave the lighthouse after what happened so I didn't dare go looking for him. When the morning came I made my way down here to wait for the boat.'

'What happened exactly?' James sounded exasperated. The men were working hard on the oars to keep the boat steady at the landing. 'Tell me fast so you can get going.'

'I was between shifts so I thought I'd wander around, have a look at the place.' Arthur spoke more calmly now but his breaths were still coming fast and heavy. 'I was going up to the monastery when a rock came hurtling down the steps. If I hadn't stepped off the path as quick as I did it would have taken my head clean off.'

James nodded, serious. He wouldn't like something like that to happen on his station, thought Eliza, especially when he wasn't here himself. 'There are occasional falls of rock here, it's something we have to watch for, so it's not terribly unusual. Scary, I'd imagine, but –'

'Scary? This wasn't a rock-fall, Mr Carthy. Someone threw that rock at my head. Someone, or something.'

James guffawed. 'Now, Mr Nelson. I can assure you there was not another living person on this island apart from yourself and Mr Hunter.'

'Not another living person, no, but something.' Arthur nodded his head repeatedly.

Eliza could see from his face that he believed every word he spoke. The hairs were standing up on her arms and she was sorry that the boys were hearing this. They'd be scared out of their wits.

'What are you saying, man? That a ghost threw a rock at you?' James looked at Jeremiah and Tom to join in his mockery but their faces were like stone.

'I'm not a fool, Mr Carthy. I reasoned with myself, exactly as you are now, that it was a natural event and nothing more. But as I was making my way back down the steps I was thrown to the ground.'

'You fell.' James' tone was flat.

'*I was thrown.*' Arthur clenched his fists. He was working himself up into a state again. 'The same as if someone had come up behind me and shoved me down. But there was no one there. No one at all!' His voice rose, shrill now. '*There is a presence on this island – and it means harm!*'

'Away with you into the boat now,' James snapped. 'I don't know that you're cut out to be a lightkeeper if you're going to carry on with this nonsense. For God's sake, man, a rock fell then you tripped. I'll put it in the logbook.'

James ushered him into the boat where he sat hunched, staring up at the cliff-face as though expecting to see something dreadful there. Tom pushed the boat out with his oar but his eyes were on Joanie. Ruth nudged Eliza who had to restrain herself from throwing off her arm. The young girl was clearly in distress.

'I wonder where Edmund is.' Eliza hoped her words would be wounding but Ruth just shrugged.

'We'll see him soon enough.' She turned her attention to Clara, relieving Joanie of her bundle. 'Come on, my darling, let's go see where you and your mammy will be living.'

Eliza fell into step beside James, and Joanie followed them.

'What did you make of all that?' Eliza asked.

'He's not right in the head, if you ask me. An awful load of nonsense. A 'presence'. Did you ever hear the like?' James scoffed. 'This is one of the holiest places on the face of God's earth.'

'But they do say the monks came out here to fight the devil.' Joanie piped up behind them.

James stopped walking and regarded the pale young girl.

'Joanie, you're welcome to Skellig Michael. But you need to put all those silly ideas out of your head now like a good girl and we'll all get along fine.'

The atmosphere was sombre as they made their way along the lighthouse road. The breeze whirled around their heads, making conversation pointless.

James carried a tired Peter as far as the front door then left them to go to the lighthouse.

'I'd better go see can I track down my Assistant Keeper.'

Chapter 16

Inside Eliza stripped the boys of the extra clothing that had kept them warm on the boat ride and lit the stove. Peter stretched out on the bench beside it and dropped straight off to sleep.

The door flew open just as she was about to serve their tea. It was James with Edmund, whose arm was draped around James' shoulder.

'Eliza, give me a hand!'

She rushed to close the door behind him.

'What's happened? Is he hurt?'

'Dead drunk. I found him on the floor of the outhouse with an empty bottle of whiskey beside him. Can you move Peter so I can put him there to sleep it off?'

'Why didn't you take him to the lighthouse? Or take him back to his own wife?'

'It's against the rules. No person under the influence is allowed in the lighthouse. And I figured I'd better bring him here to sober up or Ruth would be packing her bags again.' He groaned. 'Can you just move the child?'

Eliza clenched her jaw. Yes, rules were rules but was it proper for him to be left in her house? In this state? She did not feel comfortable after how he behaved last time but of course James knew nothing of that. She brushed the curls out of Peter's eyes, gently calling his name. She didn't want to startle him. Although he'd surely get a shock at the sight of Edmund and the state of him. Her hand went to Peter's forehead. It was burning hot. She called his name again, louder this time. He opened his eyes for a moment before they sank shut again. Eliza scooped him up into her arms and headed for the downstairs bedroom. He'd be cooler there. It was probably the heat from the stove, she reassured herself. She could hear James groaning as he relieved himself of the dead weight of Edmund who began to snore loudly.

James came to lean in the bedroom doorway. 'Can you believe this?' There was a hint of scandalised glee in his voice. 'The Dutiful Edmund Hunter, drinking on the job! Of course, I'll have to write an official account – there might have to be disciplinary action. Are you listening to me, Eliza?'

'I couldn't care less right now about Edmund Hunter and his blasted wife!' Her voice was shaking.

'What's the matter?' James moved further into the room.

'Peter's not well. He's burning up and I can't wake him.'

James placed his hand on Peter's forehead. 'Well, let's not worry. It's a bit of a fever but you've nursed the boys through those before.'

Eliza was close to tears. Yes, she had nursed the boys through fevers before. But never like this. In the middle of nowhere, with a small baby to care for and a man passed out drunk in her kitchen. She felt hopeless and angry and refused to look up as James left the room. She heard the front door shut. Edmund's snoring was interrupted by the insistent cry of Mary looking to be fed. She pulled a blanket up to Peter's chin and straightened up.

She ignored Edmund as she tended to Mary, put Joseph to bed and kept an eye on Peter. He hadn't moved since but he was sleeping soundly. James was right, she needed to have more faith in herself. It was just a fever, a chill from the damp drizzle that had coated them on the journey out. She sank into the chair beside the stove, the fire long since extinguished from lack of attention. She hadn't had a chance to keep it lit and remembered now that not a bite nor a sup had passed her lips since they got home. She thought about getting up again to prepare some food but the tiredness won out. She closed her eyes, tempted to just rest where she was.

'Oh Eliza, what must you think of me?'

She sat up with a jolt.

Edmund. She'd almost forgotten he was there since he stopped snoring. He swung his feet to the ground and dragged himself into an upright position, smacking his lips and grimacing. She could smell the stale whiskey from where she was sitting. He lowered his head onto his hands and groaned.

She felt not a jot of sympathy for him. If his stomach heaved and his head pounded, he'd brought it on himself. She had a child in bed ill, through no fault of his own.

'*What have I done? What have I done? Catherine!*' He bit down hard on his lip and released a shuddering sigh.

Eliza stared at him in disbelief. Had he forgotten her name? As he sat in her kitchen sobering up after too much whiskey?

'I'm sorry,' he said. 'You must allow me to explain.'

'I require no explanation from you, Edmund.' She just wanted him to leave. If you owe anyone an explanation, she thought, it is your wife next door with the baby you've yet to meet.

'No. I must.' He looked up, his eyes pleading with hers. 'I suppose James will write a report? This is terrible. Terrible! I've ruined everything. I swear to you, Eliza, I am not a drinker.'

'James will give you a fair hearing.' She stood up, trying to indicate to him that their conversation was over.

But he appeared intent on continuing. 'He will. He's a fair man.' His voice shook. He took a deep breath then rose to his feet and leaned heavily on the mantel.

'When you left. You all left. And Jeremiah had no letter for me.' He shook his head. 'I thought, I'll be alone forever.' He turned to face her, hands outstretched and shaking. 'I was left before, Eliza. By someone I loved.' He pressed his hand to his heart as if the love, or the hurt, was still there, buried deep. 'May God forgive me, I loved her more than I have ever loved Ruth.' He squeezed his eyes shut. 'Catherine. She worked in one of the big houses and we took to walking home together by the shore. She was light and free and Ruth started to look dull and heavy to me. She weighed me down, while Catherine allowed me to soar. I was all set to break off my engagement.'

He opened his eyes again and Eliza could see he was close to tears.

'But Catherine came to me one evening with the news that her family had bought passage to Canada and she was going with them. She knew my people would never accept her and she believed she was saving me from a lifetime of grief. I was a coward.' He struck his chest with his clenched fist. 'I didn't fight for her, I just let her go. I married Ruth and I convinced myself that the best thing, the most important thing, I could do in my life was my duty. I had to make my head rule my heart.' He stopped pacing and sat back down on the settle bed. 'But now there is a child, my child. And I want to love my child. Here is someone I can love with no falseness, and it is also my duty to do so, and isn't that just perfect?'

He lifted his gaze and stared into Eliza's eyes.

She breathed out slowly. She had been holding her breath throughout. What could she say? Yes, she knew what it was to love her children but the rest of it was foreign to her. Love in her mind, and in her life, was a simple, untarnished thing.

'You know,' he continued, his voice low, 'it has crossed my mind more than once how like her you are. In your looks and your ways.'

Eliza looked away, sickened. He shouldn't say these things to her.

He took a step towards her suddenly and pulled her into his arms. He put his hand on her chin to force her face towards his. Her stomach churned at the nearness of him and the stench of stale whiskey, and her heart thumped. She pushed hard against him and he stumbled back onto the bench.

She was shaking. Neither of them spoke. Into the silence came a barking cough that repeated and repeated, then a pitiful call of '*Mammy!*'.

Eliza turned away. '*Get out, Edmund!*'

Peter needed her. And this foolish man before her needed to face his wife.

A few hours later Eliza woke to light creeping in around the shuttered windows. She stretched, her neck and shoulders tight and stiff. She had fallen asleep when Peter settled. Her mind had been whirling with worry about him and the turmoil that Edmund had created, but the deep silence of the island had drawn her down into a dreamless sleep. Peter was sleeping easily now that the worst had passed. Illness was always at its most menacing in the dead of night. He had coughed for hours, gasping for breath in between, crying with the pain brought on by the racking fits. She had tended to him as best she could, rubbed his back, fed him warm drinks to soothe his throat. But she could not breathe for him.

With a pang of guilt she recalled the sound of Mary crying, wanting her, but she hadn't left his side. He had gripped her hand, pincer-like in his terror, his face beetroot-red and furrowed like an old man's. She'd had to stay. Eventually exhaustion had got the better of him and he'd fallen asleep. She could see now, by the last of the candlelight, that his face was grey and sheathed in sweat. Her mother had always said a fever is nothing to fear – the body has to fight its own battles. But that was before the famine fever took so many and she learned how much there was to fear and how quickly a body could succumb. She knew that Peter didn't have famine fever, he had croup. Joseph had a mild dose of it when he was younger but nothing like this. The cold, damp weather would be no help. She hoped they would get a few clean, crisp days to kill off the germs.

The door to the bedroom creaked open. Eliza put a finger to her lips to quieten whoever it was but Peter didn't stir.

James stood, silhouetted by the dawn light, with Mary in his arms. He handed Eliza the soiled, sodden baby.

'How is he?' he asked.

'Better now, sleeping at least.'

'That's good. It looks like someone else needs you now.'

Mary was trying to manoeuvre herself into position for a feed. Eliza felt another rush of guilt. How could she care for them all? She was just one woman.

'Edmund arrived for work as I was finishing my shift. I wasn't sure if he would. A new man, all scrubbed up and shiny. He apologised but we said no more. I have to decide now what action I must take, if any. But I need to get my thoughts clear first. A couple of hours in bed will help. I'm as tired as a dog.' He kissed Mary on the forehead. 'Be good for Mammy.'

Then he left, shutting the door behind him.

Eliza bit her lip. Why hadn't she said anything about Edmund's behaviour towards her? That was the moment to say it. But she was so exhausted, her thoughts were like dandelion seeds on the breeze. She would tell him later. And she would tell him about Christmas Eve as well. She should have done it sooner. Her stomach flipped. Would he think it odd that she hadn't? Would he hold her responsible?

Joseph stuck to her like a limpet all morning and Mary was insatiable. Eliza could hardly stand by the time James rose again, refreshed. He looked in on Peter who was awake now but quiet, staring at the ceiling, sipping shallow breaths.

'Has he eaten?'

'He won't. I'd say his throat is raw from all that coughing.'

'Will you manage? I need to go up again. Why don't I call in to Ruth on the way and let her know? She might give you a hand.'

Eliza closed her eyes. She didn't want anyone coming in but she knew she needed help. She was fit to fall down and there was a long day to go yet.

'Yes, please,' she said quietly.

James kissed her on the cheek and left.

She had just finished feeding Mary again when there was a soft knock at the door. She opened it to find Ruth and Joanie outside. Ruth was holding Clara who was sporting an oversized bonnet that threatened to launch itself onto the Atlantic breeze that blew hard at their backs. Joanie peered into the house over Ruth's shoulder.

'We didn't want to disturb anyone sleeping,' Ruth said. 'But James said you might need a hand.'

As Eliza stood back to let them in, Joseph arrived to see who was calling.

'Toe-toes,' he announced, pointing at Joanie's feet.

Eliza looked down and saw that, indeed, Joanie was barefoot.

Ruth rolled her eyes to heaven as Joanie giggled. 'That's right, wee man. This silly girl will not wear shoes or boots around the place. And I wouldn't mind but she has a fine pair given to her by Mrs Godfrey. Mind you, that's not where her silliness begins or ends, is it, Joanie? Here!'

She thrust Clara into Joanie's arms and removed her cloak. Clara began to squawk and writhe.

'Can you not settle her for two minutes?' Ruth admonished the girl. 'Here, give her back to me now. We'll find another use for you. Go on into the kitchen and see if there's anything to be done.'

Joanie tossed her head and left the room, trailed by Joseph.

'May the Lord preserve me, Eliza! That girl has me driven mad already.' She fussed at Clara's bonnet. 'Now, will we look in at the patient?'

'Really, Ruth, there's no need.' Eliza felt as though a winter storm had blown right through her house. She had neither energy nor patience for Ruth's squabbles with Joanie. The Hunters were taking up far too much of her time.

'Nonsense! Anyone with two eyes in their head can see that there's a need. You've black rings under your eyes, you're as white as a sheet and …' Ruth's eyes scanned the untidy room, 'you could do with an extra pair of hands. Just for a while to help you keep on top of things. I'm happy to give you Joanie for a few days if she's any good to you.'

I bet you are, thought Eliza. Out of your hair and into mine. She tried to rein in the unkind thoughts – after all, Ruth was making a genuine offer of help.

'How is Peter?' Ruth asked.

'He has croup. Joseph had it before so I know how it will go but the night was bad.'

Their exchange was interrupted by a hoarse, weak voice calling.

Eliza rushed to the room, followed by Ruth who lingered by the doorway. She doesn't want to bring Clara in, Eliza thought, for fear she'll catch it.

Peter was sitting up, looking much brighter.

Eliza pulled the curtains and the room flooded with spring light.

'I hungry,' Peter said, looking from Eliza to Ruth. His hair was stuck to the top of his head from sweating but his eyes were clearer in his pale face.

'Good boy.' Eliza put her hand to his forehead. There was heat still but not as bad. 'I'll make you something now.'

'Why don't you let Joanie do that? She's not a bad cook. It's one of the few things she can do right. *Joanie!*'

They could hear the slip-slap of her bare feet approaching. When she got to the door she froze and blessed herself, muttering a prayer under her breath.

'I'd rather not come in, Mrs, if that's alright.'

'Will you knock off that nonsense now?'

Eliza blinked at Ruth's hypocrisy.

'The child has a cough, that's all,' said Ruth. 'And a sore throat from it. Go and make him something warm to eat.'

Eliza felt a pang of sympathy for the girl. She'd made no secret of the fact that she didn't want to come to the island and Ruth seemed to enjoy being a demanding mistress.

'I'll leave you to it, Eliza. I hope she's some help to you. Edmund should be down shortly so I'd best go back home.'

'He must be happy to have you and Clara home?' Eliza asked. It was forward of her but, seeing as she and Ruth were sharing a housegirl and Edmund was baring his soul to her, she didn't really care anymore.

Ruth stiffened. 'I haven't seen him yet. I must have been sleeping when he came in. He was at the lighthouse late and gone again early this morning.'

He was not, thought Eliza. She considered for a moment telling Ruth the truth of where Edmund had been. But she wanted no part of their troubles. She had enough of her own to contend with.

Joanie returned with a steaming bowl of oatmeal and goat's milk and Joseph carrying a spoon, proud of his efforts.

'Oh good girl, Joanie, thank you.' Eliza took the bowl from her. 'And aren't you a great boy now, Joseph, helping your brother?'

Joseph grinned and traipsed out after Joanie again. Eliza could hear him peppering her with questions.

'Don't spoil her now,' Ruth warned. 'You're not used to having a housegirl. It doesn't pay to be too good to them, you know.'

'I'll keep that in mind.'

Eliza turned her attentions to Peter, leaving Ruth to show herself out. She blew on a spoonful of porridge to cool it, then placed it into his mouth. He gobbled it down but cried out in agony as the food slid down his raw throat. He started to sob, tormented by his hunger and the pain preventing him from eating. He turned his head away, refusing to try another bite. After a few attempts, Eliza gave up. She hated to see him not eating but he had enough flesh on his bones to get him through a day or two. Please God by then he'd be well enough and she could fatten him up again. He was falling asleep now. She closed the curtains to darken the room and left him to rest.

Chapter 17

Even though Joanie never stopped nattering, Eliza had to admit she was glad of the company. It was a welcome distraction and she was good with Joseph.

'He likes you,' Eliza remarked as Joseph shadowed Joanie around the kitchen. 'You're good with small children.'

'Better than with babies anyway,' Joanie said. 'Or at least that one next door. That missus makes out like I'm useless with her but I swear to you none of the women at Beaulieu could get good of that child. Roaring and bawling day and night unless she's stuck to her mother. 'Tis all the same to me but how will she make out if she has another one? You'd swear there was only the two of them in the world and no father for the child. I may be only a young one but I know enough to know it takes two to have a baby.'

Joanie looked over her shoulder at Eliza as if to check how her comments had landed. Eliza was speechless. How had her innocent remark unleashed this torrent? Ruth was correct in her assumption that Eliza had never had a housegirl before but she had a strong feeling that Joanie shouldn't speak so freely of her employer. She was about to say so when Joanie took off again. She leaned back on the counter where she had been washing the dishes and wiped her hands on her apron.

'I'm sorry, missus. I know I shouldn't talk that way but, Mary Mother of God, I was like a clam in that big house. You couldn't open your mouth and it was all 'yes, ma'am' and 'no, sir' and whispering behind closed doors. Even the young ones. 'Tis unnatural. Children going about the place like Lords of the Manor. Like they don't sit down to shit like the rest of us. And your lady next door turning up out of the blue with her big belly. I nearly fell down with the shock of it. I mightn't have all the manners and what-have-you but 'tisn't right for a married woman to be going off like that without her husband. I heard Mrs Godfrey saying as much to her one night, you know. The time himself here sent her the letter. And Mrs Hunter was "I know" and "of course". But I'd swear she'd no notion coming back here at all until then. What's he like? I heard in the village that he's a bit odd. If he is, they're well-matched. There's a pair of 'em in it. I hope you don't mind me talking but I could burst with the months of holding it in.'

Eliza didn't know whether to laugh or throw her out of the house. She didn't think she'd ever met anyone who spoke her mind like this without first weighing the effects of her words.

She didn't have the heart to reprimand her but thought it would be best to change the subject.

'Have you brothers and sisters yourself, Joanie?'

Joanie grew still. She turned back again to her work, her face hidden.

'No, 'tis just myself now. Relying on the kindness of strangers. So I'd better learn to keep my trap shut.'

Eliza felt sorry for her. All alone in the world. A thought came to her ... maybe Joanie needn't be alone.

'I'd say Tom Trant is fond of you.'

Joanie tutted and tossed her head. 'That fella? Talk about notions! He's tried me a few times but sure 'twould be like stepping out with this, for all he'd say!' She held aloft a wooden spoon and Eliza laughed. 'When he said to me the last day how I didn't have to stay here, I said to myself "Now, Joanie. You can take your chances on this island, stuck in the middle of nowhere with a screaming baby and her scald of a mother or you can take your chances with Tom Trant." I was out of that boat fairly lively, I tell you!'

Eliza was laughing more than she had in months. She felt as though her cheeks would crack from it. Proper or not, she wasn't going to censor this girl – she was a tonic.

'Anyways, his mother wouldn't have me so he's as well off.'

Eliza thought of Edmund and the echoes of his story in what Joanie had just said. Who'd have thought they'd have anything in common? The difference of course was that Joanie felt nothing for Tom Trant.

'I was scared for my life though, missus. I don't mind telling you. That old Kiely woman on the quay put the fear of God into me. And then yer man ranting and raving about a presence! No good will come of that yet.'

Eliza was conscious of Joseph who had come back into the room, trying to get Joanie's attention. He paused at the seriousness of her words and expression.

Joanie glanced in the direction of Peter's room. 'He's gone awful quiet. Is he alright?'

The hairs stood up on the back of Eliza's neck. She didn't like the thread that Joanie was pulling between the woman wailing for the dead and her sick little boy. She swallowed the chill of fear that coursed through her.

'I'm sure he's fine. Joseph had the same thing when he was younger. Actually, do you know what I've just remembered? A mustard plaster worked wonders for him that time. Do you know how to make one?'

Joanie's expression cleared, the worry gone. 'I do. Have you the powder?'

Eliza showed her where to find it and left her to the task. She tiptoed in to check on Peter. She stood a moment in the quiet of the room, listening to his breathing. There was a struggle in it for sure but the sleep should do him good. She could hear Joseph and Joanie chatting in the kitchen. Mary was gone down for her afternoon nap. She lay onto the bed beside Peter, taking care not to disturb him. She closed her eyes and uttered a silent prayer that he'd be soon mended, then she drifted off to sleep holding his small, clammy hand.

The slam of a door jolted her awake. She dragged her eyes open, struggling to understand where she was. Peter had kicked off his blanket and felt cooler to the touch. She brought it back over him and sat up. A figure filled the doorway. It was Joanie with Mary.

'Is he still sleeping, the *cratur*?'

'Yes.' Eliza rubbed at her face. 'What time is it? Where's Joseph?'

'It's late. Joseph is gone away to bed. He's tired out from following me around all day.'

'You must be tired too, Joanie. Thank you, you've been a great help.'

Joanie smiled and brought Mary to Eliza.

'This little lady is hungry now and God knows I'm no good to her. I've the paste made up for the plaster. Will I leave it awhile? I don't want to disturb him.'

Eliza put Mary to her breast and watched Peter's breathing. His tiny chest was moving up and down rapidly and with every intake of breath the fragile bones of his ribcage were made visible. She listened to hear how it sounded over Mary's suckling. There was a catch there still. It worried her.

'Bring it in now please, Joanie. I'd like to try and clear his chest.'

Eliza's hand on the back of Mary's warm head reminded her of the many small hours she had passed feeding Peter. He had always been ravenous in the dead of night. She wished it was as simple as that now. Him hungry and her able to satisfy him. Not this sick child that she was struggling to help. She was trying her best to stay calm and she knew she probably appeared so to Joanie and maybe even James. They probably thought she knew what to do. But she didn't. Peter was worsening and she was lost.

The doorway darkened again. This time it was James.

'How is he?'

'The same.'

James sat on the bed, chewing on his lip and watched Peter. Then he rubbed his hands over his own face.

He is tired, she thought, we're all tired.

'Was that you I heard coming in?'

'I came in a bit loud. Sorry. I thought of it the minute the door banged. I've a lot on my mind.'

Eliza knew how he felt. 'He'll be alright, I think.' She was trying to reassure James with a confidence she didn't feel herself.

'Peter? Sure, I know he's in good hands. No, it's not that.'

'What is it then?' Eliza couldn't imagine any other thing on the earth that could be a bigger worry.

'Edmund. There's something up with him. I don't know what exactly. But he's no good to me. He's mooching around the lighthouse like he's trying to find something he's lost. If I knew no better I'd swear he's in love.'

Eliza's stomach churned. She had to say something. She opened her mouth to speak but James sat bolt upright and glanced at the door. He whispered, just loud enough for Eliza to hear. 'God almighty, Eliza! You don't think he's fallen for that one with the bare feet, do you?'

Eliza tutted. 'Stop that! Sure, he's hardly laid eyes on her since she arrived.'

'Well, there's something up, that's for sure.' James leaned closer to her and lowered his voice. 'He was all apologies for being found drunk on duty and nearly encouraging me to report it, like he wanted to be punished. I wasn't going to but he's been behaving so strangely since, I thought I'd better make a record of it at least. In case there's anything more. I wrote up a letter to the Commissioner but I can do no more until Jeremiah comes and I might not even send it then.' He threw his hands up in the air. 'I don't know what to do, Eliza. If he's transferred out in disgrace he'll lose everything. I don't want to do that to another man.'

He looked at her as though she could solve this problem for him.

Eliza sat in silence. She didn't know what to say. Should she reveal what Edmund had told her? The way he had been towards her? It didn't feel right to keep it to herself but what would be gained from telling it? They needed Edmund here, on the island. And Peter's illness was her priority for now. She frowned, annoyed that James was giving this his attention instead.

'Life is tough here, James. He made a mistake but now that Ruth and Clara are back I'm sure he'll straighten out again.' She hoped this was true.

'I hope you're right, Eliza. You have a kind heart,' he shook his head, 'but maybe that's why women are mothers and men run the lighthouses. Sometimes hard decisions have to be made.'

Eliza focused on Mary's last few sucks. She was full and ready to sleep.

'I'm going to head to bed for a few hours.' James rose.

Eliza nodded goodnight without catching his eye. Joanie arrived with the mustard plaster and stood aside to let him pass. Eliza saw the quick look she made, sizing up the tension in the room that James himself seemed oblivious to. She was embarrassed to think Joanie might have sensed a disagreement between them. Before she could say anything Eliza followed James to their bedroom in silence and settled Mary in her cradle.

When she returned Joanie was applying the warm plaster, humming as she did. Peter was awake, staring at her, but he didn't make a sound. Eliza thought he'd complain about the smell or the hot touch on his skin. The fact that he didn't was all the more concerning. When the plaster cooled Eliza peeled it off and tucked

Peter under his blanket again. He was no better but, she reassured herself, no worse either.

'Will I sit with him awhile, missus, so you can rest?' Joanie hovered at his bedside.

'No need, Joanie. Why don't you go on home for the night? I'll send for you in the morning if I need you.'

'Home?'

Eliza realised that Joanie didn't really have one. Shunted from aunt to Beaulieu to Skellig Michael but nowhere to call her own and never among her own people. Eliza hoped Ruth would grow kinder in her treatment.

'Next door.'

'If you're sure? I'll call so in the morning.'

She shut the door behind her, leaving Eliza in the dark listening to Peter's breathing, like a ship's captain adrift in the fog, straining to hear a signal.

Chapter 18

Morning came but Eliza couldn't say if she had slept. For most of the night she had been aware of Peter's scratchy breath. Each one cost him more energy. She had got up in the middle of the night and boiled pots of water to fill the room with steam, to no avail. Her body was stiff now and her eyes burned with exhaustion. She dreaded the thought of another day. Would Peter turn a corner? Back in Ballinacourty she would have sent for the doctor or the herb woman by now. Eliza stretched out of the bed quietly so as not to disturb Peter.

A sullen Joseph and James were having breakfast together. She kissed the top of Joseph's head and sank down into the chair beside James, hoping he'd pour her a cup of tea.

No one spoke and no tea appeared.

'Where's Mary?' she asked.

'She's sleeping still,' James said. 'She had a great sleep, unlike some.' He frowned in Joseph's direction.

'Were you not feeling well?' Eliza put her hand on Joseph's forehead, a sick fear washing through her that she might have two children to tend to.

'There's not a bother on him but I'm afraid the Hunters' housegirl filled his head with *ráméis* and it kept him up half the night.'

'Joanie? What did she say?'

'Mammy,' Joseph's bottom lip trembled, 'she said once a man fell off a ship and lived in a hut in the monastery and –' he cast a look in James' direction and his next statement was ripe with dread and wonder, 'she said his skin was blacker than coal.'

'So this lad couldn't sleep,' James explained. 'Because every time he shut his eyes he saw the man with the black skin. And I didn't get a wink either. Yourself and Peter had a good night?'

With a surge of annoyance Eliza realised this was the first time he'd asked about Peter. Was he feeling sorry for himself having to look after Joseph for one night? While she was run ragged trying to care for Peter and keep Joseph and Mary going too?

She scraped her chair back from the table and started to clatter the breakfast things off the table.

'He slept. But he's a long way off being better.'

She dumped the crockery into the sink.

James stood behind her, finishing off his last sup of tea.

'Will you have a word?' he yawned.

'With Joseph?'

'No, with Joanie. She can't be scaring Joseph like that. She needs to control her tongue. All that drama on the boat and now this.'

Eliza didn't respond. Joanie had been so good, so helpful, more than James this last while now she thought of it. If she had a word with her it would be a gentle one.

'I need my rest. The work at the lighthouse is never-ending and now I have this situation with Edmund.' He reached around to put his cup in with the other dishes and leaned his chin on her shoulder. 'You know I need my sleep, Eliza, or I get very grumpy. That's what you get for marrying an older man.'

She slid out from under him and wiped her hands on a cloth. 'I'll speak to her.'

As if summoned by their words the front door banged.

'Good morning, Joseph! Where's your Mammy?'

'*In here!*' Eliza answered from the kitchen.

'You've a fine fire going,' Joanie continued. 'I'm chilled to the bone from the crowd next door. They've the fire lit as well but you wouldn't know it. They're as frosty with each other, like two strangers – oh! Good morning, Mr Carthy.' Her cheeks reddened as she realised that James was there too. She stared down at her bare toes.

'Good morning, Joanie.' He put on his coat and shot a stern look in Eliza's direction. 'I'll see you all later.'

I'll have a word with Joanie, Eliza thought, but first I want to know what was going on next door.

'Oh God, Mrs Carthy, me and my big mouth! Mr Carthy didn't look a bit happy.'

'Come on in and give me a hand with the dishes. Joseph, you stay here and play and maybe Joanie can take you for a walk soon.'

He grinned at Joanie whose face brightened.

'Is there trouble with the Hunters?' Eliza asked quietly.

'Nothing but, I'd say! When I went in last night the two of them were sitting together. Mrs Hunter told me to sit down and tell her all about Peter. He didn't open his mouth. She had me tidy up then after their tea and I swear to God not a word passed between them. But it was the loudest silence I ever heard.'

Eliza said nothing but it made sense. There was so much left unsaid between them.

'Then, before bed, after she fed the baby, she went handing her to me. Mr Hunter said he'd hold her. Well, she nearly took the head off him. "You will *not*!" she said. "She's not used to you yet." He said, "How will she ever get used to me if you won't let me near her?" and she said back to him "She doesn't know you". He roared at her, "*And who's the cause of that?*" I swear I nearly jumped out of my skin. He went out then and slammed the door. Jesus, Mary and Joseph, I didn't know where to put myself. I'd have gone up the chimney if I could. Imagine! She was mad then that I seen the two of them carrying on like that so she's taking it out on me all morning. I can do no right by her. And she said,' Joanie faltered, glancing at Eliza from under her eyelashes, 'she said I'm not to dilly-dally in here today, she has need of me and if you want a housegirl you should get one!'

Eliza laughed aloud. No doubt Joanie's tongue would get her into untold trouble one day but it was a breath of fresh air and Eliza was grateful for her. And at least she knew the truth of Ruth's feelings. She pitied poor Joanie having to put up with her and decided to say nothing about Joseph's sleepless night. He'd soon forget all about it.

Joseph slunk into the kitchen. 'Mammy, is Peter going to be better?'

'Ah, pet – he will, of course. Do you know you had this sickness too when you were small and aren't you fine now? A big, strong lad. Don't be worrying. Peter will be back playing with you again before you know it.'

His features relaxed. But he had more to say. 'I went in to see does he want to play but he wouldn't wake up. Will he be sleeping all day?'

Eliza dropped the cup she was holding into the basin and raced from the room. The image of Peter not waking up terrified her. She sank to her knees at his bedside and listened. He was breathing, but only just. A breath, silence, a suck of air, silence. The silences in between were too long. He was weakening.

'*Joanie!*' she cried out, trying but failing to keep the fear from her voice.

Joanie came running but stopped at the threshold and blessed herself. Eliza beat back the urge to scream at her.

'*Go next door! Tell Mrs Hunter he's no better and to please come in. She might know of some remedy I could try. Please, Joanie!*'

Joanie left without another word.

Joseph was in the doorway, his little face creased with fright and worry. She took a deep breath to steady her voice before she spoke.

'Come in, Joseph. Let's say a few prayers for your brother.'

Joseph stayed with her for longer that she thought he would, kneeling beside his brother's bed, echoing the words of Eliza's prayers. When he tired of that he played quietly on the floor and never left. Eliza's mind raced, trying to think what else she could do for Peter. What knowledge was she forgetting that would bring him back around to good health?

Her heart lifted at a knock on the door. Ruth, with some better remedies, she hoped.

'Go and tell her come in, Joseph.' She shooed him from the sickroom. She heard him open the door to greet their neighbour but it was a male voice that responded. Not Ruth, or Joanie, but Edmund. Eliza frowned. She hadn't expected Ruth to ignore a plea for help. The comments about Eliza getting her own housegirl came back to her. It was a mean-hearted and bitter thing to say, now that she reflected on it again.

Edmund knocked on the doorjamb and cleared his throat.

'How is he?' His eyes swept across Peter's slight body, tucked in tight under the blankets, then moved to Eliza. 'How are you? You must be worn out.'

The concern in his voice unnerved Eliza. It was too intimate and completely wrong. She had a strong desire to get him out and close the bedroom door and not have to hear it but she needed whatever he had brought.

'No better.' Her voice caught on the last syllable and she had to swallow hard to keep from crying. When she could trust herself to speak again, she asked, 'Could Ruth not come?'

'No, she was up the night with the baby and she needs a rest. Joanie is with the baby now but she'll be in to you again later, she said.'

Eliza noted how he spoke of his own daughter as though she was a visitor in his home. She looked to see what he had brought. His fist was closed and as he unfurled it she saw it was a bulb of garlic. She looked at him, her eyes forming a question.

He focused on his hand, shame-faced.

'Ruth said to try this. It works well for a cold if you boil it and drink the water. Or with a drop of whiskey even.'

Eliza couldn't speak. This was what Ruth had sent? Her hopes were dashed. She had hoped that Ruth, with her preference for scientific methods, might have brought something medicinal back from the mainland, something effective, something better than garlic.

'A cold? He does not have a cold. The child is in bed, fighting for every breath, *not troubled with a mere sniffle!*' Her voice had risen with each word and the last came out with a screech.

Edmund moved towards her, arms outstretched as if intending to hold her. 'Eliza.'

She moved fast, putting herself on the opposite side so that the bed was between them. She had no more to say to him but still he continued.

'You are a wonderful mother. I see you every day, how well you look after them all.'

The empty words churned the pit of her stomach. What did he know of mothers? Or of her? She had a mind to tell him to keep his eyes on his own wife but right now what she wanted most was for him to leave. If she was to be alone in the care of her sick child then that was what she would be – alone.

'Please leave us.' Her words were delivered cold and she kept her eyes on Peter. Tears pricked in them and she bowed her head so that Edmund wouldn't see. 'I want him to rest.'

'Aye, you should too. When you can. I'm going up to the lighthouse now. We've a rough night ahead. The pressure has been dropping the last few hours and it looks like a bad storm is going to come at us from the west. It might be a while before James is down.'

Eliza nodded. The idea of a storm matched the whirling in her mind. She felt her resolve grow. It would be a bad night, no doubt, but she was ready to battle it.

Once Edmund had let himself out again she left the bedroom to rouse the faltering fire. The bulb of garlic was on the table, mocking her with its uselessness. She threw it to the floor and stamped down hard. The skin split and wet cloves burst, spilling their juices. She took a breath, feeling immediately foolish. She scooped up the pungent pulp and threw it into the blaze. Already the flame was flattening and flaring with the pull and suck of the rising wind outside.

As the evening drew in she circled the house. From Peter's bedroom to the front room to the kitchen, feeding Joseph and Mary, filling the fire, lighting candles and placing a hand on Peter's head, hoping his fever would dissipate. She watched his chest rising and falling, willing his heart to be strong. As she tucked Joseph into bed for the night and kissed his closed eyelids, she realised that Peter had not opened his once that day. She carried a chair to his bedside and tucked his small hand into hers. Her heart clenched with fear as she saw the blue tinge at the base of his fingernails. Her finger traced down from his thumb, instinctively resting on his pulse. It was there, but only just. She lowered her ear to his mouth to listen for his breath. She could feel it coming out in hot puffs.

The windows rattled in their frames, pelted by the wind-driven rain and hail and the noise filled her head so that she couldn't straighten her thoughts. What must she do? This waiting, this watching was going to drive her crazy. She wanted to be doing, fixing. She went to the kitchen and returned with a bowl of cold water. She wet her fingertips and dabbed at Peter's dry, cracked lips. Nothing had passed between them today. The sight of his small body, oblivious to her presence and her efforts, taut and tense in its fight for survival, filled her heart with an intensity of love so strong she thought it would burst. Why could she not take on this battle for him? She would withstand it ten times over if she had to.

Peter shivered violently. One shudder, two, passing through him from head to toe, like an electric charge. It was the fever, she knew, but on instinct she wanted to warm him. She folded back the blanket, just enough to climb in, then pulled him close, wrapping her arms around him, humming a rhyme that both boys loved, then she spoke to him.

'Joseph can't wait to play with you, you know? All day long he's been asking. There's a big storm tonight and Daddy is above at the lighthouse. Ye could go down to the cove tomorrow to see what's washed in. You never know what you might find. Daddy will take ye, if you're good. Of course you're good. You're a great boy.'

She buried her face in his hair, choking back frightened tears then eased herself out of the bed again. Peter had stopped shivering. He was breathing with rapid, shallow gasps. She put her hand on his chest. His heart was pounding like a runaway horse, she could see the thump of it through his papery skin. She stood, feeling the urge to be on the move again, but not knowing where she should go. She thought of her family in Waterford and the nights she'd been aware, as a child, of a vigil going on, the men and women of the area gathered together to pray for some ailing neighbour. The memory compelled her to act. She took the stairs two at a time, then, reminding herself that Mary was sleeping, slowed and crept into her room, lifting her mother's wooden rosary beads from the mirror. The last time she'd held them was the night Mary was born. Eliza admonished herself and promised God that she'd use them more often and pray more often. If he helped her now, helped her boy. She moved quickly back to Peter's room, realising that the storm had quietened. Either it had blown away faster than Edmund and James had thought or this was the eerie pause that often fooled people that the worst had passed.

She knelt at the side of Peter's bed and blessed herself. Then her mind went blank. What was the next part, the opening prayer? She felt it was there, right at the edge of her thoughts, but it wouldn't come to her. Then, as she searched she realised that there was a silence. The room was completely still. And silent. She jumped up, the wooden beads clattering to the floor. She put her hand to Peter's face, his chest, his heart, she climbed onto the bed and put her ear to his mouth to feel his breath. But it wasn't there, not any more. Just as the storm had slipped out to sea her boy, her beautiful darling boy, had slipped away from her. She fell forward, her body covering the length of his, and sobbed. Her mind careened from disbelief to the heart-breaking starkness of the unmoving body beneath her. She half-stood, half-fell from the bed and dragged the blanket off. She scanned Peter's body and put her hand on every part, searching for any sign of life – a beat, a flutter, a sigh. But, nothing. There was nothing.

She ran to the front door, wrenching it open and screamed out into the inky blackness *'Peter!'*

Chapter 19

Eliza was on her knees just inside the open door, oblivious to the driving rain that soaked through to her skin or the hand tugging at her elbow, half-lifting, half-dragging her inside. Her world was one sensation, one searing knowledge of loss that she couldn't form into words. Not even inside her own mind. Not yet.

'Oh Jesus! Missus, you'll catch your death!' Joanie rubbed at her with a cloth. 'Mr Carthy is coming. I ran for him when I heard you. I roared for him to come. He's on his way but I didn't wait for him, I ran back down to you to see could I do anything.'

Eliza heard the words but they fell on her ears like the pellets of hail against the impenetrable glass.

'Is it bad news? Oh God, of course it is, Joanie! Shut up, you fool! Is the small boy gone, missus? The poor, small boy!'

She sank to the floor beside Eliza, buried her face in the cloth and sobbed.

Eliza looked on, unmoved. Her own grief had burrowed deep within her already. A parasite worming its way down to her soul. It would lie in wait and ambush her in time but for now there was just numbness. She stood, shut the door and moved towards Peter's room. There was something she needed to do, if she could just think of it. Before she got there the front door banged open again.

James, coatless, hatless, wild-eyed. Eliza took in his appearance. She felt a sudden urge to laugh and put her hand to her mouth to stop it. The urge subsided and liquid acid surged up her throat. She was going to be sick. She swallowed hard.

James spoke. 'What's happened? What is it? Eliza! Joanie! Is it Peter?'

At the mention of his name Joanie dissolved once more, wailing now.

Eliza took a step towards him.

'*Shush.*' She raised a finger to her lips. She could take no more noise. All must now be silent, be still.

He stalked past her, eyes wide with fear. She shut hers as he roared out, the pain in his voice echoed around her vacant body. She stepped inside the room and leaned back against the wall to stop herself from falling down. If she fell down she would never get up.

James buried his face into his son's chest, fists bunching the blankets.

'*No, no, no, no, no!*'

He dragged himself off his son's body, taking the blanket with him. He tore at it, ripping it. Then he looked at his hands as if shocked by what they had just done. Peter's body was defenceless, stripped of its covers. His skinny white legs, feet splayed sideways. His grazed knees, his soft stomach.

Eliza drank it in but could go no further. She couldn't bring herself to look upon his face, his open, unseeing eyes. Not yet.

James fell to his knees beside the bed.

'I'm sorry, my *buachaill!* I'm sorry, Peter. I took your blanket off you and it's a bad night. You must be cold. Let me put it around you again.' His voice was a hoarse whisper as he tucked the blanket around Peter's feet, legs, torso. It looked like a shroud. 'Now so!'

James straightened then looked for Eliza. He offered his hand to her from the far side of the bed, like a lost child, but she couldn't reach for it. He was marooned on his island and she on hers and that was where she needed to stay for now. He staggered from the room and she sat beside Peter, running her fingers through his dark hair. He'd had such a head of curls when he was younger. It was only lately they'd started to straighten, taking his baby look with them. That's all he still was really. A baby. And she hadn't been able to keep him from harm.

'Mrs Carthy, I can help you. I've seen it done.'

Joanie entered the room, a watchful eye on Eliza. She blessed herself and knelt at the foot of the bed. She was shaking but the ritual of the prayer seemed to calm her. She moved to the window next and opened it a crack.

'For the soul to go out,' she said and paused. When Eliza didn't react she returned to the bedside and took Peter's hand. 'Such a lovely boy. I know I only just met him but ... poor Joseph! He'll be heartbroken.' She began to cry again.

Her words stirred Eliza. Whatever was to be done needed to be finished before Joseph came down. She stood and took Joanie's hand.

'You'll help me, so?'

The winds had quieted and day was creeping in as Eliza lifted Peter, allowing Joanie to pull off his sweat-stiffened nightgown.

Both women were gentle with him, not wanting to cause hurt. Eliza murmured to him under her breath, the same words she'd said so often before.

'Hands up now, good boy. There you go. Lie down now for Mammy.'

She could feel Joanie's eyes on her. She didn't care. She needed to look after her boy.

Joanie reached up to shut the window. Eliza was glad. She was so cold her hands no longer felt like her own.

'His soul will have left by now.' Joanie wiped the bottom of his feet with a wet cloth. The cloth came away blackened and Eliza's heart cracked open at the thought of his little bare feet, pattering through the house and the yard outside, gathering dust as they went.

'Souls that don't cross over do be tortured for eternity, they say,' Joanie continued.

'Joanie!' Eliza snapped. Foolish girl, had she not a scrap of sense in her head to be talking like this? 'Give that here.' She gestured at the basin of water. It bothered her how rough Joanie was, wiping her boy down. There was no tenderness, no love. Oh but, she would show him love. She turned her back to Joanie and lifted his small hand, turning it over to clean the sticky palm. She dipped the cloth into the basin. The water was stone cold.

She turned to Joanie who stood, aimless, at the end of the bed, and spoke through gritted teeth. '*This water is freezing.*'

'Well, I – I,' Joanie stuttered, 'I didn't see the need to ... warm it.' Her voice broke on the last words.

Eliza flinched. She understood her meaning. What good was warm water to Peter now? What harm cold water when he couldn't feel it? She passed her the basin without looking up.

'Fresh water. And warm it.'

Joanie scuttled from the room and Eliza covered Peter with the blanket. When Joanie returned, Eliza took the basin and started anew the task of washing her boy. She could feel Joanie watching her again and was overtaken by a longing to be alone.

'Leave me be,' she said.

'Oh God, missus. That's not proper. Sure it shouldn't even be you doing this. In the normal way of things there'd be neighbour women helping you.'

Eliza took a deep breath to quell the rising anger. She straightened, reluctantly taking her eyes off her boy for a moment to regard Joanie.

'I want to be alone. You can gather whatever else we need but leave me be.'

She waited until Joanie had left and shut the door. Then she took the cloth and wiped Peter's feet again, then his hands, his neck, his face, taking her time over each part, committing it to memory as she went. She propped him up to ease a new gown over his head, pulled it down, then laid him back on the pillow, smoothing his hair with her hand.

She could hear Joanie creeping about outside and when she went to the door she found a collection of items.

Eliza stripped the blanket from the bed and fluttered a fresh white, linen sheet across her boy, tucking it in tight around him. She lit two candles, put one at the top and one at the foot of the bed. She'd need James to turn the bed so that the end of it faced east, to meet the rising sun. She became aware of something under her foot. She looked down and saw the rosary beads where she had dropped them. When? Hours ago? Days? Then, all was chaos. Now, all was stillness. She picked them up, kissed the small cross that hung from them and wound them around Peter's small hands, posed as if in prayer. A memory rushed at her sideways, the first ambush. Peter, copying his big brother blessing himself and ending up almost tangled in his own limbs, creased with laughter.

As if the memory had summoned him, she heard Joseph's voice outside. She opened the door, torn between the boy in the bed who no longer needed her and the boy who was staggering into the room now, sleep-fuddled, still carrying the warm scent of his bed. She lifted him into her arms. His legs dangled for a moment almost to her knees then wrapped around her waist. He nuzzled into her neck, suspended between sleep and wakefulness. James was sitting by the stove, his head in his hands. Joanie was standing, stock still, in front of the mirror she had just covered. The silence in the room was crushing.

Joseph jolted to alertness.

'Where's Peter?'

Eliza squeezed him tight for a moment. She wished she could make it last forever, the last time in his life that he would have without the loss, the grief of a dead baby brother. She swallowed hard. He needed her now. James hadn't moved and Joanie kept her eyes to the floor, shoulders shaking.

Eliza put him on his feet, then crouched in front of him, looking straight into his blue eyes, his father's eyes. 'Peter was very sick, you know, Joseph, and he's gone now to live with God, in Heaven.'

'Gone?'

'Yes, pet. He's not with us anymore.'

A look of panic flitted across Joseph's face. He scanned the room but found no answers there. He turned back to his mother. 'Is he coming back?'

His eyes filled with tears as if he already knew what she must say.

Eliza couldn't speak. The hard lump that had formed in her throat wouldn't allow it. She looked in desperation at James. Couldn't he come to her aid now? His whole body was shuddering. Eliza took Joseph by the hand. She wanted him out of this room before he saw his father grieving. It wouldn't do him any good to witness that.

'Do you want to see?'

Everything in his expression said, 'No', but he nodded.

She led him to the room where Peter was laid out. He faltered at the door, feet refusing to cross the threshold.

'Come on,' she urged in a soft voice.

He allowed her to bring him into the room, close enough to see Peter in the bed.

'*Oh!*'

He took in the whole scene, the white sheet, the candles, the rosary beads, the unmoving brother. This brother who clamoured and climbed and crowed and could never sit still. Now, like a stone.

'Is he sleeping?'

There was some hope in his voice but, mostly, doubt. This could never be taken as sleep. Eliza put her arm around his shoulders.

'Sort of. Some people call this 'eternal rest' and that means you are asleep forever.'

'Will he just stay in this bed, so?'

Eliza's mind shifted. She hadn't thought of the next step. It had been enough just to get to here. But of course there would have to be a burial. How could she explain that to Joseph?

'No, he won't.' James' voice was too loud in the room.

She hadn't heard him come in but now he was walking over to join them at the bedside. She felt herself on the precipice, a ship on the rocks, about to keel. One kind word, one moment of respite and she would be gone, dissolved.

James took her hand and held it tight. She steadied herself again.

'We can only keep him for a little while, Joseph,' James said. 'And he's not really here, just his body. His soul is with God already.'

'So where will his body go?'

'We ...'

Eliza could see that this was James' first thought of burial as well. She came to his rescue.

'Joseph, we'll talk about that later. You need to say goodbye to your brother now.'

'Goodbye? But why does God want him? Can't he send him back?'

The tears spilled over onto his cheeks now. Despite his young years he had grasped that his brother was gone, forever.

'What do I do?' he asked.

Eliza sniffed, her own tears falling unchecked. When had they begun? She led Joseph to the pillow. She kissed Peter on the forehead and he followed suit, their tears mingling on Peter's skin.

'Do you want to say something to him?'

Joseph nodded. He looked older suddenly.

'Goodbye, Peter. I'll mind the train and we can play with it when I come to Heaven.' He nodded again, his piece said. Then he turned and buried his face in Eliza's stomach. No sound came from him but she could feel his whole body, convulsed.

James' sobs filled the room. She teetered for a moment, then she too was gone, swept under.

Chapter 20

Eliza washed up on a chair by Peter's bed. She had no memory of where the chair had come from, who had sat her on it or who had put the cup of tea in her hand. It was untouched and cold now so she put it on the floor and lay her head down on the bed. She felt nothing now and there was a peace in that. That, and being left alone with her boy. The solitude was welcome but it called to her mind other wakes she had attended back home. The house would be heaving. Men talking and smoking pipes, recalling anecdotes of the dead person. Women competing in the kitchen to churn out table-loads of food and pots of tea. The keening women wailing in unison to remind the revellers of the loss. The bottle of whiskey or *poitín* passed around on the sly and young people taking advantage of the racket to advance their courtship in dark corners. She had always loved the way the house of the deceased would be crammed to the rafters with life in the days after their passing. When the wake ended and propriety was restored, the priest would come to say the prayers and accompany the body to the church and graveyard.

There was none of that now, no racket, no priest. Only the storm-washed rocks glinting in the shrill light of day and the caw of the seabirds released from their shelter. Eliza was glad. There was no one to busy her away from where she wanted to be, right beside her precious boy for the short while that was left to her.

The door opened and a hesitant Joanie entered with Mary in her arms.

'I'm sorry, I don't mean to bother you, but she's looking for a feed.'

Eliza stretched out her arms and put the baby to her breast, not taking her eyes from Peter. Mary latched on, guzzling. The sound of the feeding brought Eliza back to the world – the slurp and swallow, the little grunting noises as Mary strove to satisfy herself. Eliza resented it. She fought the urge to push the baby away. She was an affront to this situation, with her hunger, her greed, her drive for survival. Eliza allowed her to finish, then called for Joanie to take her away. Mary grizzled at the disappearance of her mother's warm bosom as they left.

Eliza felt a pang of guilt but her thoughts were interrupted by the reappearance of Joanie.

'I'm sorry again, missus, but Mrs Hunter is here and she –' Before she could finish Ruth pushed in past her.

'Move out of my way! Oh Eliza! I'm so sorry for your loss.'

She took Eliza's hand and turned to Peter. The sight of him silenced her. She bowed her head in prayer and when she spoke again she was calm, sincere.

'How can you bear it, Eliza? I can't even imagine.'

Eliza looked at her. Was this a question she was meant to answer? How could she bear it? She had no proof that she could.

'How is James? And Joseph? Oh God, he'll be lost without him.' Ruth started to cry.

Eliza watched her curiously. Why was she crying? This wasn't her loss.

Ruth composed herself and called for Joanie to bring another chair. She admonished her for not thinking of it sooner.

'Other people will want to sit with the body. Surely you know that?'

Eliza glanced up in alarm. Other people? No. This was her station. Hers alone. The body? Did she mean Peter?

'*Peter.*'

She said the word aloud. It was starting to feel strange on her tongue, foreign. In the future when she said this word it would have to be explained. *My son who ... I had another son but he ...*

She wondered numbly where Joseph was now. He was avoiding the room with the same intensity that he'd displayed when he sat for hours playing by Peter's sickbed. Sickbed. Deathbed. Eliza sighed deeply.

Ruth was still talking. '... and of course make arrangements. The sooner the better. It will do you no good to wallow. You must think on the children you have with you still and the ones you'll be blessed with in the future, please God.'

Eliza struggled to make sense of these words but her mind skittered away from them.

'Edmund will help, if he's allowed to. I do hope himself and James can resolve their differences.'

Eliza frowned. She didn't care what happened between the two men. Ruth was taking up too much of the room. Her big skirt and her strident accent and her non-stop blabber. Eliza could take no more of it. Her sense of Peter was fading.

'I need you to go, Ruth.'

'Eliza! Surely whatever disagreement the men have needn't come between us?' Ruth looked aghast.

Eliza stared into her eyes, unwavering. In a heartbeat all the words she could say flashed through her mind. You begrudged me the help of your housegirl. You sent me garlic to save my boy's life. You left me to fight for him alone.

'Get out!' was all she said.

Ruth stood and gathered her skirts, huffing and red-faced with anger.

'I will make an allowance for your rudeness, Eliza. I understand you are grieving.'

She swept out of the room, calling to Joanie to bring Clara to her. The bang of the front door announced her departure and Eliza released her breath. She unclenched her hands that had been gripping the edge of her seat.

'Mrs Carthy?' Joanie edged inside the door.

Eliza lifted the second chair, handed it out to her, then shut the door and resumed her position by the bed.

She slept in the chair, her eyes flickering open every few minutes to her new reality. James had come to join her at some point and the candles in the room had been replaced, their flames brighter and higher than before. The world outside was in darkness and Eliza was glad. It felt right. But her heart tore at the knowledge that this would be her last night with Peter. The part of her mind that was still capable of rational thought knew that he could not stay, must be buried. She couldn't think past that word and all it meant. She pulled her chair close to the bed, reaching for Peter's hand, then retracting. It wouldn't feel like his hand anymore. She needed to remember her smiling, soft, warm boy, not the waxen creature he now was. Instead James' hand found hers.

'Eliza, I have a place for him.'

She looked up at her husband's face, suddenly lined and drawn. She had never paid much heed to the difference in their ages but this was an old man before her now. She shook her head, not getting his meaning, not wanting it.

'It is the holiest place on the island. It seems to me the right place to – for him.'

When Eliza didn't ask he continued, as though driven to fill the silence.

'The monastery. There are already some graves there and the church is holy ground. I've been up to look at it and the ground is soft so it should be easy enough to ...'

He stopped but it was too late. The image had already formed in her mind. He would climb the steps, with a shovel in hand. He would dig a hole in the dark earth. He would put their boy into the hole and he would pile the earth over him. She knew it must be done but she hated James for it. For the thinking of it and the planning of it and the doing of it. She pulled her hand away and placed it over her eyes.

'I'll do a good job for him. You'll see.'

After a few more minutes of silence he left the room. The front door opened. James leaving? No, now there were two male voices. Edmund. She heard 'pay my respects', and braced herself for another intrusion. The room brightened with the opening of the door, a harsh light cast over Peter's greying skin. He looked less and less like himself.

Edmund entered and nodded in her direction.

'Eliza.'

He stood at the end of the bed, head bowed in prayer.

Eliza watched him. This strange man. What could he say to her in this moment? He turned to her and twisted his cap in his hands, drawing breath as if to speak, then shook his head. Finally, he found the words.

'I am so sorry, Eliza,' he said, his eyes on the ground.

The words were weighty and she felt as though they carried more than one sentiment. Sorry for her. Sorry for Peter. Sorry for himself. What difference? It changed nothing. Her eyes swam with hot tears as a thought formed. Was Peter's death a punishment for her? For keeping Edmund's behaviour towards her a secret? She stared at him as he backed out of the room. He began speaking quietly to James in the front room, their voices too low to decipher. Then louder.

'*No, Edmund, I said no.*'

'But I mean only to help.'

'I see that. But I will do this alone.'

'James, I know we have things to discuss —'

'*No! Not here. Not now.*'

'You mean to ruin me?'

'*Do you mean to dishonour my dead child? Get out of my house!*'

James voice had risen to a roar.

It was followed by the slam of the door, then silence.

Eliza closed her eyes. She eased into the knowledge that they would be disturbed no more. Tomorrow, she would deal with when it came.

She was watching the sun slip into the morning sky when James passed by the window. His collar turned up against the dawn breeze, cap pulled down tight on his head and his fist gripping the handle of a shovel. He marched out of the yard. His demeanour put Eliza in mind of a man going to war. She left the room.

Joanie was in the front room with Joseph. They looked up at her as if she was a phantom and Joanie rose to her feet.

'Can I get you something, Mrs Carthy?'

Eliza smiled weakly. She was grateful to this young girl, barely fifteen years old, who'd had the sense to give her the time she needed and to take care of Joseph and Mary for her. Eliza found her voice, strained and raw.

'I must prepare.'

'Of course. I will stay with Peter until you are ready.'

Eliza hadn't thought of it but she was glad he wouldn't be left alone.

As she climbed the stairs she heard Joanie ask, 'Do you want to come with me, Joseph?'

His small voice whispered, 'No'.

Eliza rubbed at her eyes. She must attend to Joseph more today. She had been neglectful of him, her mind and heart full of only one child.

She changed into the darkest dress that fit her new shape. How could she be a new mother and a bereaved mother in the same instant? None of this made sense and her mind felt as though it was underwater, slipping out of her grasp. She found her small bottle of holy water and paused to look around the room. What else? Nothing. There was nothing left to do for her boy.

Joanie got to her feet when Eliza returned. She crept towards the door but Eliza stopped her, taking her hand.

'Will you stay?' she asked.

'If you have need of me,' Joanie replied.

Eliza lifted the linen sheet that was covering Peter and with Joanie's help she slipped it under him. She had never made a shroud before, but she had seen it done. She had no idea about Joanie. Had she prepared her parents for burial or looked on while some neighbours performed the task? No matter, they both did what was to be done. Eliza traced the Sign of the Cross on his forehead, then leaned down for one last kiss. His skin was cold to the touch, her boy wasn't there anymore. She hesitated before placing the sheet over his face. James might want to see him one last time. She covered him, but left it untied. She looked at Joanie, unsure what came next.

Joanie looked as lost as her but moved to act.

'You'll need something in your stomach, missus. To see you through the day.'

Eliza's stomach felt like a stone. Food or sustenance of any kind were of no concern. She didn't care if she never ate again. But the girl was right, she had to keep her strength up to feed Mary and to make the climb to the monastery.

Joanie brought her a hot cup of sweet tea and some bread.

An uncertain Joseph trailed behind her, eyeing Eliza from the doorway. His whole world must feel changed, she thought, and beckoned him in. When he was within reach she gathered him into her arms, holding him tight, trying to keep herself together.

'Will you stay with me awhile?' she asked.

He climbed onto her lap and lay back against her chest.

'Where's Peter going?'

'We'll take him up to the monastery. It's a holy place, close to God.' Eliza was amazed how easily her words came and how they seemed to satisfy Joseph when they sat lifeless on her ears. What did any of it mean? Did she believe in it herself? Of course, she always thought of her mother and father and others in the afterlife. But now that it was her own child it seemed so wrong.

Joseph sat with her in silence, staring at his shrouded brother in the bed. A shadow passed the window, James returning.

Eliza eased Joseph off her lap and went to the doorway.

James leaned on the mantel to slide off his boots, his shoulders rounded almost to meeting. When he lifted his head she could see the tracks made by tears through the dirt on his cheeks. His hands were blackened from the soil, red welts standing out where he'd gripped the shovel. He has lost the battle, she thought.

He looked at her and nodded. It was done. It was time.

Chapter 21

James came back downstairs, cleaned and dressed in full uniform of navy trousers, waistcoat, double-breasted jacket and cap with the silver Principal Keeper's badge. Eliza, Joseph and Mary were assembled in the front room, waiting. It struck Eliza that they made a deceptive, though sombre, tableau – a family, dressed and ready as if for an outing. James took a deep breath, straightened himself and went into Peter's room. Eliza sat in silence with Mary on her chest and Joseph huddled in close to her. She concentrated on the sound of her own breathing, trying not to hear James' farewell to his son. She couldn't make out the words but the tenor of his grief was unmistakable. When it grew quiet again she eased the children over to Joanie and went to join him. He was tying the last fastening on the shroud with shaking hands.

'We'll make a start,' he said, his voice hoarse and low.

A thought struck Eliza. 'How will we take him there?'

'I'll carry him.'

She was about to say more about the distance, the climb, the weight. The dead weight. But she stopped herself. Let James do what he had to do.

Eliza secured Mary in her shawl, took Joseph's hand and they followed James out the front door. He carried Peter in his arms, head cradled to his chest, like many times before when Peter had fallen asleep and needed to be put to bed. Eliza looked away. If she was to survive the day she would have to guard herself against these thoughts. Her eyes settled on the sea, the waves rolling in, one after another after another, futile, incessant, ignorant of her loss. She felt their pull. Under their churning, roiling foam she would see nothing, think nothing, feel nothing. She watched a gull hovering, diving, coming up empty. It toyed with the breeze, swooping and wheeling, allowing itself to be swept away on a gust. She envied its easy freedom, longed for a strong, steady air to whisk her away into the vast emptiness of sky and horizon.

Joseph gripped her hand, pulling her back to earth.

The Hunters stood outside their door, Edmund in his full uniform, heads bowed as their little cortège moved along the yard. Edmund moved towards James.

'Let me help with the carrying.' He put his hands on the shroud where Peter's feet were. James stopped, a ripple of tension traversing his shoulders.

'No.'

Edmund hesitated but didn't insist.

Ruth spoke, puncturing the fraught air. 'Joanie, you'll stay behind with Clara. It's no day for her to be out. Especially up there, she'll catch her –' She caught her words, glancing at Eliza, then away again, holding her baby out to Joanie who didn't move.

Eliza knew she was torn. She had to do as she was told to preserve her position but had fully intended accompanying them. Eliza nodded to release her from the burden of having to choose.

The group moved as one, out of the yard, James at the head of the procession and the Hunters bringing up the rear. The only sounds they made were from the exertion of the climb. Eliza's thighs ached from the effort and she wished she could just sit down. Sit down and never move again. Let the sea salt coat her and the lichen and moss grow up around her, turning her to stone.

As the steps got steeper James had to stop to catch his breath. Eliza could see from the shaking of his arms the strain he was under.

They continued to climb.

A light, insistent rain began to fall as they reached the summit and the monastery. Eliza covered Mary's head but left her own bare to the elements, daring them to do their worst. As they progressed into the monastery Eliza realised they hadn't even said a prayer yet. The pilgrims of old would have recited hundreds of prayers on their ascent but she had said nothing. Had they failed Peter? Again? She wished they could retrace their steps.

They followed James into the shell of the medieval church that stood, incongruous, all sharp angles and corners among the rounded beehive huts. At one time it had a timber roof but today the brooding sky was their only canopy. Eliza's eyes landed on the gaping wound in the earth that was meant for her boy and every bit of her recoiled. She looked anew at the stone walls, the neat dwellings and tidy passageways, all crafted by men. Holy men, yes, but just men. She could find no trace of God here, only an earthly hole waiting to receive her son where his only protection from the worms would be a thin, linen sheet. James placed Peter on the ground beside the grave, sliding his hand out carefully from under his head. Eliza wanted to cry out that the ground was wet. She could see patches of damp creeping up the linen.

James stayed on his knees, head down, lost to the moment. Then he looked up and found her eyes. She could see he didn't know what to do next. They lacked a priest who could lead them through this with a steady, seasoned hand.

She stepped forward, letting go of Joseph's grip as he refused to move with her. She blessed herself. Edmund and Ruth waited for her to begin.

'Our Father –' She started, then stopped. That wasn't the one. There was something else she was supposed to say but her mind refused to deliver it to her. She clasped her hands together, rain sliding down the bridge of her nose.

Into the silence Edmund spoke, his voice too loud to her ears, his words unfamiliar.

'*We pray, oh Lord, for those who sleep.*' He looked over at James, then Eliza. When no one responded he continued. '*By thy infinite mercies vouchsafe to bring us, with those that are dead in Thee ...*' he faltered and Ruth's voice chimed in, carrying him along, '*to rejoice together before Thee.*'

James lowered the small bundle into the open grave, staring after it, then got to his feet. Ruth and Edmund looked at Eliza. She should say something. James should too. But the only words that would come to her were those of the priest who had churched her, '*The Blessed Virgin Mary who has given thee the fruitfulness of offspring*'. Why give her Peter only to take him from her?

James started to fill in the grave, taking care to lower each shovelful of dirt onto the shroud gently. Eliza looked away. How could he do it? Their baby boy. How could he put him in the ground? Up here? So far from them. This cold church of stone and dead monks was no place for a small boy. She was his mother. It was her he needed to be close to. The anger gave her strength. She turned and walked away. Her legs burned with pent-up energy and she quickened her pace. She wanted to run but there was nowhere to run to on this cursed island. She could run all day and all night and never get off it.

'Mammy! Wait!'

A voice called to her. For one beautiful moment she allowed herself to think that it was Peter. She tasted the joy of it even though she knew it was false. She turned as Joseph caught up to her. She bent and held him close. His eyes were full of questions but he kept them to himself. She led him down the steps in silence. There was nothing to say.

They had nearly reached the end of the steps when Eliza heard voices. She wondered if they were in her head. But as she and Joseph rounded the turn at the foot of the staircase she saw two familiar figures making their way up the lighthouse road ahead of them.

'Mammy, that's Jeremiah!'

She was exhausted. It would take all the strength she had left just to drag her feet back inside her own door. Every cell in her body was screaming out for dark solitude. Let me pull the curtains and climb into my bed and never leave it, she thought. She was in no way able to speak to these men. Why had they come? They weren't expected for a while yet – a few weeks they had said when they'd left them a few days ago. Four days? Another lifetime.

When she reached the yard there was no sign of them but the Hunters' door was open. They had found Joanie then.

Eliza had almost made it to the sanctuary of her own door when they appeared, Jeremiah's eyes red.

He approached her without hesitation, shook her hand solemnly and declared, with more sincerity than she'd ever known, 'I'm very sorry for your loss, missus.'

He kept his eyes on hers. She understood. He wanted her to know the depths of his sentiment.

She found her voice. 'Thank you, Jeremiah. He was very fond of you. And you were good to him always.'

He released her hand and shook his head. ''Tis a desperate business. To think of him so full of life only a few days ago.'

He shook Joseph's hand too. 'You'll miss your little brother, you poor lad.'

Jeremiah cleared his throat. Tom came over and shook her hand, unable to meet her eyes but she caught his muttered condolences. They were shocked, she could tell. They'd had no advance warning of what would greet them on the island today.

'Ye were above? At the monastery?' Jeremiah asked.

Eliza didn't answer. He already knew.

They looked at the ground, their words dried up.

'You must be wondering what brought us out?' Jeremiah said.

She didn't care. The thought had crossed her mind idly but she felt she'd never again be curious about anything. What was the point?

'Tom was worried for the young O'Sullivan girl,' he continued. 'Between the storm and the way she was when we left ye. I said to him she'll get used to it but it wouldn't do him. He plagued me until I agreed to row out. He had a sense of something not being right. But God Almighty, we'd never have thought of something like this. A desperate, sad thing.'

Tom stood back from them, the tips of his ears reddening.

Joanie emerged from the Hunters' house. She had her shawl on, and the famous boots. Her small bundle of belongings betrayed her intentions. She glanced at Tom, then spoke to Eliza.

'I won't stay. I've decided.' Her voice wobbled. 'Tom says he can get me a position at one of the cable houses. I'm sorry to leave you, missus. And Joseph. But I can't stay. It's too awful.'

She broke down, weeping into her sleeve. Tom moved closer to her but hung back, not touching her. She pulled herself together, wiped her nose and looked at Eliza, as if waiting for her response.

Eliza said nothing. If Joanie went or stayed what was it to her? She'd been a good help to her. She'd helped her lay out her dead child. But Eliza couldn't find the words to say that now. Maybe she should go too. She tried to let her mind explore the possibility of gathering her things and taking Joseph and Mary off the island. But it refused to be deflected from the knowledge that her little boy was in a grave at the pinnacle of this place. The silence that grew in the space between them was interrupted by the sound of footsteps.

Ruth took in the scene before her in a glance as she entered the yard.

'*Where do you think you're going? Where's Clara?*' she spat at Joanie.

Joanie gestured towards the house. 'She's sleeping, Mrs Hunter. And I'm leaving.'

Ruth's face reddened. She looked around at the small gathering as if looking for someone to explain this or someone to blame. Her eyes settled on Tom.

'I suppose you're the cause of this! It's a disgrace. Courting a young girl out of a respectable position. What have you to offer her in its place?'

Tom kept his head down and said nothing.

Joanie spoke up. 'Tom is only here as my friend, Mrs Hunter. He's found a position for me in Valentia. Thank you for taking me on but it hasn't worked out for me and …' Her voice trailed off, her courage faded.

Ruth stalked past her into the house, pausing to look her up and down one last time and firing off a venomous '*Good riddance!*' before she slammed the door.

Joanie bent to hug Joseph and when she was finished Eliza took her hand. 'Thank you' was all she could manage. She watched them walk out of the yard.

James came against them, his jacket off and sleeves rolled up, still sweating from his task. Eliza saw Jeremiah shaking his hand, offering his condolences, followed by Tom, and then they were gone. Joseph peeled away from her side to watch their departure. Eliza stayed where she was. She might never move again. Her feet felt like they had taken root here.

James came to stand in front of her but didn't speak.

'Joanie's gone,' she said eventually.

'Yes.' He turned and stared out over the wall at the sea. 'Maybe it's for the best. All her tall tales and carrying stories, it was only going to lead to trouble.'

Eliza's eyes filled with tears. 'I don't want to be on my own,' she said, although she knew it wasn't Joanie she was crying for.

James turned to face her. He moved as if to hold her but then gripped the handle of the shovel instead.

'I'm away to the lighthouse,' he said. 'There's things I need to do.'

'Now?'

'We have to go on, Eliza,' he said, walking away from her and out of the yard. He leaned the shovel against the stone wall, its metal blade glinting in the fading sunlight.

Chapter 22

Eliza struggled on. But there were days that passed in longing for her bed from the moment she stepped out of it. She lay awake until the early hours of the morning, listening through the nocturnal silence for something. What, she couldn't say. Then sleep would grab her in the hour before the children woke, pulling her into a dreamless respite. She resented Joseph pawing at her, climbing in beside her with his cold feet, shocking her into a wakefulness she abhorred. There were days when she couldn't say how she had spent her hours. She found Mary in a soiled, sodden nappy when she could have sworn she had changed her. Joseph complained of hunger when she was sure she had given him dinner. She had to fight hard to keep pulling her mind back into her reality. Where did it keep slipping off to? She didn't know but she preferred it there, in the numbness. She hated it here, the absence of his voice and his footsteps, the silence of Joseph with no playmate, the empty seat at the table on the rare occasion they sat together.

James was seldom home, busying himself with work although the night shifts were getting shorter with the lengthening days. Ruth knocked at her door a few times but Eliza ignored her, hiding in the room where Peter had died, holding her breath until she heard Ruth's front door closing again.

Eliza began to sleep in this room every night and every moment she could snatch in the day. She told herself she could still feel him there. But really she could feel nothing. Staying in this room kept her out of the one she shared with James. She couldn't bear the thought of him putting his hands on her, the same hands that had put their son in the ground. The arrangement seemed to suit him too. He worked and slept, chewed and swallowed his meals in silence as fast as he could before disappearing again to his bed or the lighthouse. The only person who got more than this from him was Joseph. He would sit with him for a few minutes, trying to talk to him about his games. But Joseph was lost for words. Where before, his and Peter's games were intricate, rule-bound sagas now there was only one player in a flat landscape, devoid of imagination. James would accept defeat, pat Joseph on the head, then leave.

Eliza would sometimes hear Joseph pretending that Peter was still there.

'You can be the train driver, Peter.'

But never for long. Joseph could not conjure him either. He was well and truly gone.

Eliza roused with a start in the chair by the stove. She hadn't slept a wink all night and hadn't been aware of falling asleep now. She licked at the corner of her lips where some drool had hardened. Mary was napping still in her cradle by the stove and Joseph played quietly at the kitchen table. She stretched the stiffness out of her limbs then became aware of an insistent tapping noise. It was coming from the bedroom, Peter's room, as she now thought of it. The room where he had died. Her mind went immediately to the keening woman on the pier and Joanie's words about souls getting trapped. She shook her head to steady herself. Probably a loose shutter. She opened the door of the room slowly then shrieked as a flutter of wings brushed her face. She slammed the door shut again, her hands trembling.

'What is it, Mammy?' Joseph ran to her.

Eliza took a deep breath and laughed nervously. 'It's just a bird, Joseph. It gave me a fright. I'll have to try and get it out.'

He clung to her arm in terror, refusing to release his grip. Eliza crouched down beside him.

'Joseph, Mammy needs you to mind Mary for a minute. Can you do that?'

He nodded, ready to take on his big-brother duties again, his serious face pulling at her heartstrings. He walked to Mary's cradle, keeping his eyes fixed on Eliza and reached a hand in to stroke his sister's cheek. Eliza gave him a smile that was all for show.

She crept into the room again, blessing herself and wishing she had thought to grab the broom. The white-and-grey bird, a fulmar, had settled in a corner of the room where it trembled, poised to take flight again. Eliza crept towards the window, opening it wider without a sound, speaking gentle words all the while to the bird. Her mother had always told her that the fulmars were spiritual messengers. She stood and waited for the bird to sense the drift of air from the open window, its escape route. It unfurled its grey wings and rose up. Its wingspan seemed to dominate the room and Eliza took a step back so that she was flat against the wall. The bird flapped its wings once and came to hover directly in front of her, level with her eyes. She didn't dare blink. She stared into its dark, beady eye, almost prepared for it to speak to her. Then it turned and with one more flap flew out the window.

Eliza breathed out. Her legs were shaking but she rushed to close the window.

Joseph was outside the door when she opened it.

'Is it gone, Mammy?'

She nodded then jumped as another tap sounded. This time it was her front door. A fresh-looking Ruth and Clara entered. Eliza patted at her clothes – she dreaded to think how she looked.

'Eliza? I hope you don't mind us calling. We thought you might like some company. Oh, goodness! You're very pale.'

Ruth took a seat, with Clara perched in her lap, and Eliza recounted her adventure with the bird.

'Dirty things!' Ruth asserted. 'I hope it didn't mess up the room.' She wrinkled her nose.

Eliza made tea and struggled to keep up with Ruth's incessant chatter. She was making an effort to be friendly but it was giving her a dull, throbbing headache right behind her eyes. She longed to lie down again, in a dark room. After Ruth had mentioned Edmund for the umpteenth time a thought, that had been scratching unformed at Eliza's brain, finally surfaced. When had Ruth and Edmund become such firm allies? Less than a month ago they were at odds and Ruth had been intent on keeping Clara all to herself.

'Relations between yourself and Edmund are good?' she asked.

Ruth paused for a moment, then gave a thin laugh. 'Oh well, they weren't all that bad. I fear my emotions got the better of me when I was expecting. It can happen.'

Eliza raised her eyebrows. Did Ruth expect her to swallow that? She had seen the coolness between them with her own eyes. And what was it Joanie had said about them? That they were like two strangers. When had they reconciled? She cast her mind back. It was only a few weeks since she and Ruth had returned from the mainland even though it felt like a lifetime. It must have been around the time of Peter's passing, maybe after Joanie had left.

'I suppose, Eliza, if I'm to be honest, it did take us a while to reacquaint ourselves, after my absence. But we are firmly bound together now in a common purpose.'

'What is that?'

Eliza thought she knew the answer. She could feel the hum of ambition from Ruth. They wanted James' position. Ever since they got here they had felt it was their entitlement. For a moment she welcomed the idea. It might get James off the island. But she sensed the danger of it too. What were they capable of doing to achieve this common purpose?

Ruth had ignored Eliza's question so she asked it again.

'What common purpose?'

'Oh, you know.' Ruth's tone was bright, giddy. She kept her eyes on her baby. 'Just to give this little lady a good life. And maybe some brothers or sisters if we are blessed with them.' She looked up. 'You look tired, Eliza. Why don't you have a rest while Mary is sleeping? I'll sit with Joseph.'

Eliza rose from her seat with a terse 'Thank you'. She wasn't tired, no more than usual, but she didn't want to spend another moment in Ruth's company.

She went to her room with a heavy step and lay on top of her bed, fully dressed. Her mind was a whirlpool of half-formed thoughts and unanswered questions.

Frustrated with tossing and turning she rose, threw a shawl across her shoulders and crept downstairs. She could hear Ruth in the front room, talking to a silent Joseph in a rushed, low voice. Eliza couldn't make out the words but her skin prickled at the sound. She was tempted to leave without saying anything but thought better of it.

'I'm going to get some fresh air, Ruth.'

'Oh! What a pity the girls are napping or we could have all joined you.'

'That's alright,' Eliza said, relieved that she could go alone. 'I won't be long.'

She backed out the door, feeling a pang of guilt at the lonely figure of Joseph playing in the far corner.

She moved quickly across the yard and found herself once more ascending the steps towards Christ's Saddle. A light drizzle coated her but she didn't care. She was enlivened by the fresh air and distracted by the physical effort of the climb. It was good to punish her body by pushing it hard. When she arrived she was breathless and her thigh muscles felt tight. She paced, getting her breath back, then turned her face to the sky, mouth open, allowing the rain to fall in. She screamed. A long, high sound that didn't feel like it had come from within her, not from any place that she knew of. The scream released something within her and she fell to her knees in the wet grass and mud, sobbing out the pent-up grief until her stomach muscles ached and her fingertips were raw from scrabbling at the soil. Sated, she rocked back on her heels, gasping like an athlete at the finish line. The world around her was utterly unchanged, the rocks unmoved, the rolling waves beneath still charging in and the seabirds twirling noisily above. She thought how little change the waves wrought on the cliff-face. Minute after minute, year after year, crashing their full force against it only to make the smallest mark, a faint erosion. This is what my grief is. My broken heart is this rock and it will never change. She sat in silence another while, then pulled herself up, brushing the muck from her knees. She wiped at her face with her shawl and braced herself to return, to be again around people.

There was another voice in the front room. James. Had she lost all track of time? Was his shift ended? She heard him speak.

'I'll go and look for her.'

Then the door opened and he was in front of her.

'*Oh my God, Eliza! Where were you? You scared us half to death!*' Joseph ran past him, flinging himself at her. '*Mammy!*'

James stepped back and Eliza moved inside, Joseph still hanging on to her.

Ruth came and took her by the hand. 'Oh, my goodness! You're soaked through. And look at your skirts. Did you have a fall? *Oh!*'

Ruth lifted Eliza's hand so that her fingertips were visible, raw, torn, broken. Ruth put a hand to her mouth and turned to James with a look of distress. She was dressed in her outdoor clothes, as was Clara.

'I don't mean to intrude, James. Maybe it's best if I go,' she said.

'Not at all, Ruth. But I don't want to take up any more of your time. You've been very kind.'

Ruth nodded. 'Take care, Eliza.' Her face was soft with sorrow.

She left, followed by James. Eliza could hear their hushed conference by the door but couldn't make out what they were saying.

James came back in.

'Joseph, leave us,' he said. 'Go upstairs.'

Unquestioning, Joseph peeled himself off Eliza, his big brown eyes brimming with tears. James closed the door then stood with his hands on his hips, shaking his head.

'Eliza, what were you thinking?'

She frowned. What was all the fuss about? 'What's the problem, James? I just needed to go out for some fresh air.'

'Without telling anyone? Leaving Joseph and Mary here on their own?'

'*I did not!*' Eliza stepped forward, indignant. 'I mean, I left ...' She took a breath to steady herself and untangle her words. 'Ruth was here with them. I told her I was going.'

James pursed his lips and frowned. 'Is that so? Then how do you explain Edmund coming to find me at the lighthouse to tell me you were missing?'

'Missing? I wasn't missing. I ...'

'*Nobody knew where you were!*' he was shouting now. '*Poor Joseph has been crying his eyes out!*'

'Ask Joseph. He'll tell you Ruth was here with him.'

'Joseph is distraught, Eliza. All he said to me was, "Mammy went away".'

'So go and ask him now!'

Eliza sat down hard in the armchair and put her head in her hands. What was happening? This didn't make any sense. She remembered Ruth whispering to Joseph. What lies had she put into his head?

'James, Ruth came over, we had tea.' She gestured at the table, expecting to see their cups and plates but it shone, clean and empty. 'She must have tidied it away.' Her voice faltered.

'Eliza ...' James sighed. 'Ruth said she has been at home all afternoon resting with Clara because they had a fitful night. They were just going out for a walk when she heard a scream.'

Eliza reddened. Could Ruth have heard her?

'She was worried about you,' James continued. 'Even more so when you didn't answer the door to her. So she let herself in to find Joseph here alone, terrified, and Mary bawling in her cradle. She sent Edmund to tell me. The two houses have been in turmoil because of you, Eliza. *What possessed you?*' He banged a fist against the doorjamb, making her jump.

She started to cry, a low keening sound, and James came to her side. He crouched beside the chair, cradling her sore fingers and spoke quietly.

'I know you've been struggling, Eliza. Ruth was saying maybe you need to see a doctor. Or some time away in a place to rest. Until your mind is strong again.'

Eliza blinked, her tears drying up. Suddenly the pieces fell into place. This was all their doing, Ruth and Edmund. She turned to

James. She needed to see his face and she needed him to hear that she was telling the truth. She put her hands on his cheeks, forcing him to look at her, to see her.

'It's them, James. They're lying. They want you to think I'm going mad. Or maybe they mean to drive me mad.'

He pushed her hands away and rose to his full height.

'Enough!' he roared. He paused, then continued in a calmer tone but there was no doubting his seriousness. 'No more nonsense, Eliza. Or I'll have to send you ashore the next time Jeremiah comes. Ruth has agreed to keep an eye on you for now. We're lucky to have her as a friend. Now if you think you can stay and take care of our children without vanishing again, I have work to do.'

He turned away and stormed from the room, leaving Eliza trembling.

Chapter 23

Two weeks after Peter's passing Eliza was lying in his room. It was a bright April afternoon but the curtains were shut tight against the glaring sun, all light and no warmth. Her eyes were closed, hoping she might drift off for a few blessed moments. When she heard the bedroom door opening she recognised James' footsteps but didn't stir. If he thinks I'm sleeping, she thought, he'll leave me be. But he put his hand on her arm, giving it a gentle shake.

'Eliza, wake up!'

Her skin flared. This was the first time he'd touched her since their argument and every cell and pore was repelled by it. Against her will she opened her eyes.

James paced to the window and yanked the curtains open. The sunlight streamed into the room through the salt-flecked glass.

'Oh God! The cut of the windows!' He froze, then shook the notion away. 'Never mind, they'll have to do.'

Eliza watched him as she slowly got to her feet. Who was he talking to? What was he talking about?

He ran a hand through his hair, then tugged at the hem of his jacket, pulling it straight.

'You have to get moving, Eliza. Right away. The supply boat is here. Edmund saw it from the lighthouse, approaching from the

Dursey side. He had a look with the telescope and he's pretty sure the inspectors are on board. He raced over to tell me. I'd say we have twenty minutes, maybe thirty if we're lucky, to get things right.'

He pulled at the bed covering, attempting to straighten it, to erase the imprint of her recently prone body. The more he flapped about, the less inclined she was to move herself to action. The Commissioners, an inspection. So what? In normal times they'd have been in a constant state of readiness. Spick and span and shipshape. Especially at this time of year when the newness of spring shone an unforgiving light on all that had gone awry in the winter months. But these were not normal times. She didn't care that a man she'd never seen before was coming to run his judgmental white-gloved finger across the dusty surfaces of her life. Let him. Neither did she care that her husband was working himself into a state over it. Would he tell them what he'd done? Were there regulations in their rule book for burying your child?

James gripped her arms. 'Listen. I know this isn't easy. But it is important. As Principal Keeper I am responsible for everything being just so on this island. Ruth is next door putting the place straight. Edmund is seeing to the light but I need to go up now and prepare. Will you do this? Can you do it for me? Can you try?'

He must have seen something in her face that suggested she would because he pecked her on the cheek and was gone.

Eliza eyed the bed covetously then dragged her feet out to the front room. Where to start?

The stove was lit, a kettle boiling on the hob and the table set for tea when a knock at the door announced the arrival of the inspectors.

Eliza managed a weak smile for Joseph who sat, miserable, in the cleanest shirt she could find. There was a smudge of dirt beneath his left ear that she had missed in her hasty wiping. Too late now. She hoisted Mary onto her hip, hoping the baby would distract from the scruffiness of her own clothes. She was suddenly aware of her body odour and lank hair. When last had she washed? She opened the door. Two tall men in crisp Irish Lights uniforms stood before her. They raised their caps in greeting.

'Mrs Carthy. May I present Mr Keane and myself, Mr Duffy.'

'Pleased to meet you. Do come in.' Eliza moved aside, permitting them room to enter.

Already their eyes were roving about, taking stock of her housekeeping efforts or the lack thereof.

'We won't keep you, Mrs Carthy. Just a quick look around is all that's necessary.'

'But won't you be taking tea?' Eliza gestured at the table where she had set the Irish Lights crockery.

The two men exchanged a glance.

Mr Keane spoke. His voice was softer, apologetic. 'That's very good of you but Mrs Hunter has prepared tea for us. She thought that might be for the best. In the circumstances.'

Eliza bridled. As Principal Keeper's wife it was her place to cater for the inspectors, not Ruth's. The feeling passed, followed by relief. This meant they'd leave her be sooner and maybe she could rest again.

Mr Duffy removed his cap and Mr Keane followed suit.

'May I offer our sincere condolences, Mrs Carthy. Of course, we knew nothing of your loss until our arrival. It's not unheard of, unfortunately. Life on these rock stations poses certain challenges.'

Eliza's eyes pricked with tears. He spoke of it so matter-of-factly as though it was an irritation, an inconvenience one had to contend with, rather than having one's heart and soul ripped out. Her eyes were drawn to the glinting brass button on his sleeve, imprinted with the motto, *'In Salutem Omnium'* – For the Safety of All. Not for Peter, she thought. The Irish Lights couldn't guarantee the safety of my boy.

'But you have two lovely children and you are young. Please God, you'll be blessed with more. Now, I will take a quick look into the rooms and Mr Keane will check the inventory.'

Eliza sat down heavily on the fireside chair. By right she should show the man around but his cruel words had punctured her. To think that she could just replace Peter with another child. Her eyes slid to the door of what she now thought of as Peter's room. She couldn't bear the thought of a stranger poking about in there. She sat stock still, trying not to hear the thud of his steps overhead or the muttering of the man counting spoons and saucers in her kitchen. She laughed to herself. This wasn't her kitchen, or her house for that matter. It was theirs. She stood up, hoisting Mary higher.

'Come on, Joseph. We'll leave these men to their work.'

He looked startled but took her hand and allowed himself to be led out the door.

Eliza headed down the lighthouse road without thinking, panting with the effort of carrying Mary and pulling Joseph along behind her. He dragged his feet, tugging on her hand and whining.

'Where are we going, Mammy?'

Eliza stopped, wiping the sweat from her brow. She caught her breath and tried to still her mind. They were at the base of the steps. Where was she going? Up to the monastery? No. Not now with her two small children and the evening closing in. She had no desire to return to her house either. So where? Where could she go? They could go up to Christ's Saddle. It had a good vantage point and was, now that she thought about it, midway between their house and Peter's grave. Seized by decision, she started up the stone steps. It took a long time to coax Joseph along but finally they reached it.

She took off her shawl and spread it on the ground. 'Here. Let's sit a while.'

Joseph settled beside her. She kept her gaze out to sea but was aware of him peeking up at her from uncertain eyes. So much new territory for him to cross, for them all. They sat in silence for a while, watching the seabirds diving for fish.

Eliza fed Mary under her shawl and watched Joseph as he built an elaborate castle of stones topped with a feather from a gannet.

Joseph got to his feet and pointed. 'Look, Mammy, the boat!'

He was right. The supply boat carrying the inspectors was in open water, pulling away from them towards the mainland, the white flag with the prominent red cross still visible. They hadn't delayed with Ruth obviously. Eliza breathed a sigh of relief. She felt a vague sense of victory, like the monks of old watching a Viking ship leave their shore, plundered but alive. Survivors, if nothing else. She pulled Joseph down again, happier to have him seated.

'I like it up here,' she said to him. 'Maybe we'll come again tomorrow if the weather holds.'

She was at peace for a moment but it was illusory, pierced in the next breath by guilt. How could she be making plans like nothing had happened? Her eyes flooded with tears and through the watery veil she saw the silhouette of James stalking towards them.

Eliza got to her feet, cradling Mary to her chest.

'*What are you at, woman?*' he shouted.

Eliza took a step back in shock as James reached them. He was red-faced, sweating from the climb, and spitting fire.

'*Why aren't you below looking after the Commissioners? You are the Principal Keeper's wife and you're lolling about up here like it's a holiday!*'

Eliza gestured at the open sea below them. 'They're gone,' she said.

'I know they're gone! I saw them off. Do you have any idea how embarrassed I was? What could I say? What possible reason could I give them for having to take their tea in the Assistant Keepers' house?'

'But Ruth asked –'

'I know well she did. And thank God! She took one look at the cut of you and she knew you weren't up to it. But to add insult to injury, then you take off while they are inspecting our house. *You just walked out, without a by-your-leave!*'

'It's not our house,' she responded under her breath but he heard. It stopped him in his tracks.

'What? What are you on about?'

Eliza was aware of Joseph, crouched behind her, stock still. She had never seen James in a rage like this before, not once, in all the time she'd known him. She didn't want to anger him by saying more but it would make matters worse to offer nothing by way of explanation.

'Well,' she straightened and looked him right in the eye, 'it's not our house. How can it be when strange men can traipse in and out of it, poking their noses into every corner, putting on their white gloves to point their fingers at a dusty mantel or dirty floor?'

'*Eliza, have you gone mad? You're a lightkeeper's wife. You know about inspections. We've had them before. What's changed?*'

She recoiled. When she answered her voice was shrill. '*What's changed? Everything has changed!* Nothing on this cursed island is ours truly except what we brought with us. We've already lost a most precious piece of ourselves. I'm not like you, James. I can't pretend that Peter isn't dead and just go on with life like before!'

He stepped back from her and surveyed the grass at his feet. Had her words given him pause for thought?

'It is unfortunate that ...' He took a breath then continued more calmly. 'It is unfortunate that the Commissioners came so soon, after ... But we have a job to do, Eliza, no matter what the circumstances. You owe Ruth your gratitude. Her and Edmund both. They did us a great favour today. The Commissioners spoke highly to me of Ruth's hospitality and Edmund's professionalism. In fact, it has decided me not to file the report on Edmund's mishap. We are indebted to them after today.'

Eliza couldn't believe what she was hearing. This was what he wanted to say to her?

'What if it wasn't a single mishap?' She took a step towards him, lowering her voice so that Joseph wouldn't hear. 'What do you really know about your Assistant Keeper, James? You spend so much time with your head in your logbooks and your instruments you don't even see what's right under your nose.'

James' eyes darted left and right. She could tell she had unnerved him. She wanted to hurt him, to mortally wound him with her words.

'Do you know that Edmund only married Ruth out of a sense of duty? That he loved another woman?' She sliced her words at him through gritted teeth.

'Eliza, this idle gossip is beneath you. What business is it of yours or mine?'

'Do you know that he told me I remind him of the woman he once loved? That night you left him, drunk, in our front room. I didn't say anything at the time because of Peter. He put his hands on me, James. He tried to kiss me. Can't you see how he has been undermining you? Him and Ruth? And you want me to go down there and show them my gratitude?'

She spun on her heel, returned to her shawl and sat down, her eyes on the horizon. There was no taking it back now, the damage was done.

James stood a moment longer, looking like a man whose world had been rocked, then he took off down the steps at speed.

Eliza fought back the tears and the rising tide of panic that replaced her anger. She shivered, her limbs tight around her. She held Mary tighter, trying to draw warmth from her and wished she could gather her words back. Why had she said anything? What trouble had she started? After a while she pulled herself upright, announced to Joseph that it was time to go home, and half-dragged him back down the steps. She would speak to James, she needed to speak to him before he met Edmund.

He was at the foot of the lighthouse.

'*James!*'

He shook his head and stalked into their house. She followed him, her every nerve jangling. Had she caught him in time? She laid Mary in her cradle.

'Joseph, stay with your sister.'

Eliza followed James to their bedroom, a room distasteful to her now.

James had his back to her, unbuttoning his formal jacket.

'James.' Her voice sounded uncertain to her own ears. She took a deep breath as he turned a stony face to her. Now that she had his attention, she didn't know what to say. What had she come here to say? 'I didn't mean to. I mean I don't want you to ...'

What did she want? She wanted peace. She wanted nothing to happen and for her real world to fade from her vision so that she could wander among happy memories.

'I already spoke to Edmund.' James' face betrayed nothing. 'In the lighthouse, just now. He says you are mistaken, Eliza. He never had any such exchange with you. I'm inclined to take him at his word. I believe him to be a truthful man, too truthful in fact. And I'm sorry, but you are changed, Eliza.'

Eliza breathed in sharply. Was he calling her a liar?

'Edmund spoke sense. He said that grief can muddle the mind and when I see how you are this past while I think he's right.'

Eliza sat down hard at the edge of the bed, all strength gone from her. She hadn't wanted James to do anything about it. But for him to doubt her word, her mind, was cruel.

'You need more time, Eliza. I see that. I'm not a hard man. But I need to do my job. And I need you not to make that difficult for me with tall tales and inventions.'

She said nothing, so he continued.

'You will return to this bedroom also. It's not natural for a man and wife to be apart under the same roof. And it will be better for you not to be in the room where Peter died. You will move on more quickly.'

She looked at James. He had changed into his everyday shirt and trousers, more familiar to her, and yet his words made him a stranger. Where was his warmth, his compassion? He took a step towards her and planted a kiss on her forehead, his cool lips on her skin a moment too long, then he was gone.

Eliza released the bunched blanket from her clenched fists, the ground under her feet like shifting sands. Had she imagined it all? Were James and Edmund right to say she had invented it? She needed to speak to Edmund herself. But she needed to see him alone. She took up position by the front window where she could watch for his return from the lighthouse once James relieved him.

Chapter 24

The sky was dark and the first stars were creeping out when Eliza heard footsteps in the yard. She rushed back to the window to check. Yes, it was Edmund. She smoothed down her hair and brushed at her skirts. If he was making her out to be a madwoman she'd be sure not to look like one. She opened the door as quietly as she could and slipped out.

'*Edmund!*' she whispered, loud enough for him to hear in the dead silence of the night. The only other sounds were the waves shushing at the rocks and a late seabird skating by on the light breeze to its night-time perch. A rising moon bathed the yard with light.

The sound of her voice had stopped him. Now he turned and walked back towards her, his face watchful and wary.

She stepped to the side of her porch, where they wouldn't be seen from the lighthouse if James happened to look their way. With a glance up at the light, he joined her there.

'Eliza, what are you doing out here? You'll get cold. There's going to be a hard frost tonight.'

She raised a hand to silence him. She only had a few minutes before she was sure to be interrupted by Joseph or Mary and she didn't want to alert Ruth.

'What did you say to James?' It was blunt but she was past caring.

'What did I say? About what?' A smirk skirted his lips.

He wasn't going to make this easy for her. She could feel her thoughts scattering. She had played the conversation over in her mind while she was watching for him but now it was all confusion.

'You told him lies.'

'Did I? I don't know, Eliza. It seems to me you might be the one inventing tall tales. I didn't know what he was on about. Lost loves and longing looks.' He snorted in derision. 'It was embarrassing for us both but for him particularly. Being Principal Keeper is a hard job, Eliza. And a Principal Keeper needs a good wife with a strong mind. I fear yours has been weakened by your loss.' His cold, green eyes stared into hers, unblinking.

She could not think what to say. How to defend herself. She tried to recall the exact words he had said to her that night but her memory was blurred. And it wasn't just the words that mattered. It was his tone and the way he'd looked at her. He had tried to kiss her, for God's sake! She was sure of it. Hadn't he? Oh God! Horror seeped through her bones. Had she misunderstood him? But no, she remembered now the name of the girl, Catherine.

'*Catherine*,' she said it out loud, hoping to shock him but he remained unmoved, his lips pursed and his dark eyebrows softened in an expression of pity.

'*Catherine*,' she said it again. 'That was the girl you loved. The one who went away. To Canada.'

Edmund nodded and looked down. 'I knew a girl by that name, alright. She was a bit soft in the head, poor thing.' He tapped his temple with his forefinger. 'She was a wee bit infatuated with me, following me around and waiting for me when my shift was done. There was no more to it. She did go away. But not to Canada. That's what the family said to hide the shame of it. No, she went away to a place for those with weak minds. Poor girl.'

Eliza drew back. Her memory of that night was incomplete, perforated by what had come after it, but she was sure none of this was true. She knew it. She stepped closer to Edmund again so that her next words could be no more than a whisper.

'You put your hands on me!'

He couldn't see, she was sure, but she could feel her cheeks burning.

Edmund stood back from her, hands raised in defence.

'Eliza, I have no difficulty saying I was in the wrong. I drank too much and had no business being in your house that night. In truth, I don't know what James was thinking to bring me there. But that's all there is to it. If I staggered and put a hand out to steady myself, maybe. But I have no memory of that and you need to get a hold of your mind. We'll help you if we can, Ruth and myself.'

He looked over her right shoulder. She turned. The silhouette of Ruth was visible in the darkness of their front window. She was there, watching, and made no move to conceal it. What had she heard?

'As we are speaking frankly, Eliza, I'll say this.' He took a step closer, his voice deep and steady. 'You let your husband down today. A Principal Keeper needs to know that his wife is rock solid and steady. If not, he won't be long for the job and someone else will take his place.'

Edmund moved past her and entered his house.

She gulped in handfuls of the bitter night air. The moon was starting its ascent and the cold, white light from it cast the jagged rocks of Skellig Michael into a deeper darkness. She felt as though she was surrounded by sharpened knives, ready to wound her.

As she turned to go inside a sound froze her to the spot. Laughter. Behind their closed door Edmund and Ruth were laughing like children.

Eliza lay in the room she shared with James. She had returned reluctantly, to appease him. All night she tossed and turned, trying to still her thumping heart, wanting to scream out that she was telling the truth. Wasn't she?

The next day she couldn't settle her mind to any task. The screech of the seagulls set her nerves on edge and she longed for some quiet just to get her thoughts straight.

She started at the sound of a knock on her front door. She answered it. Ruth was standing there with Clara in her arms, wrapped up against the fresh spring breeze and looking ready to go somewhere.

'Eliza, how are you? I was just heading out but I wanted to check on you. After yesterday.'

'Heading out?'

'Yes,' Ruth replied, giving no indication of where she might be going. Just to the lighthouse, Eliza supposed, or a walk to Blind

Man's Cove. Where else was there to go? She was hardly going to climb to the monastery.

Ruth shifted Clara to her other hip. In the expectant silence Eliza felt wrong-footed again, under pressure to speak, but not sure where to start. How to answer that question, 'How are you?'

Ruth took the lead. 'There's no need to be embarrassed and no need to thank me, Eliza. I just rose to the occasion when it was called for.' She gifted Eliza a serene smile but there was no warmth in her eyes. 'It's understandable that you didn't feel up to the inspectors' visit. Although when you're a lightkeeper's wife there's no such thing, is there? You have to be willing and able to meet the demands of the position, no matter what. Edmund has taught me a lot about duty.'

She stared at Eliza. She knows, Eliza thought. Before she had time to decide on the right way forward the words were out of her mouth.

'Ruth, did Edmund ever speak to you of a girl by the name of Catherine?'

'Catherine? No, I don't think that rings any bells. Who is she?' Ruth's expression betrayed nothing beyond mild curiosity.

Who is she, thought Eliza. A lost love of Edmund's? A crazy woman? A figment of a crazy woman's imagination?

'She – he told me – the night you returned from the mainland – do you know he was in my house? Drunk?'

Ruth's cheeks coloured a touch. She sighed. 'Yes, the silly man! I am sorry, Eliza. I'm sure it was an awful nuisance. I meant to come and apologise but then Peter was so sick.'

Eliza recoiled at the sound of Peter's name coming from Ruth's mouth.

Ruth smiled coyly. 'Edmund said he missed me an awful lot while I was gone. He thought he'd lost me forever. Of course, he shouldn't have sought solace in a bottle of whiskey or whatever it was.' She laughed.

'He was quite ... improper ...' Eliza stumbled over the last word. None of it was coming out right. Tears filled her eyes and she lowered her head, not wanting Ruth to see.

'I agree. It was not at all right for him to be drunk in your house. I don't know why in the name of God James didn't just bring him here.'

'James was trying to help.' Eliza had allowed that same thought to run through her mind more than once. Why had James put her in that position? But she could not allow Ruth to question his authority.

'He has a soft heart,' Ruth said. 'But, in all honesty, I don't think that was the right thing to do. However, I owe him my gratitude for not making a record of Edmund's misstep. I'm not sure many Principal Keepers would have made the same decision. Promising careers have floundered on less.'

Eliza heard the threat in those words. They echoed Edmund's warning of the night before. Suddenly she was exhausted. Ruth and Edmund had closed ranks and James didn't believe her.

A sob escaped and Ruth put a hand on her arm.

'Oh, Eliza! You've been through so much. And so soon after a baby too. I've known women who became very melancholy after a birth and they never recovered properly, poor things. They had to be put away, for their own sakes.'

Eliza looked up. Ruth's face was close to hers and she could see the hardness in her eyes. A cold river of fear flooded Eliza's veins.

'I hope you feel you can rely on me whenever you need to.'

Eliza couldn't find the energy to respond to her false offer of friendship. Ruth gave her arm a little squeeze and turned from the door.

Eliza closed her door and dragged her feet back to the downstairs bed.

James came from the lighthouse just as she was rousing Mary from her nap.

'You spoke to Ruth?' he asked. 'I met her on the way and she said ye had a chat.'

Eliza nodded.

'Good, that was the right thing. I hope you thanked her.' He took Mary from her arms. 'Please God, the next time the inspectors come we'll all be on top form.'

Later that night Eliza ran out of reasons not to go to bed. Joseph and Mary had settled hours before. She had tidied away all traces of their evening meal and even attempted some darning, although her shaking hands made her work clumsy. She had breathed a sigh of relief when James stretched and said he was going to bed. That was nearly an hour ago and Eliza could feel her eyes growing heavy.

As she climbed the stairs she said a silent prayer that James would be sleeping but she heard him stir as she let herself in. She removed her clothes, pulled her nightgown on and slipped under the blanket. She thought of this as his bed now, not hers, not theirs. She squeezed her eyes shut, slowing her breathing to give the impression of falling asleep. The heft of his bed-warm body turned towards her. His hand was on her shoulder, then smoothing the hair away from the nape of her neck and kissing her there. In the past this had always thrilled her, his rough skin and hot breath on the softness. But now she felt nothing. She was suspended, external. She could shrug him off, say she was tired. Or she could turn to him and try to find herself in his embraces.

She turned onto her back and he climbed on top of her, his hands becoming frenzied now, running over her breasts, hardening her nipples through the light cotton of her nightgown. He pushed his knee between her legs, parting them, then he pushed himself inside her.

Eliza winced – his rough entry hurt her. Salty tears sprang from her eyes but James was lost in his own pleasure, thrusting and grunting to his conclusion. He slumped on her chest, panting.

'I've missed you, Eliza!' He kissed her cheek hard. 'I'm glad you've come back to me.'

But Eliza was not there. She had not found herself. She was not in this room, or this house. She was on a flat point of the island, halfway to the monastery.

Chapter 25

James' mood remained unpredictable despite their reunion. He shouted at Joseph for running through the house, causing the door to slam and waking him. Joseph had rarely had a cross word from his father before this and Eliza's heart broke for him. She didn't know what game he'd been playing when the door banged. She didn't care either. He could break every door and window in the place if it meant he was able to have fun again.

One morning James stormed around the house, angered at not being able to find his uniform jacket.

'For God's sake, Eliza! It has to be here somewhere.'

He had the house nearly torn asunder.

'Do you really need it today?' Eliza ventured.

Her hands shook as she opened doors to peer inside cupboards and drawers, knowing full well that it wouldn't be there. She remembered quite clearly when last she had seen it but she was afraid to tell him. She had taken it from the chair in their bedroom days after the inspectors' visit and hung it on the line to air in the spring sunshine. She was sure that's where she'd seen it last, wasn't she? But what had she done with it then? She racked her brain but could find no trace of that memory.

'That's beside the point!' James' voice was quivering with temper.

'Well, it can't have vanished. I'll keep looking for it while you're at the lighthouse.'

His answer to this was a slammed door, the bang ricocheting through the silent house.

After he left Eliza gathered together food and blankets and whisked Mary and Joseph off to what she now thought of as their place. It was peaceful on Christ's Saddle and they whiled away many hours watching for passing fishing boats and spying on the little seabirds that hopped about, pecking at the greening ground. She could relax here. Far from the gloomy orbit of her angry husband and her devious, scheming neighbours. The respite allowed her to brace for whatever tense hours stood between her and sleep.

She was returning when she saw Ruth at her door. She stopped, tempted for a moment to hide behind the high wall until she left. But Joseph towed her onwards, anxious for his tea. Ruth was tapping lightly on the door and spun around when she heard their footsteps.

'There you are. I thought I might need to send out a search party again.' Ruth's laugh faded as Eliza remained stony-faced. 'Goodness, you'll be frozen. It's getting cold. I've my stove blazing inside.'

Ruth's eyes flicked to Eliza's chimney. There was no smoke and Eliza's heart sank as she realised she hadn't banked the fire before they left. She'd have to light it again when she went in and that meant a cold tea for Joseph. She uttered a silent prayer that James wouldn't return until it was going strong. She was afraid he would look poorly on her keeping the children out this late and bringing them back to a cold house. Ruth was watching her closely. Was there anything this blasted woman didn't know about her comings and goings? And did she have to comment on it all? Eliza remained silent. She longed to give full force to the hatred she had for this woman but understood the importance of not letting her emotions show. Edmund and Ruth would love another opportunity to show James how unstable she was, no doubt. Neither would she give Ruth the satisfaction of asking what she wanted now. She hoped she felt awkward.

Then, from under her shawl Ruth produced a piece of clothing.

'Anyway, I won't keep you out in the cold. I just wanted to bring this back to you.'

Eliza stared in disbelief. What was Ruth doing with James' jacket?

She managed to find her voice. 'Where did you get that?'

'Oh you are funny, Eliza!' Ruth laughed then grew serious. 'You remember you asked me to mend the button? See here, the second from last. It should be secure now but –'

'*You took this from my line!*' Eliza's grip on the navy material tightened as her voice shook. She knew she needed to stay in control but every cell in her body wanted to reach out and slap Ruth.

'Eliza, how could you say such a thing? I'm sorry, I will not allow you to accuse me in this way.' She took a deep breath then narrowed her eyes. 'No, I'm worried actually. You don't recall asking me? Is everything alright? I heard shouting this morning. I would never interfere in private affairs but I have to admit I am concerned.'

Eliza nudged Joseph. He was hanging off her, following every word of their conversation. 'Go on in, Joseph.' He hesitated. 'Go on!' She managed a thin smile. 'I'll be in after you.'

When he was gone she stepped closer to Ruth. She examined her face. Was that a smirk flirting around her lips?

She pointed at her. 'Why would I ask *you* to mend a button?'

'Eliza!' Ruth sighed as if the effort of the explanation was a burden to her. 'You said you couldn't steady your hand to do it.' She looked at the outstretched finger.

Eliza snatched it away and stowed it behind her back but they had both seen the tremor.

'I don't know what you think you're doing.' Eliza's voice was one she'd never heard before. It was flinty sharp. '*But you need to stop – now!*'

Ruth looked shocked but the smirk lingered. 'I don't know what you mean, Eliza. I'm just trying to be a good neighbour.'

She pulled her shawl tighter around her and stepped away.

Eliza stayed where she was, her hand a pincer-grip on the jacket, until Joseph reappeared and she had to go in.

She was still awake when James returned from the lighthouse. She had spent the last few hours willing herself to sleep, staring wide-eyed at the ceiling as her mind raced. Was she going crazy? Had she given the jacket to Ruth to mend? *No.* She played and replayed the scene, like retracing her steps to find a lost item. She could see herself carrying the basket of washing outside and pegging the jacket to the line. She racked her brain to recall bringing the clothes back in but found only a blank. Her days were a whirlwind of feeding and changing and cleaning and she often found at the end of a day she couldn't remember how she had spent it.

She closed her eyes when she heard James' heavy step on the stairs. She was far too exhausted to endure another row or even a strained conversation. She slowed her breathing. He came in quietly and she heard him undressing. She cracked her eyes open a sliver and saw him turning to lay his folded clothes on the bedroom chair like always. He saw the jacket where she had hung it.

'Oh,' he said under his breath. 'You found it.'

He sighed and a moment later the mattress sank under his weight. Eliza tensed her muscles to counteract the gravity that would move her towards him. But he leaned over her. His breath was on her ear, then a whisper, 'I'm sorry', and he turned away from her onto his side. Within a minute his snoring filled every corner of the room and she eventually surrendered to sleep.

The morning brought some relief. Eliza had slept well and her heart was soothed by Joseph cuddling into bed between her and James. She braced herself for tension when Joseph woke his father but James just laughed and tickled his squealing son into hysteria. Eliza allowed herself to smile as she went to the kitchen to prepare their breakfast.

Ruth's deviousness troubled her still but in the newness of the morning she decided it wouldn't serve her to dwell on it.

James kissed her cheek once he'd finished his food and she could hear him whistling as he crossed the yard.

Eliza had a strong sensation of a mishap avoided, a fresh start. As her eyes alighted on the dust and cobwebs in the front room she knew how she would spend this day. It was time for a spring clean. It would do them all good and for the first time since Peter died she had the energy for it.

Joseph was happy to amuse himself with a basin of water and a rag and within hours Eliza was standing back to admire her work. She had even managed to rub the cloth around the window in the room where Peter had died. She felt a pang of loneliness in that moment for Joanie – her impudent company would be welcome and she would be an ally.

Her back and knees ached from scrubbing the floor, her hands were cracked and red from being immersed in water and she dreaded to think how she looked. But she had a sensation that had been missing for many weeks, since Peter first sickened. She was at peace and proud of having accomplished something. Her little house shone from top to bottom, and now, when the spring sunshine hit the windows they were transparent.

She was just bringing Joseph inside to change him out of his sodden clothes when she saw James entering the yard. Her heart gave a little skip at the thought of him seeing her efforts and being pleased with her, but it sank again when she saw the hunch of his shoulders, his stiff gait and the dark cloud that shrouded his face. He wasn't whistling now.

On instinct she slipped into the house before he saw her, herding Joseph ahead of her, and watched James' approach through a crack in the door. He walked, like a man on a serious mission, straight to Ruth's door and knocked decisively. It opened and Eliza strained to hear what was being said but she could decipher only James' serious tone and Ruth's soft murmuring, followed by a tinkle of laughter.

Ruth's door closed and Eliza leapt back from her own as if it had burned her. She hurried to the kitchen, cast around and seized upon a brush by the stove. When James came in, banging the door behind him, she was stooped by the stove, sweeping at non-existent dust. She stood, smoothing her skirts and her hair, and feigned surprise.

'Oh, I didn't hear you coming,' she said brightly.

Joseph ran at James, no doubt expecting the same warmth as the morning but James stopped him in his tracks.

'Go and wash up, Joseph. You look like a chimney sweep.'

Joseph's face fell. It was true, thought Eliza, his face was smeared and grubby, but he was happy. Could James not see that?

James waited until Joseph left, then he stood, straight as a rod and stony-faced, before her.

'I called on Ruth,' he declared.

'Oh?' Eliza's confusion was genuine. What was this about?

'I was due to make my inspection of their house but more importantly I felt I should apologise to her.'

Eliza furrowed her brow.

'For your behaviour.'

'*What?*' Eliza was incredulous. Was she really hearing this?

James cleared his throat. He had more to say. 'You accused her of stealing from us, Eliza. My Assistant Keeper had to report to me this morning that his wife was distraught.' He gritted his teeth. He jabbed a finger at Eliza, punctuating every word in his fury. *'Distraught! Because – you – called – her – a – thief!'*

Eliza sank into the chair. 'James, she had your jacket. The one you couldn't find. Why are you taking her word in this? I am your wife.'

'Well, you'd better start acting like it. Because this last while I feel like I don't even know you. The way you've been, the things you've done. No more, Eliza. I will have no more of this nonsense. I don't want to hear your reasons or the ridiculous notions you entertain. I'm telling you now. There is to be no more. I have been embarrassed. Humiliated. By your actions – and there is to be no more! What's more you could do with taking a leaf out of Ruth's book, the way she keeps that place. *You've let things slip, Eliza.*' He was shouting now, flecks of spittle flying from his angry tongue. *'You need to get them back on track now. Am I clear?'*

Eliza did not speak. She gave a slight nod.

James stormed from the room, back out the door he had come through minutes earlier. She had no idea where he was going but she was glad he was gone. His anger frightened her. Her own stomach filled with anger now as well. Ruth! She had caused this, all of it. She knew she would have to watch her. She wouldn't take her eyes off her for a moment. She understood, even if James was ignorant to it, what was behind Ruth and Edmund's deviousness. It would take everything she had in her maybe but she would keep this ship afloat. She would not allow these rats to scuttle it.

Chapter 26

Eliza moved through her days now like a hunted, skittish animal. She kept the uneasy peace in the house and played the part of the good wife. Through intense mental focus she made sure that James never wanted for a hot meal or a clean shirt. Her conversation stayed in the safe channels of the weather or harmless questions about his day. She avoided any mention of her poisonous neighbours and if James mentioned them she managed to fix her face into a convincing template of neutrality. Tears were still never far from her eyes but she let them fall only when she was sure they would go unseen and unheard. She thought about making an effort to soothe matters between herself and Ruth but it stuck in her craw. She could not bring herself to knock on that woman's door and deep within she knew Ruth would see through any attempt at peacemaking.

She felt some guilt at not having been to Peter's grave since the awful day of his burial. With the first month anniversary encroaching she steeled herself to return. If they were on the mainland they would remember him in a special Mass. Instead, she would push herself to go beyond Christ's Saddle and lay some flowers for him.

The day dawned bright and Eliza readied herself. She thought only of each action in turn and did not dare think beyond it. I will eat breakfast. I will dress Mary. I will brush my hair. In this way she managed to get herself as far as the door with Mary and Joseph, who bubbled over with nervous excitement.

'Will he be there, Mammy? Will we see him?'

Eliza crouched down to look him in the eye, balancing herself with a hand on the cool wall to counteract the weight of Mary in her shawl.

'No, pet, we won't.'

'So where's he gone? Why are we going up if he's not there?' He kicked at the floor with his boot.

Eliza stood and took his hand. 'Come on, I'll you tell all about it on the way.' She led him across the yard. 'Do you remember what we said? We all have a thing called a soul and when we die that bit goes up to God.'

Joseph watched her lips, trying to catch the meaning.

'So it's only Peter's body that's up at the monastery. We won't see him but we can think about him and say some prayers.'

Joseph nodded, somewhat mollified.

Eliza quickened her pace. She forced herself to think of the warm sun on her face and nothing more. They had just rounded the base of the lighthouse when James came against them, head down, not even seeing them.

'*Daddy!*' Joseph was thrilled at this unexpected encounter. He looked up at Eliza. 'Is Daddy coming too?'

'Coming where?' James frowned into the glare of the sun.

'We're going to see Peter,' Joseph announced.

James looked at Eliza, surprise on his face. She reddened. She hadn't mentioned it when she'd seen him last night and was embarrassed to be caught out in her secret.

'You never said.' James looked hurt.

Maybe she should have told him. He'd like to go too perhaps but the thought of seeing Peter's grave again for the first time filled her with such dread that she needed to be alone, without being observed. She looked away, trying to keep the lie from her eyes.

'I hadn't decided really until this morning. I wanted to see would the weather hold.'

She looked up at the blue sky, untroubled by cloud. If ever there was perfect weather to sit by your dead son's grave, this was it.

She looked back at James. His wounded expression irritated her. Why was he making this about him? It was about Peter.

'It's his month's mind, you know – today,' she said. The words came out harsh, an accusation.

'You think I don't know that, Eliza?' His blue eyes stared her down, forcing her to concede.

'No, of course you know. I just thought you'd be too busy to come with us anyway.'

She gestured at the glinting, revolving light behind them.

James glanced in its direction and nodded. 'Maybe so.' He sighed. 'I could go with you only Edmund is after spotting a problem. He reckons the lamp oil might be dirty ...' He stared up at the light as if it might offer up the information he needed. He shook his head. 'I'll have to leave ye at it. Mind yourselves up there. I'll go up later when I'm able.'

He looked at them for a moment. There was an unspoken message but the gap between them was too wide and Eliza couldn't decipher it. He walked away, glancing up at the light, and they continued on.

As they reached the base of the monastery steps Eliza heard someone calling her name. She turned to see Ruth coming down the road with Clara in her arms. Eliza cursed under her breath but made sure to fix a smile onto her face by the time Ruth had caught up with them.

'Are you off for a picnic?'

There was a sprightliness about Ruth that Eliza found grating.

'No,' Eliza responded.

'We're going up to see Peter,' Joseph said.

Ruth's face turned serious and she raised a hand to her mouth. 'Is James not going with you?'

Ruth's question stirred something in Eliza that she hadn't known was even there. She wanted him by her side. But the James who would support her, help her through this ordeal. Not the James who would watch for any signs of erratic behaviour and judge her for it.

'No, he's not able to.' Eliza fussed at the shawl securing Mary so she could hide her expression from Ruth. 'Some problem with the light.' She gestured towards the lighthouse.

'That's a shame. But duty calls, I suppose. I could come with you. If you'd like some company?'

Eliza was struck dumb. She could think of nothing she would like less than to have Ruth intruding on her grief. But how to say it without causing offence and sending her running to Edmund and James with her complaints? The lingering silence spoke volumes and Ruth tutted.

'Now, Eliza, I hope there isn't going to be awkwardness between us. After all, if I am willing to forgive and forget then ... I do understand, you know. You've been under a lot of strain. It's easy to see how you might get confused.' She stared at Eliza, unflinching.

Eliza wanted to scream at her. She was not confused. In fact, her eyes were wide open to what Ruth was trying to do. But she plastered a smile on her face instead. 'Thank you, Ruth. I hope you'll understand as well if I say I'd rather go alone today. It is my first visit ... since ... and ...'

Ruth took a step forward and placed a hand on Eliza's arm. 'Of course,' she said. 'I will call in later, to see how you are.' She smiled beatifically as Eliza mounted the first step.

Eliza made herself put one foot in front of the other, resisting the urge to turn around and check if Ruth was watching their ascent. She was exhausted from it all and she still had the endless steps and Peter's grave to confront.

When they finally reached the monastery the effort had robbed Joseph of his chatter and Eliza was glad. The spring sun had an intense warmth at this height. She paused to catch her breath and stretched her head back to gaze at the endless blue sky disrupted by an occasional wheeling bird. The monastery hummed with the energy of bees and birds and Eliza's eyes swam with tears. She would give everything she had in the world to have her little boy back again but if he had to have a final resting place she could see now that this wasn't so bad.

She approached the grave. It was less raw than a month before – already there were signs of nature reclaiming it. She knelt beside it and sighed. 'Hello, Peter, pet,' she said, patting at the soil as if he could feel her caress.

Joseph stood behind her, twisting his fingers into her hair, as he did when he needed comfort. She reached back and drew him up beside her. He stared at the grave, then whispered. 'Didn't you say Peter isn't in there, Mammy?'

'I did, love. Only his body is here. Your little brother is above in Heaven with God now.'

'But why does his body have to be up here? Why can't we have him down near us?'

Eliza thought for a moment. 'Well, this is a holy place, Joseph. The monks built it so that they could be nearer to God. So that means Peter's resting place is near to God too.' It was the right answer but she still didn't feel it to be true. Was Peter nearer to God? She had no sense of that, could take no comfort from it, the loss of him still too cavernous.

He was silent, mulling it over. 'But why can't we go see him in Heaven so?'

Eliza could see that she had confused him but she was at a loss to explain this new reality to herself, never mind her child. The plain truth was that Peter was gone. The grave served as cold comfort to those left behind.

'We're not allowed to go to Heaven, Joseph. Not yet.'

'But, if we want to be near Peter we come up here?'

'Yes.' Eliza felt a pang of guilt that this was her first visit. She had dreaded it but now that she was here she could stay forever. She would come often now, she resolved. 'We can come up whenever you like. I'll tell you what would be nice. Will you try to find some nice shiny stones or little flowers to put here to show Peter how we love him?'

Joseph nodded and set to his task, head down, rigid with concentration. Eliza freed Mary from her shawl and fed her, smiling at Joseph whenever he delivered his bounty to her. Her mind wandered to memories: him and Peter playing together, tucking them in at night, both still giggling but stupid with tiredness and asleep within seconds. She reined her thoughts in before they upset her. She wasn't ready for them yet. With Joseph's assistance she arranged some daisies and quartz stones around the grave then said a few prayers.

Joseph was bored with it now and Eliza marvelled at the easy acceptance of children.

She led the way back down the steps. The weight of Mary on her front made her feel all the time like she could topple forward. Joseph skipped ahead, from step to step. She breathed a sigh of relief when they finally reached the road at the bottom.

As they neared the yard she heard voices. They belonged to Jeremiah and Tom. They tipped their caps when they saw her and Joseph set off at full speed, crashing into Jeremiah who caught him up and swung him around.

'God almighty, what are ye feeding this lad? He's a ton weight. He'll be catching up to us in no time at all. Tom, see can you lift him!'

Tom made a big performance of trying and failing to lift Joseph off the ground. Eliza's heart swelled with gratitude for these warm men as Joseph dissolved into fits of giggles.

'Now, I have something for you.' Jeremiah reached into his pocket. 'But it's not from me at all. Tell me, have you a sweetheart?'

Joseph shook his head, unable to speak for laughing.

With a flourish Jeremiah produced a small ball. ''Tis from Joanie. Are you sure she's not your girlfriend?'

Joseph took off, bouncing the small rubber ball with delight, and tossed a cheeky 'No!' back at them.

'Thank you, Jeremiah. You're too kind. Can I get ye a drink of something?'

'No, you're fine out. Mrs Hunter is looking after us.'

As if on cue Ruth emerged from within her own house with two enamel mugs.

'Are you sure you're happy with water? I can make tea, no bother,' she said, playing the hostess.

Eliza marvelled at her brazenness. The last time Ruth had seen these men she had taken the head clean off Tom over Joanie leaving. She watched for Jeremiah's reaction but his expression and tone gave nothing away.

'No, no, this is lovely now. Thank you. We're parched from the rowing.' Jeremiah drank long and deep as they stood in silence.

'How is Joanie?' Eliza asked.

Tom reddened and slurped at his water.

'She's good, thanks be to God,' Jeremiah said. 'The new place is working out well for her. She's close enough to Portmagee and she's happy out with the family. They're from the South of England and they have two boys and a girl. Lively enough but hardy, she said. 'Twas from one of them she got the ball. He was done with it and she asked could she have it for the small man here. She's been feeling awful bad for him.'

He drank again, not meeting Eliza or Ruth's eyes. Two boys and a girl. The words echoed in Eliza's mind. That was what she should have.

'How are the Godfreys?' Ruth asked archly.

Trust her to remind everyone of her lofty connections, thought Eliza.

'Oh, there's a bit of bad news from there, I'm afraid.' Jeremiah shook his head and lowered his voice. 'Bella, the second girl. She's after being taken away to the Killarney hospital – the asylum they call it.'

'Oh!' Ruth blanched.

Jeremiah continued. 'Yerra, she hasn't been right in the head for a while, the poor girl. It do come and go in spells but they say she's lost it altogether now. Accusing the workers in the house of all sorts and causing fierce upset.'

'Well, hopefully she'll come right. The doctors there can help her surely. She might just need the rest. For her own good.'

Ruth's eyes settled on Eliza's and the message was clear. You see, it said. People do get sent away for acting crazy.

Eliza's head spun and she had to lean her back against the wall to steady herself.

Ruth took the mug from Tom.

'Ye made out alright with the Commissioners so?' Jeremiah asked.

Ruth's hand paused in mid-air as it reached for his mug. She cast an almost furtive look at Eliza then took the mug and said, 'We did indeed. They were most happy with everything.' She bid the men a curt goodbye and retreated to her house.

Eliza was relieved she was gone but she was trying to make sense of Ruth's reaction to Jeremiah's question. 'You heard about the Commissioners' visit?' she asked Jeremiah.

'Ah, I knew before they came at all. I got wind in the village that they were down the south coast. I said it to Edmund, the day Joanie came away with us. I told him ye could be expecting them any day. It was terrible bad timing for ye, he said it himself, but sure isn't that the way of things?'

'Would you take another cup of water?' Eliza offered, her voice tremulous.

Edmund had known all along that the Commissioners were due and he hadn't told them. She remembered now that Edmund had spotted the boat approaching from the lighthouse and told James he could see the inspectors onboard. But he had known long before that. They had set a trap for her and James. But would he even believe her if she told him?

'No, we're grand now, but thank you.'

Tom wandered over to join Joseph in his game. Jeremiah watched them bouncing the ball against the stone wall and catching it.

Eliza turned to study his face. Could he be an ally to her? She decided to test the waters.

'That Ruth is some piece of work. Butter wouldn't melt today and she taking the head off ye the last day.'

Jeremiah looked at her and threw his eyes to heaven. 'It takes all sorts, I suppose.'

Eliza smiled. He wouldn't be drawn into criticising Ruth. For a moment she was ashamed of herself for trying to involve him.

Jeremiah changed the subject deftly. 'That's a sight for sore eyes, to see Joseph happy. You know, I lost a child myself. 'Tis not uncommon. A small scrap of a girl, the first winter we were married.' He turned to face Eliza again, his eyes wet. 'No matter how many children you have, the ones you lose do never leave you. There were times my heart was so sore I'd have been happy to die too. But then I'd be leaving the living ones. 'Tis a curse to always have your heart torn between the ones that are here and the ones that aren't.'

She nodded, the lump in her throat preventing her from speaking.

Jeremiah put his cap on and called to Tom.

Eliza slipped inside her front door and released the tears. She pulled herself together and started to pace. What Jeremiah had just told her was crucial. She needed to figure out what to do with the information.

Eliza headed for the lighthouse with Joseph hanging on to one hand and Mary swaddled against her chest. She needed to talk to James, to tell him what she knew. Edmund had deliberately not warned them that the Commissioners were due. He wanted them to be caught unawares, to look bad. Surely now James would see Edmund and Ruth for what they were?

The two men were outside, looking up at the light, eyes shielded by their hands. From a distance Eliza could see that Edmund was doing all the talking and James was attending to his every word. She faltered for a moment. This wouldn't work – she needed to talk to James alone. He must have sensed her presence as he turned towards her and raised his hand. She couldn't turn and leave now, she'd have to keep going.

Joseph let go of her hand and wandered off to trace a lonely circle around the base of the lighthouse, bouncing his new ball.

'Jeremiah and Tom were here.'

'We saw them.' James' words were clipped.

She heard the unspoken rejection in them.

'They had news,' she said.

She shifted from foot to foot. Neither man seemed interested in what she wanted to say.

James sighed. 'Can it wait, Eliza? We're in the middle of something here.'

She could feel her cheeks reddening. 'He was telling us about Joanie. She found a position. With a new family. And the girl of the Godfreys. There's news from there too.'

She stared at Edmund. Would he not get the message that she wanted to speak to her husband alone? Or was he well aware of the fact and deliberately staying put?

James sighed again. 'Really, Eliza, can't this wait? I don't have time to stand here listening to gossip about Joanie and some other girl that I have no interest in. We'll talk later.'

He stalked off.

Eliza and Edmund stood in silence, hearing him pound up the lighthouse stairs.

Edmund shook his head. 'That was unnecessarily brusque, if you ask me.'

'I'm not asking.' Eliza rounded on him. 'You knew about the inspection.'

'The inspection?' He smirked at her, as if she was a small child he had to humour. 'What's this about now, Eliza?'

'Jeremiah told me. He knew the inspectors were due to call because he heard it in the village and he told you. Which means you knew but you said nothing. You wanted James to be caught on the hop. You wanted him to look bad in front of them.'

'In fairness, you did a good job of that yourself. I was up here making sure everything was topnotch, not lying in bed with the curtains pulled tight in the middle of the day or wandering the clifftops like a madwoman.'

'James will believe me this time. Jeremiah will back me up.'

Edmund shielded his eyes again, this time to look out to sea where the tender boat was making its way back to the mainland. He turned to look again at Eliza. 'What has your mind dreamed up this time? What exactly are you accusing me of?'

Eliza clasped her hands together so he wouldn't see them shaking. She needed to appear strong. Not let him beat her down.

'Nothing that you don't already know full well.'

'Is that right? And you have proof of this?' He held his hands out.

'No. But I have Jeremiah's word.'

'You have Jeremiah's word that he told me something that he picked up in the village. Idle hearsay. I don't pay heed to that sort of thing. And it wouldn't go well for Jeremiah to be known as a gossip.'

Eliza looked around wildly. This wasn't what she meant. She didn't want Jeremiah to get into trouble. She shouldn't have said it to Edmund. She should have waited to speak to James, in private.

Edmund moved closer. 'A bit of advice, Mrs Carthy. I hope you will take it in the spirit it is meant. Be careful. Be very careful what you say and who you say it to. There may be unintended consequences.'

She called to Joseph then turned on her heel and hurried back to the house before he could see the effect of his words. She could try to talk to James again but he didn't seem to want to listen to her, and it would be Edmund's word against Jeremiah's and she didn't want to risk getting him into trouble. And, anyway, the fight was gone out of her. The visit was over and done with and the Hunters had got what they wanted.

Chapter 27

The island moved from spring to early summer and bit by bit nature came to life around them, frantic to cram in as much living as possible in the brief season. Buds unfurled, heathers flowered and the rocky slopes teemed with puffins. Joseph loved to watch the colourful, comical birds as they hopped about. He and Eliza made frequent visits to the monastery with Mary, taking advantage of the improved weather, and they grew to know every step and every corner of it. They watched as birds alighted, then walked through the monastery, never flying.

It broke Eliza's heart to hear him tell of the puffins' burrows they would find together when Peter came back from staying with God. Eliza had to explain again. Peter wouldn't be coming back.

'Isn't he scared up here and all of us down here together? Can we not have him down here?' Joseph persisted.

'God is minding him,' Eliza said but being honest she was inclined to agree with Joseph. She hated the thought of Peter's small, soft body lying in a grave at the pinnacle of the rock, surrounded by beehive huts that had lain empty for centuries especially on those nights when the wind screamed across the island, sending squalls of seawater chasing against the cliff-face, threatening to extinguish the precious light. On those nights Eliza carried the sleeping Joseph and Mary into her and James' bed, for their comfort or hers she couldn't say. Joseph next to the wall, Mary in the middle. Then she turned to bury her face in the pillow and sob for the child who was not there.

Peter's grave grew thick with the quartz rocks and flowers that they laid there on each visit and Eliza started to wonder if it was time to consider a headstone. It was something she needed to talk to James about but their relationship these days was cold. He never accompanied them to the monastery. She made sure to let him know when they were going but there was always something else he had to do. He spent more time at the lighthouse than was required of him and when he was home he was distant, worrying at an endless stream of problems that Edmund unearthed for him. Eliza was sad to see him labour and stress, growing older-looking by the day. His hair was entirely grey now, not a trace of the dark curls that he had been so proud of when they first met. It crossed her mind to suggest that Edmund's constant emphasis on what was going badly at the lighthouse was an attempt by him to undermine him. But she knew better than to risk seeming irrational and she never discussed the Hunters with him now if it could be avoided.

The other benefit of spending so much of the long, warm summer days at the monastery was that she could avoid Ruth who kept very much to her own house and the yard.

Mary continued to thrive and Eliza wondered at how she had sustained such a hearty baby through her grief. There were rare moments when she felt she might be past the worst of it but these were fleeting. The one thing that never left her was the tiredness and she grasped any opportunity she had to disappear behind a veil of slumber, hoping not to be troubled by dreams.

James watched as she shuffled around the kitchen, clearing the table after the midday meal. She could feel his eyes on her so she made an effort to straighten her back and brighten her face but she knew the dark circles under her eyes couldn't be hidden. She carried each cup and plate, one by one, to the sink, fearful of dropping them. As she reached for his plate James took her hand.

'Sit down, Eliza, before you fall down. I can do this.'

She smiled weakly at him and shook her head. 'I'm fine, I'll carry on.'

'You look exhausted – why don't you go for a rest? I'm here for the next few hours. I'll watch Joseph and Mary. Is she fed?'

Eliza nodded. She looked at the cradle by the stove where Mary slept hard, her chest rising and falling heavily, her face serious as if concentrating on an important task.

'Well, then. Off you go. You can't keep going in this condition.'

Hot tears filled Eliza's eyes and she turned away so he wouldn't see them. Were they because of this unexpected kindness? Or her exhaustion? Or the fact that James had just articulated what she knew? That she was not doing a good job as wife or mother? She dragged herself upstairs and surrendered to the tiredness.

Eliza woke later with a pounding heart and for a moment struggled to understand where she was. The sudden shriek of a gull outside the salt-encrusted window brought the reality home. She was on Skellig Michael. Her salty prison. She had shed so many tears on this rock that she thought surely the seas surrounding it must be higher now. Her heart pounded harder as the dream that woke her returned, wisping just out of reach past her thoughts. She had been dreaming of Peter. She tried to grasp more of the dream. He was happy and wild and free and a voice had been calling after him, laughing at first, then despairing. She swallowed the hard lump in her throat. She could not lose another day to her grief. Nearly three months had passed and she believed that only for Joseph and Mary her heart would have stopped beating. It was for their sakes that she had to keep putting one foot in front of the other.

Joseph! That was the voice in the dream. The tears fell from her eyes now unchecked. The two boys had been inseparable – deep in love and war each day. Now Joseph was a lost soul, adrift without his mate. Eliza rubbed at her cheeks and eased herself out of bed. The house was strangely silent. Had James taken the children out? She moved aside the bedroom curtain but the yard below was empty. Not a soul to be seen anywhere. Eliza shivered. She felt a strange panic that everyone had left Skellig Michael and left her behind, alone, forever. She shook her head to clear the silly notion, pulled on her boots and went downstairs.

The rooms there were empty too. The table still bore the remnants of their meal and she tutted. James had forgotten to clear it or hadn't been bothered. She didn't mind really – it was nice for a moment to have such a mundane thing to be annoyed about. She lifted a plate then put it down again. The feeling of aloneness was still with her and she felt compelled to find her children. The sound of boots being shook loose alerted her to their return.

'*Joseph!*' James called from the porch. '*Come here till I show you what I'm after finding!*'

He came into the kitchen cradling a creamy-white, cracked puffin egg in his palm.

Eliza spun around to face him.

'Why are you calling Joseph?'

'I'm after finding this and sure you know he's stone mad for –'

'But is he not with you? And Mary?'

James put the egg on the table. 'I had to send them in to Ruth while you were resting. Edmund sent her with a message that he needed me above at the lighthouse. And I didn't want to disturb you, she offered so ...' James shrugged. 'I thought she'd have brought them back by now. I'll go next door and get them.' He sat down hard into the armchair and rubbed his hand across his face. 'In a minute. I'll just take a minute off my feet.'

Eliza felt the colour draining from her cheeks. 'I'll go get them.' She didn't want to have to explain to James, he wouldn't understand, but the thought of Ruth minding her children filled her with cold dread.

She tugged on a shawl and as she left the room a plaintive cry from next door spurred her on. Mary! She pushed open Ruth's door without knocking. Ruth was jostling Mary on her knee, trying to settle her, but the baby's face was reddening and creasing more with each movement.

Eliza snatched her up into her arms, shushing her until she was soothed.

'Really, Eliza, I fear you have that child ruined! She expects to be lifted and petted every time she makes a sound.'

Ruth looked flustered and cross. Her hair was coming loose from its pins and her cheeks blazed. She won't be so quick to offer next time, Eliza thought.

'Where is Joseph?' Eliza demanded.

'Another ruined boy, if you ask me. I sent him up to his father.' Ruth stood and started to put the room back into order. She pontificated as she tidied. 'The nonsense coming out of that boy. Of course, it's not his fault. You have filled his head with some silly notions and superstitions.'

Eliza was only half listening. Her mind was racing trying to process what Ruth had said. She had sent Joseph to the lighthouse, to James? But James was next door and obviously hadn't encountered Joseph on his way down.

'You sent him to the lighthouse?'

Ruth tutted. 'He's well able! You've mollycoddled him too much. He was driving me mad asking could he go and play with Peter? That's not right, Eliza. You'll have to make him understand that his brother is gone. For once and for all. I couldn't be listening to it.'

'*Oh my God! Ruth!*'

Ruth paused her tidying at Eliza's scream.

'He's not with James. James just came down, on his own. *You damn fool!* How did you not realise?'

She moved to the door as fast as she could with Mary in her arms, calling to James as she went.

'James! James!'

He was at their front door. She thrust Mary into his arms.

'Joseph's not there! She let him go! Ruth let him go!'

'What are you saying? You're panicking. Keep your head, woman! He can't be gone far.'

'I know where he's gone. He wants to play with Peter. She didn't understand him.'

'I don't understand.'

'The monastery!'

The final word floated in Eliza's wake as she tore down the road that led away from the lighthouse. She berated herself with every stride. Why had she fallen asleep? How had she not realised that – oh God! – the voice in the dream – it was real. Joseph had been calling out to Peter. Her poor, poor boy. She could picture him sitting beside his little brother's grave, nattering away to his old friend. That was where he was now, she was sure of it. Eliza had to pause at the foot of the steps. Grief had taken away her appetite along with everything else and the effort it took to feed Mary had stripped her of her energy. She should have sent James. She surged upward.

Finally, gasping for breath, she reached the top. There was no sign of Joseph and for a moment she sagged in relief. But if he isn't here, she thought, where is he? She wiped stray strands of hair from her forehead that blew straight back into her eyes again, blinding her. The drizzle she had run through past the lighthouse was a steady fall of sleety rain up here. She shivered violently as she made her way to Peter's resting place.

'Joseph! Joseph!'

Her voice disappeared into the great nothingness that was all around and was swallowed up by the encroaching cloud moving in from the west. Peter's graveside was empty. There was no sentry, no companion. Eliza cried out, half-laughing. She had panicked. He wasn't here. He was probably below by the stove nursing his hungry belly and wondering when she'd come on and make his supper.

She began her descent, shaking her head at her own foolishness. What had led her to think that a small boy would attempt to scale these steps by himself? Especially a small boy who, frightened by the sudden loss of his brother, had become a second shadow to her. And what had Ruth been thinking, sending him to the lighthouse on his own? She was certainly going to have some strong words with her about that.

Chapter 28

The persistent rain had turned the ancient steps slippery and Eliza's right foot lost its place in the same moment that it met the stone. She grasped wildly at the air around her, then landed on her backside with a thump. Winded by the fall, she placed her hand on her racing heart. She'd always been nervous on these steps. Rough-hewn out of the rock centuries before by the monks, no two steps matched in size or scope. To the right of the steps on her descent was a grassy rock-face. To the left the ground fell away to the thrashing sea, the drop interrupted only by jagged rocks puncturing the soil.

Eliza rose to her feet with care. She couldn't resist a look to her left. It was almost a superstition, to stare straight into the face of the fate that had nearly befallen her. Through the haze of drizzle she peered down and her heart stopped beating once more.

There, among the green grass and slate-grey rock, was the worst sight her eyes could ever behold. The red woollen vest, knitted by her own hands, and tangled white limbs of her eldest child.

Her screams bounced off the rock, circling into the thick air with the shrieking gullies, as her heart ruptured. Her mind rebelled. Reared back from what lay before her. She started to scramble down the rock-face, oblivious to the coarse stones cutting her skin.

The moment she laid her hands on Joseph she knew he was gone. A bright crimson ribbon flowed from under his head. His body was still warm but she recognised the emptiness, the lack that she remembered too well from Peter. Her hands shook as she sought a place to put them that could trick her mind into thinking he was still there. She pulled at the hem of his vest, already getting too short for him, he was growing so fast. Then she heard a voice calling. It was James. She couldn't face him. How could they meet again over the dead body of their child? He would blame her. She clambered back up to the steps and cast about wildly for escape. She looked towards the monastery. No. Not there. As her thoughts wheeled and whirred she heard a roar from below.

'*No! Joseph!*'

It was an animal sound. All the injustices and cruelties since time began compressed into those two words. She turned and ran away from the monastery steps, losing her shawl as the ground slipped away underfoot. A conical peak rose before her and she scaled it, feet skidding on loose stone, hands scrabbling at grass and sea campion. She was compelled, driven, to go up. *Up.*

She came to an impasse. A large slab of stone blocked her ascent but still she had to go on. She squeezed her body into the narrow cleft between the stone and the rock-face and heaved herself through it, bracing herself against its heft and using her hands and feet to propel herself upward. She emerged gasping, her muscles screaming but still she had to go on. *Up. Away. To the ends of the earth.*

The ground levelled and in the fading light she could see the remains of a shelter. It was not unlike the huts at the monastery on the other peak but this one had not fared as well. Only two walls remained. She took refuge inside them, leaning her head against the cold, rough stone, closing her eyes, giving her breath and her heart a chance to settle. She opened her eyes. She could survey all from here but she was apart, invisible, unreachable. Some hundred feet below her was the monastery on the northern peak. To her right a small ribbon of the lighthouse road was visible. She fixed her gaze on it. Suddenly there was a blur of activity as two men dashed along the road. It was fleeting, surreal. She watched on, a motionless sentinel. Time passed and finally they returned, carrying a bundle. An unmoving shape wrapped tight in a blanket. It was a pained procession. Feet trudged and over the movement there was a sound. Barely audible from her lofty perch, brushing lightly against her with the evening breeze and cacophony of roosting birds. It didn't penetrate. Not her mind nor her heart nor her soul. But she grasped its meaning from the cooling air.

James was petitioning his God. Wanting to know why? How? She spat on the ground.

This cursed island.

This 'holy' place.

It had taught her only loss and suffering.

It had taken everything from her.

A well of hatred cascaded through her and she turned her eyes from what she could not comprehend. She beat her fists against the stone walls until they were marked with her own blood. She longed to tear it all down stone by stone. First this hut. Then the island. Then the world. She sank to the ground, numb, and by some grace slipped into blankness.

When next she opened her eyes the edges of the sky above her were tinged with light. Her body was stiff from the cold and coated in dew that soaked her to the skin. Was it dusk? Or dawn? Where was she? Then she remembered. The southern peak. The edge of the world. The limits of her pain. She felt around for her shawl but couldn't find it. A quiet rustling noise outside the wall pulled at her attention. She dragged herself upright and peered out. It was a small, light-brown rabbit, ears pinned back, alert to danger, nibbling industriously and watching her with a dispassionate stare. I must seem very out of place to him, she thought. The walls surrounding her were testament to the fact that people had traversed this part of the island before but that time was long past. She smiled. Joseph would love to see this little fellow. Then she was staggering to her feet as it all rushed in on her. Joseph, fallen, lying, still, her shawl lost, the climb. She shook her head trying to rid it of its knowledge and the rabbit bolted for cover. She grabbed great gulps of air. The fading stars in the sky overhead twinkled, winking, mocking her. Far below she could hear the waves rolling in and out. The natural world all around was stirring, embracing a new day as if nothing at all had happened and it was all wrong.

I don't understand it. How is it possible that the sun can rise and the world can keep turning? she thought. There has to be an answer.

The cold morning air stung her hands. They were bloody and torn from the assault on the hut. A sob escaped from somewhere deep within her as she turned in frantic circles, her head craned back to face the sky and tears running free. *I was so numb before. After Peter. Now I feel everything and I cannot bear it. How am I to bear it? To lose them both!* She stalked to the edge of the rocky outcrop, balancing on the balls of her feet, tempting the movement into being. *I can find no answers on this earth. I tried to beat them from the rock last night but they weren't there. Maybe I am to look for them elsewhere. I must turn to God.* She understood now why in her flight she had pushed herself higher and higher. Like the monks who sought His proximity, she too needed his audience. His penance. His damnation. *What sin have I committed to be condemned to such heartbreak? I will petition. I will atone. I will do anything.*

Eliza headed for the narrow summit of the peak. The morning sun was still below the horizon but light was bleeding in from the edges. Her passage to the top was unimpeded and when she reached it, panting, she fell to her knees and tried to gather her thoughts but nothing came to her. The formulaic words of generation-worn prayers meant nothing in this moment. *Ár n'Athair*: Our Father. No. He was unlike any father she had ever known. She turned her face to the sky. This needed to be a conversation, a confrontation.

'Why?'

The word came from her raspy and weak. She cleared her throat to continue. God would know what was behind that one word but she needed to say it out loud. To make it real for herself if nothing else.

'Why did you take my boys? My heart was broken when Peter went. Now you've taken Joseph. Like that!' She snapped her fingers, the sound falling heavy in the silence of the dawn. 'The same way I might kill a house fly. Why would you do that? To punish me? What are my sins? What did I do?'

Her voice rose and cracked on the question. She waited, listened, heard only her own uneven breath. She hung her head. What did she expect? She rose from the ground, pushing her weary body up to standing. She had nothing left in her. No fight. Nothing. As she stood the sun crested over the horizon. She felt it before she saw it. A bare touch of warmth chasing the last chill of the night. The orange disc sailed higher, fingers of light reaching out to caress the world. *Méara Dé*: God's fingers. She'd seen them often before, not just at dawn, but now they stopped her in her tracks and brought tears spilling down her cheeks. The rays of light settled upon a long fragment of rock, perched at the end of a narrow path. She could make out a crude cross carved on it. Her heart slowed and she knew. She would make her way to the cross. It was her test.

Eliza inched her way down from the summit to the start of the narrow path. She put her foot on it, then drew back, filled with terror. Now that she was confronted by it she could see it was not a path but a ridge, barely two feet wide with no protection on either side. Far below, in the churning, white-foamed spray and jagged rocks, was certain death.

Eliza faltered, but only for a moment, to still the tremor in her limbs. She was on the precipice, hovering between life and death but she had to do this. She crouched down, unlaced her boots and removed them, then straddled the rock. Her skirts caught under her and she wished she'd thought to remove them too. She closed her eyes, hugged her arms and legs around the rock and started to inch forward. She could hear the crash of the swell below. The wet rush of it. The birds were waking in their perches and as they stirred the air thickened around her with their cries. The shrill, nasal call of the kittiwake saying its own name unnerved her and she stopped moving. She needed to focus but it was as if the island was rousing to thwart her. She took a deep breath and started to hum a tune that she had taught to Joseph. The familiar notes reverberated in her ears, sufficient to repel the riotousness around her. When she reached the end of the tune she paused and opened her eyes. She was halfway across.

Without thinking she straightened up so that only the grip of her knees was keeping her in place. Behind her was the island and all it meant to her. Before her was the stone slab. Beneath her was sweet oblivion. No one knew where she was. They would search for her, would have found her shawl on Christ's Saddle, would have probably decided the worst by now. It was tempting, magnetic. The ease of it. She could just let go. Just release. She relaxed the muscles in her thighs. It was freeing. Nothing held her now. She swayed slightly, testing the motion, the pendular over-and-back. At what point would it pull her over? And down? It was an idle thought, a curiosity, an abandonment of all her burdens, toying with her life. She stretched her arms out either side of her, like a bird. She could be like one of them and just swoop down and glide. It would be just one movement, one free flight, but it would be enough. She lowered her arms. They were tired now.

Her legs too.

Her body was weary.

She shuddered a sigh.

The waves below rolled and crashed.

Shattering themselves on the rocks.

She could let go now. Go and be free of this pain. Then, unbidden, she felt a prickling in her breasts. A hot needling as they filled with milk. Her mind filled with the reality of her living child and she threw herself forward onto the rock, terrified now of the risk. She could not fall. She had an urge to go back, to her baby. But first she had no choice but to go on. Finish what she'd started. Trembling, her hands slick with sweat, she pulled herself to the end of the path. She put her hand out and touched the base of the slab. She kissed the palm of her hand and pressed it against the solitary, stony recluse. It was done. She didn't dare to linger or to turn around so she reversed, her mouth filled with acid fear. Finally, the ground widened behind her and she pushed back onto her knees. She collapsed and pressed her forehead to the ground and did not move until the sun climbed high into the sky.

Chapter 29

When she got to her feet again she was utterly exhausted. Gravity and instinct led her back down the way she had come, staggering and stumbling, her bare feet scratched and torn. She had left her boots at the hermitage. Pieces of her all over the island. The ground levelled out beneath her and she was back on Christ's Saddle, her corner, where she had spent hours watching Joseph play. A movement near the top of the steps stopped her heart and for a moment she thought maybe this had all been a mistake. Maybe Joseph was here, alive, looking for her. Then a silver, curled head appeared. It was James. She stood, motionless, as he called her name and ran to her side and gathered her fiercely into his arms. She was limp, unable to return his embrace but she was glad of it. The solidity of him. He led her down the steps and carried her home. Over their silent threshold and upstairs to the marital bedroom. A macabre bride. She raised her arms and lifted her feet as he tugged off her skirts and her blouse, damp from sweat and rain and stiffened with dried milk. She closed her eyes while he pulled her nightgown over her head and didn't open them again. The room darkened and cooled when he closed the curtains and she allowed herself to disappear into an exhausted sleep when he pulled the blanket up over her. The mattress sank under his weight and he lay behind her, an arm around her, pinning her here. His cheeks were wet as he leaned to whisper in her ear.

'I thought I'd lost you too.'

Then she slipped under.

Eliza was alone when she woke, confused. The bright sunshine peeping around the curtains suggested morning. I must have slept through, she thought. She lay still and listened. The silence of the house was unnerving, a thrumming vibration that had a physical presence. She eased her body from the bed and pulled a blanket around her. Her head swam and she was shivering. She moved one curtain aside. The yard below looked empty but then she heard voices. *James. Ruth.* The scrape of metal being placed on stone. Her front door below opened and heavy steps entered. She froze, held her breath, listened. Then exhaled. Just one set of footsteps. James was on his own. She crept down the stairs, not wanting to disturb the very silence that was gnawing at her nerves.

James was washing his hands at the kitchen sink, shirt sleeves rolled up, a large sweat stain spreading across his back.

'James.'

He spun around at the sound of her voice, startled. His features softened and he reached for a cloth to dry his hands. Neither of them spoke. She felt like she was seeing him for the first time in a long time. She noted how thin he had become, his cheekbones sharpened, dark, deep hollows under his eyes. He avoided her eyes as the many words unsaid between them clamoured to be aired. She scanned his clothes. Muddy boots, soiled, old trousers and shirt. What work had he been doing?

Her heart thumped and she looked again at his face. Why was he avoiding her gaze? She spun away from him and pushed open the door of the bedroom where she had laid Peter out. It was empty. Through the wall she could hear the thin cry of a baby. Clara? Now it was joined by another cry, louder, more persistent. She went back to face her husband.

'James. Where is Joseph? And Mary?'

Confusion flitted across his face and his chin crumpled. He shut his eyes for a moment then looked directly at her, frowning.

'Joseph fell, Eliza. Surely you remember?'

'I know that!' Her voice had risen, shrill now with panic. 'But where is he? His –?' She reared back from the word. *Body. Corpse.* She gestured at the empty room.

James regarded her in silence, nodding, as if coming to an agreement with himself about what to tell her. He wiped his palms along his trouser legs then inspected one, worrying at a cut or callus he'd found there.

'At the monastery ... Ruth and Edmund thought ... we talked ... decided it would be for the best.'

'You buried him.'

It was a statement, not a question. A cold, hard fact that lay, insurmountable, between them.

'How could you? Without me? I didn't even get to say goodbye.'

'You weren't here!' James raised his voice, his face red. 'We couldn't find you, Eliza. We found your shawl. I was going out of my mind thinking that you were – you had – that I'd lost you too!'

She stared at him, breathing hard. It was true. She hadn't been there. But she was now. He could have waited, for one more day even.

'I came back. Why didn't you wait for me, James?'

'I didn't want to put you through all that again. Last time – after Peter – you – you weren't well, Eliza. It was too much for you. Ruth thought it hadn't been good for you to see Peter being buried, to have spent so much time with him. It nearly broke you.'

Eliza let out a bitter laugh. 'That's not what nearly broke me. What broke me was that my baby boy died. *Whatever bloody Ruth thinks!*'

She grabbed a plate from the kitchen table and hurled it at the wall, the Irish Lights motif shattering. She hoped the smash would be heard by Ruth on the other side.

'*Stop it, Eliza!*' James shouted. 'You'll be heard — what will they think?' He looked panicked. His eyes slid to the table where two days of unwashed crockery had gathered.

Eliza picked up a cup and smashed it on the floor. She had his attention now.

'*I don't care what they think!* It's me you should be listening to, discussing things with, making decisions with. I'm your wife, James! They are liars. Edmund knew the Commisioners were coming. He got word of it from Jeremiah.' She fired three more dishes at the wall in quick succession, punctuating her words. '*They – set – you – up!*' she screamed. '*And it's her fault that Joseph is dead!*'

'Eliza, no more!'

James clamped her arms to her side and she couldn't shrug him off. His face was so close to hers she could feel the spatter of spit when he spoke again, between gritted teeth.

'You're not the only one suffering, you know. You think my heart isn't breaking as well? I have lost my two sons.'

His face collapsed and dissolved into tears. He released her arms, pushed her away and turned his back. Eliza couldn't bring herself to put her hand on him, to comfort him. You still have a daughter, she thought. She felt a sudden wave of nausea. She'd already registered that Mary wasn't in the house but her veins flooded with dread now.

'Mary?' she asked.

He turned to face her again, his hands trembling.

'I didn't know what to do, how to look after her. Ruth has her.'

Eliza fled from the room and out the front door.

―――⁂―――

Eliza burst through the door of Ruth's house. She was standing near the stove, cradling a baby. Mary? No. Eliza could see that this baby was bigger. Where was she?

Ruth looked shocked at the intrusion. Her face was pale and drawn.

'Eliza, shush! I'm trying to settle Clara!' she said in a loud whisper.

Eliza stalked around the room, ignoring her. *'Where is she? Where's my baby?'*

Ruth pointed to the ceiling then put her finger to her lips. Eliza threw her a look full of hate and pounded up the stairs. She pushed open the first door she came to but the room was empty. She opened the next door. There. There was something familiar. In a cradle at the foot of the bed was her baby, a tuft of wispy hair just visible. Eliza's eyes filled with tears. She crept closer, not wanting to disturb her even though she was aching to hold her. She was buried under too many blankets, her tiny fist bunched on her cheek. Eliza could see a sheen of sweat across her forehead. Her eyebrow furrowed and Eliza's heart clenched. Was she having a bad dream? Still trying not to wake her, she started to peel back the blankets. It sickened her to see Mary in this strange bed, dressed in clothes that weren't her own. What had James been thinking? He'd said he didn't know how to look after her. Suddenly, Eliza had an awful thought. Her mind filled with an image of Ruth breast-feeding Mary and her mouth filled with bile. Surely not! Wet nurses were not uncommon but how could James have handed over care of their daughter to this woman?

The floorboards behind her creaked. Ruth stood in the doorway.

'*Eliza,*' she whispered, beckoning her out to the hallway.

Eliza went reluctantly. Ruth pulled the door shut behind them, then spoke.

'I do not appreciate you bursting into my home in this way. You have been through an ordeal and I'm glad to see you returned but really –'

Eliza stiffened. 'Are you? Glad to see me?' She stepped closer to Ruth. '*I'm sure you'd have loved it if I'd never come back.*'

Ruth gasped and leaned one hand on the banister. 'How could you say that? I was so relieved when James told us. He was frantic with worry. That was an awful thing to do to him. It is good that he found you, even if –'

'What? Even if what?'

'Well,' Ruth smirked, 'you don't seem too happy about it. I heard the unpleasantness. It was impossible not to.'

Eliza's face reddened. She clenched her fists and raised herself to her full height. 'Then you'll have heard what I said. *I don't give a damn what you think of me!*'

'Such ingratitude!' Ruth spat back. 'I am here trying to care for your child, as if I don't have enough to do with my own. *Here!*'

Ruth pushed a glass bottle at her. It had a brown rubbery teat on top, sourness wafting from it.

'If you are quite done with your nerves you may take on your responsibilities again. I am not a cruel woman. It is beyond awful that you have to bear the loss of another child. I cannot imagine how it must feel. But ...' her voice wobbled, 'I have hardly slept these past two days trying to keep your baby from fading away. If I were in your shoes I would be thanking me.'

'What do you mean?'

'I tried to give her pap. Then I remembered that Mrs Godfrey had gifted me this bottle in case I needed it. So I tried to give her some warmed milk. But she would take nothing. No matter what I did. She refused everything.'

Eliza took the bottle. Her mind whirled. If Ruth was telling the truth then nothing had passed Mary's lips since the afternoon of Joseph's fall. Two days! She pushed past Ruth, into the bedroom, letting the bottle fall and roll across the wooden floorboards. She lifted Mary gently from the cradle and perched on the edge of the bed. Mary stiffened, then relaxed again, still fast asleep. Eliza could see now that her lips were pale and dry. She pulled at the front of her blouse, freed her breast and raised Mary's head to her nipple. The milk was starting to flow and her breasts hardened. Droplets of milk sat on Mary's closed, pursed lips but Eliza could not get her to suck. Her eyes wouldn't open and her head lolled. Eliza tried again and again but to no avail. Blinking back tears she stumbled from the room, clutching Mary to her chest, not stopping to retie her blouse. She needed to get her home. She needed to tend to her little girl. She had to fight for her.

Ruth blocked her exit. 'Eliza, I have something I need to say.'

Eliza stood still, refusing to look at Ruth, trying to quell the desire to shove her out of her way. She held her breath as Ruth continued.

'I feel that you may hold me responsible in some way for what happened – for Joseph. And really, I can't allow it. I had no way of knowing that he would run off like that. How could I have known? And, believe me, I feel just terrible about it all. I have been praying for his soul. And for yours. That you might find some peace.'

Eliza coughed out a bitter laugh. 'Peace? I won't ever know peace, Ruth. I have lost another part of my heart, my soul. I would throw myself into the ocean if it wasn't for Mary.' She held her baby tighter. 'I *will* hold you responsible for Joseph's death for as long as there is breath in my body. You are the reason he is dead. I know that. And I think you know it too.'

Ruth breathed in sharply and took a step back. She's afraid of me, thought Eliza. Me, the madwoman, what I might do to her. She savoured the power this gave her and took a step towards Ruth, summoning up all the anger and hurt inside her to pour venom into her words.

'I will pray for you too. I will pray that the knowledge of what you allowed to happen to my little boy worms its way into your heart and soul and eats away at you for the rest of your life. I will pray that you live for a very long time and I hope that you are trapped on this island forever. I am leaving here. I hope you never do. I hope you have to live every remaining day of your life knowing that there is a small boy lying in a grave because of you.'

She took another step towards Ruth, forcing her out of her path and fled down the stairs.

Chapter 30

Eliza persevered all day until finally Mary roused enough to take a small feed. She veered between elation at this tiny victory and despair when her little head lolled to the side, the precious milk dribbling out of her mouth. But she had taken some. Eliza was sure of that. There was a healthier pink tinge to her cheeks now and she was sleeping more comfortably. The house darkened around Eliza but she sat, unmoving, beside the unlit stove, not willing to let her baby out of her arms. She worried at the question that echoed off the emptiness all around and inside her. *What should I do?* Every time the same answer. *You have to go.*

James hadn't returned since morning. She had heard Edmund coming and going next door. The sound of him and Ruth conversing enraged her. Were they discussing her? If she left the island, did that mean the Hunters had won? That they would get what they wanted? James' position? Eliza shook the thought from her mind. They were welcome to it. She wanted none of it. All she wanted was to get her baby away from the island, to safety.

She wrapped Mary into her shawl and stepped out into the evening air. There was a stillness blanketing the island as it settled for the night. A sliver of moon was ascending over an inky sea, painting a thin path of silvery white that she longed to follow ashore. She took in a breath, a lungful of salt, seaweed, flowers and earth. The calm beauty contrasted with her jagged thoughts as she crossed the yard and circled up the spiral stairs inside the lighthouse. When she reached the lantern room she was blinded for a moment. James had just lit the lamp. The darkness outside was illuminated ferociously as the light beamed its signal to the watery domain around them. Sailors from up to eighteen miles away would see it and know they were safe, there was someone here to watch over their passage. She envied them. The bright light caught James' face as if captured in a daguerreotype. He looked so peaceful, observing his light, unaware of her presence. It reminded her of how she liked to watch the children for a few moments after they fell asleep. The children.

Eliza wrapped an arm around Mary, snug in her cocoon.

'James.' Her voice was an echoey intrusion.

He started.

'We need to talk.' She descended to the landing halfway down the stairs, his footsteps treading heavy behind her.

'How is she? Ruth said she wouldn't take any milk for her.'

Eliza shook her head. She didn't know the answer yet. There was a time when she would have trusted her maternal instincts to know how her child was, what she might need. But that was gone now, along with so much else. She turned to look out the high window. She could see swathes of endless ocean beneath her, lit up by the beam of the light. Strange, how that light can communicate with unknown seamen with just one signal. Yet here I am with so much to say but unable to think of how to be heard.

She turned to face James, leaning back on the sill for support.

'We need to leave.'

James nodded. 'I understand. That will do you good. Didn't it do wonders for Ruth that time? Where will you stay?'

Eliza stared at him. He had misunderstood her. He thought she was suggesting a break, a holiday, then a return. To leave and come back? No.

'No, James. We need to leave Skellig Michael. Together. Forever.'

He froze, open-mouthed.

'We can't stay here. Surely you can see that yourself. It's no place for us, our family.' Her voice caught on the word. Their family, a tattered remnant of what it had been. 'We've suffered the deaths of our boys and now ... maybe Mary. I need to get her ashore. To see a doctor. I can't risk losing her too. We should have gone after Peter died. That should have been enough. We would still have Joseph.'

'You can go in with her.' James' voice was unsure. 'Next time Jeremiah comes. Have her seen to and when she's stronger, come back out and we –'

'*No, James!*' Her shout bounced off the curved walls of the stairwell, coming back at her. '*I am leaving. Mary is leaving. We will never return. Never! Do you hear me?* You have to come with us. Or do you want to stay here with the Hunters? You have believed them over me time and again, you have sided with them against me. Now you must choose. Either way, I am leaving.'

'What do you want me to do?' He paced the landing. 'Just up and go?'

Eliza thought for a moment. She hadn't expected to have to figure this out. She had got as far as the resolution to leave but had given no thought to how it would be done. She was quite prepared to up and go, as he had said, but clearly he needed more.

'You need to write a letter,' she said, as though she had given it much thought.

'A letter?'

'Yes, a letter. Write to the Board and tell them, James. Tell them what's happened to us and that we can't stay here. Tell them why.'

'How do you think that will look, Eliza? A Principal Keeper asking to leave his station?' He shook his head furiously. 'No, that's not done. Not ever. They won't agree to it and even if they do, it will finish me.' He took a step towards her, his tone becoming desperate, softer. 'If we wait it out a little longer, they will transfer us. You'll see. They don't leave people at these rock stations forever, you know. We just have to hold tough.'

'Hold tough! I'm not staying here, James. Why can't you understand? I cannot stay. I cannot bear it. We've lost too much.'

'*I know!*' he shouted, turning away. 'I know what we've lost. And you want me to throw all this away on top of it?' He looked up to the ceiling, to his beloved light above, his breathing ragged.

Eliza stood up straight.

'I am taking my child off this island. I will do what I have to. I will tie her to my back and swim ashore if that's what it takes.'

'That's crazy talk!' he spat back.

'Is it any wonder? This place and those people have driven me to the edge, James. I swear to you I am ready to do anything. Anything! I will blow this place sky high. I know where the oil is stored. They'll see it burning from the mainland.'

She could hardly believe the words coming out of her own mouth but she had to make him see. He was staring at her, as if seeing a stranger. She took a step towards him and pointed up to the light.

'I'll smash the whole thing to pieces if I have to.'

James searched her face, his eyes wide.

'You really want to take all this from me? Everything I've worked for? I'll lose everything, Eliza.'

'We've already lost too much, James. Write the letter. Or you will lose us too.'

Eliza turned from him. Her heart was thumping as she stepped down the stairs. She paused for a moment and squeezed her eyes shut. *Please, James*, she prayed silently. *Please write it.*

Chapter 31

Eliza didn't speak another word to James in the following days. She had said all she needed to say. They circled each other in silence, slipping out of the room when the other person entered. She felt his eyes on her as she rinsed her hair over the kitchen sink but he didn't offer to help, nor did she ask him to. James continued to spend his waking hours at the lighthouse and Eliza was left to her own company. Was he waiting for her to change her mind? That wasn't going to happen. She had made her decision. She would be on Jeremiah's boat the next time he came if James didn't write the letter. She didn't allow herself to think of where she might go. A married woman and her baby, alone in the world.

She needed James to understand that she was serious about this and so she began to pack. First, Peter and Joseph's things. She cried her throat raw as she folded their little tunics and shirts into the crate. The rubber ball that Joanie had sent out to Joseph. The little wooden train carriage. Her stomach turned at the thought that they knew nothing of Joseph's death yet. She envied them, longed to be them, living a life where, as far as they knew, Joseph was still a living, breathing, running, ball-hopping boy. James threw his eye over the crate when he saw it in the hall, but said nothing.

Eliza hadn't crossed the threshold again since the day he'd found her on Christ's Saddle. She couldn't. She was gripped by a terrifying certainty that something awful would happen if she did. To Mary, or to herself, and then Mary would be left motherless and probably farmed out to some other woman if James' recent actions were anything to go by. No. She would stay here, in this house that she had grown to despise. Stuck, like a tumorous growth, to the Hunters' house next door. Trapped, forced to bear witness to the sounds of their living, their talking, chairs scraping, doors closing. Eliza wanted to block them out, to stick her fingers in her ears and scream. But she felt compelled to listen. She sat for hours, cradling Mary, trying to decipher what was being said between them. Even in the dead of night, under a heavy blanket of silence, she lay, holding her breath, in case she missed something. No, she would not leave this house until she was leaving for good. Until then her neighbours invaded her every waking moment. If she took her eyes, or her ears, off them, something terrible would happen. She was sure of it.

She rarely put Mary down. Her back and shoulders ached from the strain of it but she only felt safe when her baby was expelling her hot little breaths against her chest, tied into her shawl as she went from room to room, planning what would go with her and what she would leave behind. Mary fed a little but hadn't regained her alertness or strength, sleeping sweatily most of the time, and crying fitfully when awake, or gazing at nothing, unblinking. Eliza's heart squeezed tight when Mary refused to latch on, or didn't react to clapping hands, or wouldn't wake from her sleep. But she could not think of anything she could do for her, other than get her off the island.

Eliza was in the front room, sealing the crates, when James returned late one night. The stove was cold and she had prepared nothing for him to eat. She couldn't remember when last she had made a meal, for either of them. She picked at whatever was in the pantry whenever she remembered to eat and she presumed that was how he was getting by too. Or maybe Ruth was feeding him, keeping him sweet.

Eliza rose, her knees complaining, feeling the exhaustion of her sleepless nights and unstoppable mind crashing in on her. She closed her eyes, rubbing at them. Should she try again to convince James? Was there any point? She lifted Mary from her shawl and laid her in the cradle by the fire. The baby didn't stir and Eliza's heart squeezed again. She collapsed back into the armchair, facing James. His head was resting on the back of his chair and his eyes were closed but when she said his name he sat bolt upright. It had been days since she'd spoken to him.

'When do you think Jeremiah will come?'

He shook his head and blew out his cheeks. 'Who knows, Eliza? You're leaving, I take it?'

He gestured at the packed crate. Eliza stared at him, unbelieving. Was he going to let her go? Alone?

'Nothing has changed, James. Mary is still not right. How can you not see that?' Her voice was barely a whisper, drained of its anger and vehemence. She couldn't think what else to say. She looked at James, her eyes swimming, hoping he would see into her heart and soul.

He sighed and sat forward in his chair, as if to begin a speech. Instead he dropped his head and banged his hands on the arms of the chair.

'I don't know what to do. What do you want from me?'

His outburst woke Mary who started to wail. James jumped to his feet to lift her from the cradle but before he did her little body went rigid. Her back arched, her neck extended and her eyes rolled so that all they could see were the whites. She didn't seem to be breathing.

'What's happening? What's wrong with her?' James screamed.

Eliza felt as if she had stopped breathing herself. She was frozen, not knowing what to do. Should she touch Mary? Or not? In the next instant the baby gulped in a breath and resumed her wailing.

James collapsed to his knees beside her cradle. It was as if all the air had been sucked from the room then whooshed back in again. Eliza went to kneel beside him and turned his face so she could look at him. He would write the letter. She could see it in his eyes.

Eliza stood, put out her hand and led him to the table. She soothed Mary until her crying subsided then brought James paper, a pen and some ink. She lit a lantern and set it before him, the tremor in her hand making the flame flicker. She left him and went to stand at the window. She could do no more. She knew it hurt him but this had to be done.

'When will the boat come?' she asked. Had she said this aloud already? She couldn't remember. She could hear the scratch of the pen on the paper but did not turn, or speak, or breathe, until it was done.

Finally she heard the click of the pen on the wooden table and turned her head to look at him. He was pale, his features cast into disturbed shadows by the flickering lantern. He had the look of a man who had lost the world. What could she say to him? She searched her mind but could find only one thing. A question.

'When will the boat come, James?'

He didn't answer. She couldn't look at him anymore. His broken heart was there, on display for anyone to see. She lifted the corner of her shawl and the retching of her sobs found its way into every corner and crevice of their sad, clifftop dwelling.

Jeremiah arrived the next morning with a fresh south-westerly behind him. Eliza couldn't face him but she didn't have to. James met him alone at the landing with the letter so she was spared the telling of their sad news and the burden of his and Tom's condolences. She wondered if she should have gone herself, climbed aboard his boat and headed for shore with Mary. But she was terrified at the thought of her baby taking ill miles out at sea.

James returned carrying the provisions. Eliza stepped over the box of fresh food he dumped in the kitchen, not bothering to empty it. She hoped they would not be around long enough to need it and was superstitious that putting the items away would jinx them.

James hurried out into the yard, shouting. *'Edmund! A word!'*

Eliza crept out to the porch to listen. To her eyes the difference between the two men was marked. Edmund stood tall and tidy in his uniform, his face unruffled by cares, his fresh youth and prospects evident. James was in his rough clothes, dusty and sweating from his exertions. She couldn't see his face but his shoulders were rounded. She couldn't hear all that was being said at first, only the occasional word carried on the breeze.

Then James' voice rose.?

'Jeremiah told me!'

Edmund shrugged.

James shouted, '*You're a dirty liar, Edmund Hunter!*'

Edmund stepped back, his hands raised as if to defend himself. James shoved him on the shoulder, making him stumble backwards but he remained standing. Edmund shook his head. He had a wry smile on his face.

In that moment Eliza hated him with every fibre of her being. He didn't even care that he had been found out. The damage was already done.

She stood stock still when James came in, slamming the front door. She waited for him to say something. To tell her she was right. To tell her he was sorry. But he went past her, then she heard the bedroom door slamming. She couldn't go to him.

She stayed listening for sounds next door, excited voices or shrieks of laughter but there was nothing. Did they know she was listening? She pictured them pointing at their shared wall, mouthing their delight and victory.

Eliza took up permanent residence by daytime at the front window. How long would they be made to wait? What if the Board refused? It was filled with men, of course. Men whose interests were in regulations and procedures and steel and stone and signals. They knew nothing about pushing a baby into the world and having it taken from you. Would they understand the reason for the request? She pictured Jeremiah and Tom mooring the boat, securing the ropes, not wanting to be stranded here. She pictured them walking their slow and steady walk up the lighthouse road, in sync, as if still rowing. She could see them in her mind's eye handing an envelope to James. But nothing beyond that. She didn't dare to hope. It was a torment but she had to wait.

Her heart quickened when she saw James entering the yard days later, in his hands a cream page. His tread was slow, ponderous and his head was down. She tried to read him from afar but he was a closed book to her now. He came into the house and stood, looking at her, saying nothing. Then he nodded. Once. Handed her the paper and left.

Eliza scanned the text trying to make sense of it. In her panic, words and phrases jumped before her eyes. *'Board has considered ... grave circumstances ... unfortunate ... permission granted ...'*

She leaned back against the windowsill, straining to keep her legs from buckling beneath her. Permission granted. They were leaving.

Eliza was thrown into a maelstrom. She scurried from room to room, rinsing dishes, pulling the linen from the beds. Eventually, she came to a halt. She was finished. But she had a sensation deep within that there was something forgotten, overlooked. She sat down to feed Mary. This moment was all so strange. It contained the excitement, the frenzy of a new beginning but really it was an ending. Whatever lay before her and James now was unknown. They were about to enter the 'after'. After the island. After the boys. A memory came rushing to her of the day they arrived here. She remembered the ceaseless questions of Joseph, the solid weight of Peter in her arms. It rocked her. Suddenly she wasn't so sure she could go. She wanted to, had to, but it meant leaving her boys, leaving them behind, here, in the ground of Skellig Michael. Would she ever get to see their resting place again? Who would tend the grave? What about their headstone? Had she made a terrible mistake? Was it better to stay? Jeremiah's words about his own lost child came back to her.

''Tis a curse to always have your heart torn between the ones that are here and the ones that aren't.'

Is that how she would live the rest of her days? Rent in two? It had to be done, for the sake of the one who was here. She would take her baby ashore, get to a doctor, protect her. But first, there was somewhere she had to go.

Chapter 32

Eliza had to stop for breath halfway up the stone steps. The weight of Mary had her shoulders and lower back screaming. She wondered about carrying her on her back instead of her front but she preferred being able to see her. She could see lots of activity below. There was a man she'd never seen before heading up the lighthouse road with James. There was no sign of Jeremiah and Tom. They were probably with the boat, staying out of the way until they were needed to carry everything down to load it. The sea was restless, topped with small, white waves that chopped at the lower edges of the island. The breeze was light but fickle, blowing strands of hair into her eyes one minute then tugging at her skirt in the next. The metal-grey sky was one continuous canopy, shrouding the island in sameness. The air was sticky, heavy, with the threat of a summer storm. Even the seagulls wheeling overhead were listless, as if they were performing their duty, doing only what was expected.

Eliza struggled on. Her blouse was stuck to her spine by the time she reached the top of the steps. She entered the monastery and found a flat tuft of grass on which to lay Mary. She opened her shawl, flattened it down and put Mary on it, making sure there was no way for her to roll. She needed a moment alone with her boys.

All the while she kept her eyes averted from the grave, his grave, their grave. A fresh scar made in what was barely three months old. She steeled herself and approached. James had taken care to replace all the glittering quartz stones that she and Joseph had gathered. Eliza's head swam with the thought of Joseph's little hand bringing her his offerings.

'Look, Mammy – do you like this one?'

And now he was underneath them, covered by them. She was going to be sick. She closed her eyes and swallowed the sensation down. She didn't have much time and she needed to do this right.

She stood by the grave, then knelt, then sat, her legs stretched out childlike in front, then tucked under her. Finally she lay down, stretched out parallel to the grave of her two boys.

'Boys, I need to tell you something. I have to go. Me and Daddy and your little sister. We have to leave the island.'

She imagined them, as they would have been in life, listening to her every word, gawping, wide-eyed, Peter sucking his thumb, holding his big brother's hand. Joseph, being the big man, interrupting with questions and distractions but twiddling his hair for comfort. She squeezed her eyes shut. This was hell.

'I'm so sorry you can't come too, that we have to leave you here but Mary is sick. I have to get her help because if I lose her too I won't be able to go on. I can only barely go on as it is for her sake. Maybe it would be easier if she was gone. Then I'd come to you in a heartbeat. But who knows if I'd be able to – that's a sin – and –'

She thought back to the moment on the spit when she had toyed with the idea of letting herself fall. Of letting go. How delicious it was! But the moment had passed and she was still here.

'So, we have to go. I hope someday we'll be able to come back to visit. I want to lay a headstone and write your names on it. I want everyone to know you're here. Two beautiful boys. Brothers.'

She gulped at the humid air. This was so hard. Could she just say the words inside her mind? Would that count? No. She needed to speak them out loud. She wiped away the tears that slid from her eyes, down her cheeks, into her hair.

'I'm so sorry I didn't mind you better. If I'd known what would become of you out here I never would have stepped foot on that boat.'

She could barely speak now. She got to her knees and draped her body over the grave. She wished she could take a sharp rock, cut her heart out with it and leave it here.

'I know you're great boys. Always so good. I want you to mind each other. Joseph, take care of your little brother.'

She wept, unable to speak any longer. Over the sound of her tears a thin wail carried on the breeze. Mary needed her. She staggered upright, planting kisses on her palms and pressing them to the grave. She picked up a small piece of quartz. It had a seam of silver down the middle that made it look like two halves, bound together by nature. She squeezed it tightly in her fist and looked skyward.

'You have my boys now!' she shouted. *'Take care of them for me!'*

She pocketed the quartz, picked up Mary and secured her for the journey down. She didn't trust herself to glance back at where her boys lay. If she did she would never leave.

When she reached Christ's Saddle she saw a familiar shape, crouched low, staring out to sea. She caught her breath. Was James going to be annoyed at her for disappearing again without a word? Or cross with her for holding up the boat? She stiffened, braced for harshness as he stood and turned to face her.

'I was going to come up with you, but –' He swallowed hard and turned to face the sea again. Eliza saw a tear trickle down his cheek. She took a step towards him and put her hand on his sleeve. He turned into her then and sobbed. When he had no more tears she pulled him down to sit next to her on the scratchy grass. They sat in silence watching the gannets gliding through the air.

'Bad neighbours,' Eliza said. Her voice felt strange, like she hadn't used it in a long time. James looked at her, not getting her meaning.

She gestured. 'The gannets. The way they rob from each other to feather their nests.'

James nodded. 'You were right, Eliza. I should have listened to you.'

She pulled at a blade of grass by her feet. These words were ones she had longed for but now, hearing them, they meant nothing. It was too late.

'The day that Peter – that we lost him –' he sighed, 'Edmund got wind that I had prepared a report about him to send the Commissioner. I told you that, I know. I never sent it. I decided to give him a chance and he betrayed me. You were right about the inspection. He knew all along they were coming. Jeremiah confirmed it.'

Eliza took a deep breath. She was glad he could see it now but her heart burned with the hurt that he hadn't fully believed her. He had to get his proof, he had to hear it from Jeremiah.

James pulled a piece of paper from his trouser pocket. 'And I found this. He had a list.'

'A list?' Eliza looked at the paper, furrowing her brow.

'Of my "misdemeanours" as he called them. He'd recorded everything. He meant to ruin me. Us.'

He handed it to Eliza with a shaking hand. She scanned down through it. It was a list of dates with a brief report beside each one.

Arose late the morning of my arrival.
Malfunctioning lamps suggesting negligence.
Failed to report for duty Christmas Day.
Consumption of alcohol in the lighthouse.
Dereliction of duty for purposes of a party.
Wife of PK of unsound mind.

Eliza's head swam. *Unsound mind.* That was his description of her. Bile rose up her throat. She looked at James.

He lowered his head into his hands. 'I didn't know who to believe, Eliza. I'm sorry. I should have trusted you.'

'Yes.' Eliza kept her gaze on him until he faced her. 'You should have.' She tore the paper into tiny pieces and held her palm skyward allowing the remnants to drift into the breeze. She offered James her hand and pulled him to his feet so that they could descend together.

Edmund was waiting for them outside the lighthouse.

'*What's going on?*' His cheeks were blazing. '*Who the devil is the man who came ashore with Jeremiah?*'

James placed himself between Edmund and Eliza. He regarded Edmund coolly.

'That is the new Principal Keeper. Temporary. Until they send my permanent replacement.'

Edmund cursed. 'That's rubbish! I'm well capable of the PK job. You know that I am. I'm a better lightkeeper than you even!'

'Some might agree.' James nodded. He stepped closer to Edmund, squaring his shoulders. 'But I know you better than any, I'd say. I know how willing you are to lie and cheat your way to what you want. *And I think you are disgusting.*' He stepped back and drew Eliza to his side. 'Enjoy your time with the new PK, Edmund. It won't be for long, I'd say.'

He squeezed Eliza's hand gently as they walked away.

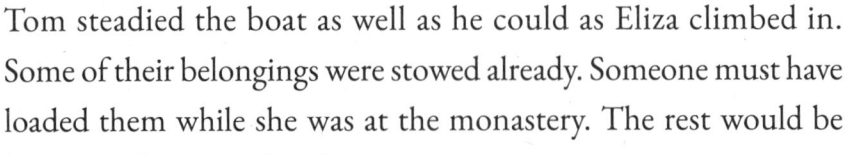

Tom steadied the boat as well as he could as Eliza climbed in. Some of their belongings were stowed already. Someone must have loaded them while she was at the monastery. The rest would be brought ashore another day.

Jeremiah helped her aboard. His shocked expression suggested to Eliza that she was a state to behold. No doubt her face was stained with tears and mud. She didn't care. He took her hand in his and shook it, then held it. She patted his hand and pulled hers away. He shook his head, unable to speak. She understood. What could anyone say to this?

Tom leaned across and extended his hand. The other oarsmen shook her hand in turn, mumbling condolences. She shook them briefly and ignored whatever they muttered at her.

She sat down and fixed her eyes on the lighthouse road, willing James to come on. The swell was getting choppier and the boat rocked against the stone of the landing. Tom nudged at it with his foot and shot a look at Jeremiah whose gaze was fixed on the sky that was growing darker now. They were anxious, she could tell. Determination surged through her. She was leaving. Today. If they had to go without James. If they had to row through a storm. She refused to spend another night here.

She released her breath as James appeared, accompanied by a strange man. James' expression was grave. He shook the hand of the stranger, imparted a few final instructions, then climbed onto the boat, avoiding her eyes.

'Are you ready?' Eliza asked.

'I am.' His voice was bereft.

Eliza looked away. Was everything ruined for them?

'No sign of the Hunters,' she said. Not that she expected them to appear. They were licking their wounds, it seemed.

James gave Eliza a wry look, a hint of his old warmth beneath it. She held his gaze a moment then looked down at her hands. She felt sorry. Sorry for James, for herself, for her lovely boys.

'There's something else, Eliza. Something I didn't say to you yet.' James put his arm around her, pulling her tight to him. He spoke quietly into her ear. 'I sent the report. About Edmund. His time here will be coming to an end too.'

She sat back so that she could see his face. It was earnest.

'The day I requested permission for us to leave I sent that off with it.'

He looked into her eyes. She could see herself there once more.

He pulled her closer and she let herself lean into him.

Tom pushed against the wall with his oar and with a few powerful pulls he and Jeremiah got them on course. The swell lifted the bow of the boat and it fell from the crest. It was rhythmic, numbing.

Eliza watched as Skellig Michael disappeared, appeared, disappeared.

THE END

Author's Note

Another place with a story, which is lost today because of rockfalls in the area, is Eliza's Corner – a spot on the roadway between the two lighthouses that was named by Portmagee tradesmen who were working on the rock over 100 years ago. Eliza Callaghan, after whom the place was called, was a beautiful young woman who used to sit out at this corner for hours on end, knitting in the sunshine. But was she a lighthouse daughter, much admired by the Portmagee men, or was she the mourning mother of the two children, Patrick and William Callaghan, who died in 1868 and 1869, aged two and four years and are buried in the medieval church ruin in the monastery? This is something I may never know.

Lavelle, Des. *The Skellig Story.* (2004)

When I first visited Skellig Michael I was moved by the grave of two young boys in the monastery on the summit of the island. As a young mother myself I could not fathom how anyone could raise a family in such a remote and hostile location, what a struggle it must have been to keep them safe from harm and what a heartbreak it must have been to lose them and have to leave them behind in their burial place.

The two boys were William and Patrick Callaghan, the sons of a lighthouse keeper and his wife.

This story is inspired by them. I have taken some liberties with the facts in order to tell it.

In 1867, there were two lighthouses in operation on Skellig Michael, the Upper Lighthouse and the Lower Lighthouse, though the upper one was closed down in 1870. This would have afforded the families living there more company and support, so I have been cruel to reduce the population to just the Hunters and the Carthys. But I have been kinder in allowing them the frequent visits from Jeremiah. In reality the Irish Lights supply boat brought the lighthouse families what they needed only twice a year, in autumn and in spring. The lighthouse keepers' wives would only have made it ashore twice a year also to make their own purchases.

All other details are as accurate as I could make them with the information available to me.

I hope the story works despite these changes and I hope in reading you pause to wonder at the strength, courage and resilience of the women of the past.

June O'Sullivan

If you enjoyed this book from Poolbeg why not visit our website

WWW.POOLBEG.COM

and get another book delivered straight to your home or to a friend's home.
<u>All books despatched within 24 hours.</u>

FREE SHIPPING on orders
over €20 in Rep. of Ireland*

Why not join our mailing list at www.poolbeg.com and get some fantastic offers, competitions, author interviews, new releases and much more?

POOLBEG ON SOCIAL MEDIA

@PoolbegBooks

poolbegbooks

www.facebook.com/poolbegpress

*Free shipping in Republic of Ireland only on orders over €20.